Darkness at the Edge of Town

By Kevin McManus

 All constructs are intentionally capitalized to denote importance.

ISBN: 978-1-7396189-1-9

Published by Book Hub Publishing, An Independent Publishing House with Offices in Galway and Limerick, Ireland.

www.bookhubpublishing.com @BookHubPublish

Book Hub Publishing is committed to inclusion and diversity. We print our books on forestry sustainable paper. Viva la forests!

CONTENTS

Chapter 1: Like Clockwork

Saturday April 22nd, 1978
Gallagher's Pub
The village of Ballygorman
North Leitrim, Ireland

The clock hanging on the wood-panelled wall to the right of Donal McCabe tocked away, its loud and melodic "tock, tock, tock" ringing through the room like an incessant reminder of time passing by. Its antique design was one that had seen many years, its metal hands and numbers covered in a thin layer of dust. The pendulum swung back and forth in a mesmerising fashion, creating an almost soothing rhythm that was hard not to focus on, a sharp noise compared to the other sounds that filled the room. It sounded like a knife against bone.

The clock was made of a deep, dark mahogany wood, its hour and minute hands crafted out of brass that shone brightly as it rose and fell across the dial. The clock face itself was a pristine cream colour with bold black Roman numerals to mark each passing hour.

Tock, tock tock.

It was definitely a tock and not a tick. It was not a thin tick sound, it was a heavy, slow and deep tock. Like the sound resonating from the throat of a primeval beast it was loud and overbearing. The pendulum swung over and back within the Gustav Becker casing and the clock defiantly tocked.

Tock, tock, tock.

It was fourteen minutes past eight on an April Saturday evening. Donal McCabe took his second mouthful of his pint of Guinness; it tasted good and he had a taste for more. The Guinness was thick and black and tasted of hops and barley.

Donal was thirty-seven years old, with thick brown hair that was lightly peppered with grey. He was tall, around six foot two, and considered by many to be an attractive man. His brown tweed trousers were pressed, and his black leather shoes were polished. He sat upright on his stool as if an invisible thread was pulling him from behind. He rubbed his fingers along the rough counter as he thought about the night before. The counter was made of a sturdy pine with rounded edges. Its white top was faded with age and bore the scars of thousands of drinks and cigarettes.

Behind him, timber sparked in the open fire as it hungrily devoured the wood. The flames snapped in the hearth as they licked the sooty walls of the chimney. The sparks ejected from the fire and burnt holes in the stained brown mat that was straddled across the lino. The old linoleum was as pale as gingerbread, with a grain like a thousand crusted corals, piled there in flakes like golden leaves. The lino was covered in stains of all kinds. Some were from spilled drinks, but most were from the mud of Leitrim's farmlands. Over the years, the lino had absorbed all the liquids and dirt from the floor, and the stains were like a map of the pub. The floor covering smelt of old beer and spirits that had been spilled over the years. The lino was silent, but the tock-tock of a clock and the crackle of the fire were all that could be heard.

DARKNESS AT THE EDGE OF TOWN

A grey and black mass of swirling smoke rose from the open fire and swirled around the room. The chairs and tables were made of dark, rough wood that had been eroded by years of use. The chairs were covered in dust, the kind of dust that builds up slowly over time from the traffic of feet. Some of the chairs were bare, some had long-forgotten cushions in tatters. Years seemed to slowly leak out of the chairs, each year slowly fading into obscurity, like snow slowly melting in a filthy winter. If you sat in the chair long enough your mouth would dry, perhaps that was what the landlord intended.

The smell of beer and whiskey was everywhere, mixed with the musty and stagnant scent of grime, soot and ash. It was a stench like a thousand wet dogs packed into a small room.

The door to Donal's left opened with a ring of a bell as a bald man squeezed through. He sat on a stool at the other end of the short counter, took out a pack of twenty major from his grey trouser pocket and threw them up on the counter in front of him. The man was bald, bald in the sense of bare and shiny, hairless, and naked. His face was red, in the sense of flushed and warm, his nose was pointed and red like a cherry, as if it had been pinched hard. His skin was leathery, like a dead-falling leaf that had been missed by the wind and was now decomposing. His eyes were small, and his chapped red lips were pursed, in the sense of tight and not moving, his face had a look of hard disgust and impatience, like he had been disappointed over and over again and had become resigned to it. He wore a navy jumper with large red diamond patterns over a grey shirt, the collar was frayed, his shirt was unbuttoned, and grey chest hair was visible below the neckline. He had the air of a barber and a priest, a man who was sorry for himself and sorry for you, but mostly sorry for himself.

He sat pensively for a moment; his brow furrowed in thought. His fingers moved to the cigarette box on the countertop and he began tapping it with a quiet urgency, his thoughts seemingly turning over in his mind. Tap, tap-tap. Tap-tap-tap. The rhythm grew louder and more insistent as he continued. Donal's gaze shifted to the man before him, his face hidden in the shadows of the dimly lit bar. The man didn't bother making eye contact as he asked, "Is himself not about?" His narrowed eyes fixed on the small fag box in his hands as if it held some mysterious answer.

"Joe was here five minutes ago, I'm not sure where he went, could be changing a barrel or something," Donal answered.

"Jasus, a man could die of thirst."

"Aye," Donal replied with a laugh.

The bald man struck a match, drawing it along the side of the box in a practiced motion. He brought the flame to his lips and lit the cigarette, taking a deep inhale. Releasing a plume of smoke from his mouth and nose, he waited impatiently for service while looking out at his surroundings with an expressionless face. The man's breathing was loud, deep and raspy, like a winded runner. The cigarette fluttered when he touched his lips. His throat gave a hissing sound as he exhaled the smoke.

"Its shockin quiet for a Saturday evening," the man hissed.

"Aye, it is, but it could be worse... it could be rainin." Donal laughed.

The man broke into a wide smile, his lips curling up at the corners and his eyes twinkling with amusement. His voice carried a hint of playfulness as he casually responded, "Yeah, I suppose."

Heavy thuds of steps accompanied by laboured breathing converged into an ominous rumble and heralded the arrival of the landlord, Joe Gallagher, behind the counter. He blew into his hands to warm them, the cold of the night having permeated every crevice in the bar. With a quick flick of his wrist, Joe grabbed a cloth and began wiping down the surface of the counter. When finished, he cast it aside into a nearby basin beneath the counter with an air of finality. "Well boys, that's a cold enough evenin."

"It's cold, there is a biting north wind there all day that would cut you," Donal said.

"Aye, cold for April, for sure," Joe replied.

"A pint of stout and a half one," the bald man at the counter interjected, his ruddy face becoming increasingly flushed with each passing minute as he impatiently listened to the long-winded conversation regarding the weather outside. His gruff and weathered voice cut through the chatter, clearly conveying that he was fed up and gasping for a pint.

"Right, you are," Joe replied as he lifted a pint glass and began to fill it.

Gallagher wore a simple white shirt and grey trousers. His white shirt was soiled, and his trousers held the same dirt stains. Both were splattered with beer and cow shite. His shirt clung to his barrel chest. The landlord was a thick-set, middle-aged man. His thinning grey hair was matted, his face red with perspiration. He wore a pungent odour of whiskey, sweat and cigarette smoke.

"You're not a Leitrim man," Joe said as he continued to pull the pint and look at the bald man sideways and engaging his curiosity. Joe's voice was coarse and gruff. The landlord liked to know everybody and everything that was happening or passing through the village of Ballygorman.

"No, I'm not," he replied.

"Not that far away?" Joe probed with a raised eyebrow.

"No," he confirmed with a shake of his head.

"Sligo, I'd say, judging from the accent," Joe guessed and looked to him for confirmation.

The bald man smiled and gave a nod in acknowledgment. "You're the sharp one."

"I have you now, you're a brother-in-law of Peggy O'Connell, I heard that Peggy had visitors up for the weekend," Joe said with a satisfied look on his face.

"Jasus, you don't miss much," the bald man said. His scalp gleamed in the light from the bar, reflecting like a beacon in the dusky, half-lit pub.

"You're very welcome to the village. My name is Joe Gallagher," Joe said as he put out his hand to offer a handshake to the customer.

"I'm Brian Reynolds from Colooney," he said as he shook the publican's hand.

"Pleased to meet you, Brian, this is Donal McCabe at the counter. He is a blow in too," Joe said with a laugh. "Donal is a Monaghan man, but he has been living here for... how long now, Donal?"

"Eight years next September," Donal answered.

"Donal is a schoolteacher in the national school," Joe said to Brian.

"Oh, right, a good pensionable job and good holidays, a handy number, that's for sure," Brian said as he took a long, deep drag from his cigarette. His expression was one of contentment and relief as the smoke filled his lungs and billowed from his nostrils in wispy white curls. His eyes seemed to soften as he exhaled the smoky grey vapor into the air around him, savouring this moment of leisurely bliss.

"What kind of work do you do, Brian?" Joe inquired.

"A bit of this, a bit of that, you know. Anything I can get my hands on; building, plumbing... but I'm not able to work at the moment. Fucked up my back pretty bad," Brian replied with a grimace as he adjusted his posture.

"Right," Joe responded. "Hopefully, you will be okay after a while."

Brian nervously rubbed the back of his thick, fleshy neck as he replied with a dubious, "Hopefully." His voice trailed off as he failed to mask his uncertainty. The clock tocked on.

A half hour had passed, and the atmosphere at Gallagher's had grown livelier. Not too crowded, of course; Joe Gallagher preferred smaller crowds that he could easily manage, not wanting to be too busy pouring drinks that he didn't have time to chat with his customers and glean information from them – the newest news, the juiciest gossip.

As people began filtering in, the conversation grew louder. There was a soothing hum surrounding Joe Gallagher, created by all the conversations happening at once. The customers were discussing sports, current affairs, their day jobs, family life and more. He listened closely to each story they shared with fascination, learning something new from every person he spoke to. There was something special about these moments – it made Joe feel like he was part of a larger community. He cherished being there in the moment, connecting with his customers.

The delicate chime of the bell above the door announced a new patron. Heads swivelled in unison as all eyes settled upon the imposing figure who stepped inside. It was Sean Breslin, whose gait was steely and determined as he made his way to an empty barstool close to Donal's. He moved confidently and with ease, his strides sure-footed as he navigated between chairs and tables toward his destination.

Sean's fair hair cascaded around his face, long and thick, its ends darkening after being caught in the rain. His skin glistened with the droplets of water, sticking to his face, neck and ears. Sean Breslin had a weathered look as if he stood out in the fields all day and worked until his hands bled. Although he was only thirty-five, his features looked worn out and aged beyond their years due to countless winters that had left their mark on him. His face was lined with wrinkles – a product of both time and life's troubles. There was a long, jagged scar on his left cheek, which he attempted to conceal with a neatly trimmed beard. His frame was lean and wiry, evidence of his physical labour as a farmer. He wore the marks of his work proudly upon him like battle scars; from the creases on the corners of his eyes from squinting against sun-glared skies. Sean smelled of earth and rain.

Conversations resumed as Sean made his way to the bar, taking a seat with a few nervous smiles thrown around. He shifted in his seat restlessly, trying to make himself comfortable before placing his right hand on the counter for balance. The skin on his hand was calloused from years of hard work – there was even a long scar stretching across the palm and edges of his fingers from too many encounters with sharp and thorny wire.

"Well Donal, any craic?"

"Not so bad, Sean, not so bad."

"How was the head this mornin, you had a late one last night."

"It was late, right enough," Donal replied with a smirk and a tired rub of his eyes.

"Must have been near four when you left," Sean said.

"Christ, was it that late." Donal sighed.

"It was, you were well steamed." Sean laughed.

"I wasn't that bad, was I," Donal said with a hint of embarrassment tinting his features.

"You were bad enough... anyway how did you get on?" Sean asked.

"What are you on about?" Donal replied defensively.

“With yer one... Patricia O’Neill, you were all over each other in the kitchen. You were looking might cosy altogether,” Sean commented, a sly smirk on his lips.

“You must have been keeping a close eye on me.”

“It was hard to avoid.” Sean laughed.

“Ahh, you are just jealous, Sean,” Donal said as he shoved Sean with his elbow.

“Not at all, would you go away with yourself,” Sean said as his face contorted into a mask of disgust.

“I know you and Patricia had a good thing going last year,” Donal said.

“Not at all, you’re dreamin’, McCabe,” Sean replied.

“Ah now, Sean, you still have a soft auld spot for her.” Donal grinned.

“I’ve no interest in the woman, you’re welcome to her,” Sean said as he took a swallow of his stout.

“I’ll make it up to you, Sean, I’ll buy you another drink,” Donal said as he beckoned towards Gallagher and nodded for two pints. "How did you get home, anyway?" he enquired, leaning in inquisitively.

"Well, somehow I managed to make it back all the way on Shank’s mare," Sean said with a wry smile, rubbing his shoulders as if still feeling the bitter cold of the night before. He continued, shaking his head slightly at his own misfortune, "Got soaked to the bone I did. Not a pleasant experience, let me tell ya."

“Jesus, it was a long walk on a bad night,” Donal said.

“Tell me about it.” Sean sighed. “I’ve aches and pains all day. I can’t get warm, no matter how many layers I put on.”

"Ah, lad, when the damp seeps into your aching bones it's impossible to get yourself warm. That's why you need a good pair of long johns," Donal advised with a smirk.

"Oh, stop taking the piss now, McCabe," Sean said.

“I would have given you a lift out home, why didn’t you give me a shout?” Donal said.

"I was aware you were occupied," Sean said with a light chuckle, "So I chose not to intrude upon your moment and disturb your peace with Patricia cozied up in your lap and you intent on exploring the far reaches of her throat with the tip of your tongue."

"Ahh, give it a rest Breslin, change the record, you're the right sore bastard."

"Fuck you, McCabe, you Monaghan blow in, up here in Leitrim, taking all our women."

"Well, somebody has to... here, drink your pint and quit your yakking," Donal said.

Sean took a large swallow of the pint and lit himself a fag.

Donal's gaze drifted upwards, settling on the colour television resting upon a shelf in the corner of the bar. "Hey Joe," he called out to the publican, "turn up the volume on that TV, will you?" The glow of its screen illuminated the dimly lit surroundings, casting an eerie hue across Donal's face as he watched.

"Why, what's on?" Joe enquired as he looked back across his shoulder while pulling a pint.

"The Eurovision song contest, our fella is coming on now," Donal replied.

"Who is he?" Joe asked.

"C.T. Wilkinson," Donal said.

"He has a good voice that fella," Sean interrupted.

"He has," Donal agreed.

"What's the song called again?" Sean asked.

"Born to sing," Donal said. "Now can you shut up for a few minutes so I can hear it."

"He's a fine-lookin' fella," Sean said admiringly.

"Really, he doesn't do much for me," Donal replied with a shrug of his shoulders.

"You know what I mean, he is sort of debonair."

"Debonair, just, that's not a word you hear every day around here," Donal quipped.

"He dresses well," Sean remarked as he took a pull of his cigarette.

"You mean that big scarf around his neck" Donal laughed, shaking his head in amusement. "You should get one of them, it would suit you. Handy when you are walking home at night from a party in the pissing rain, it would keep you warm. Actually, you look a bit like him, Breslin, with the beard and the hair and all, do you model yourself on him?"

"Would you ever shut the fuck up McCabe, you Monaghan muck savage?"

"He could win this you know, I put a fiver on at the bookies in Sligo," Donal said.

"No chance, it's a great song but there's no way it'll win," Sean declared with conviction. "The English group Coco are the ones to beat."

Donal slowly sipped his pint, studying his friend for a moment before speaking. "We shall see," he replied as he set down his pint, a twinkle in his eye and a hint of optimism in his voice.

"Doesn't it look beautiful in colour," Sean observed as he stared at the television screen. "I'm treating myself to a colour TV in the summer, it will be great for watching the football."

"You mean to watch Monaghan getting hammered as usual," Sean remarked.

"Says the Leitrim man," Donal replied.

Joe Gallagher let out a hearty chuckle and said, "Ah lads, just you wait and see. Monaghan is destined to come out on top eventually. Those Monaghan lads are hardy bustards, tough as nails."

Gallagher grabbed a hold of Donal's shoulder, his grip like a vice. His hands slammed against the counter, veins protruding from his arms and neck. The landlord's hands were coarse and beefy, fat fingers filled with grime beneath his long and dirty fingernails. His skin was thick and rough like sandpaper.

Donal slowly nodded, his face showing his agreement with Joe's words. "He's right, you know," he said. "Monaghan will have their day eventually. That's one thing I'm sure of."

Sean just rolled his eyes, taking a sip from his pint of stout. "I'll believe it when I see it," he said as he put down his glass on the bar counter.

At that moment the TV sputtered and died, its screen blanked out with static. Joe raced to the back of the set and fiddled with the wires for a few minutes in an attempt to bring it back to life, but nothing seemed to work. He sighed deeply and ran his fingers through his hair in frustration. "Ah, bollocks to it," he muttered under his breath with a shake of his head. "I'll just have to call the repairman tomorrow. I'll put on the radio, at least we can listen to the competition on it."

Donal and Sean glanced at each other with a knowing smirk and let out a soft chuckle. "Looks like C.T. Wilkinson's performance was just too powerful for the TV to cope with," Donal quipped. "He must have overloaded the tubes with his charisma."

Sean nodded in agreement as he surveyed the blank television in front of them. The conversation drifted back to the topic of Eurovision and the chances of C.T Wilkinson winning.

"I don't know," Sean said thoughtfully. "I mean, I like his song, but there are some pretty solid entries this year. But you never know – stranger things have happened!"

Joe spoke up with enthusiasm, his voice rising in excitement. "Wouldn't it be just marvellous if he actually won? What pride it would bring to our humble little corner of the world! We could be flying flags and banners proudly all summer long."

Donal and Sean continued their discussion as they sipped on their pints in anticipation of C.T Wilkinson's performance results. Joe stood behind the bar polishing glasses as he listened to their conversation with an amused grin.

At 11 pm, the results were announced.

"Well, that's it for another year, we didn't win yet again." Donal sighed resignedly.

"We came fifth, not too bad," Sean said. "Sure, there is always next year."

"That's a long way off," Donal said downheartedly.

"What's another year?" Sean remarked. "It will fly by."

“That would be a good title for a song,” Donal replied.

“What?” Sean asked.

“Never mind,” Donal said shaking his head.

"What was the winning song called again?" Sean asked.

"Aba daba doo, or something like that." Donal let out a hearty laugh.

"What the hell, was the singer Fred Flintstone?"

"Could be, he was from Israel, I think," Donal said.

"So, Israel won the Eurovision, holy fuck," Sean said shaking his head in wonder.

The boisterous laughter that had filled the air slowly died down, and the conversation turned to other matters. All the while, Joe diligently kept everyone's glasses filled up, his cheery grin growing ever wider as he could see the pound notes building up in his till.

An hour passed, then two. The TV and radio had been forgotten as everyone’s attention was firmly focused on each other’s stories. Donal and Sean continued to talk until late into the night, only stopping when Joe finally called the last orders at twelve o'clock. With their last pint downed and with sighs of reluctance, they said their goodbyes to Joe and stumbled out into the night air.

As they walked out of the pub, the cold air hit them like a slap in the face. They could see their wispy breath in the air like smoke. Donal pulled his coat tighter around him, trying to keep the chill at bay as he uttered a frustrated groan. "Jesus, it's fucking cold for April.” He looked up and saw the night sky in all its glory. The stars twinkled and glistened like diamonds on a black velvet cloth. A perfect full moon hung low in the sky, casting a blue glow onto the buildings of Ballygorman that were lit up against the dark mountains. Looking out into the desolate street, Sean took a deep breath, the crisp air filling his lungs as he pondered out loud, "Hey Donal, you ever wonder what it would be like to just leave everything behind and start fresh somewhere else? Somewhere far away from here?”

Donal gazed at him with confusion, his eyebrows slightly furrowed in curiosity. "What do you mean?"

His friend took a deep breath before replying, his voice taking on a grandiose air as if the words were carrying heavy importance. "I mean, just pick a place on the map, anywhere in the world, and just go. Shed all your obligations and responsibilities for a while and just live only for that moment."

"You are pissed, Breslin," Donal replied.

Chapter 2: Sunday Girl

Sunday April 23rd.

Sunday morning had rolled in, the bells of St Mary's church ringing out for eleven o'clock mass. Donal made his way up the main street of Ballygorman, nodding to each face he passed as they all made their way towards the looming spire of St Mary's. As headmaster, Donal knew he had a duty to set a good example and was thus obligated to attend mass every Sunday, even if he had a hangover from the night before.

The main street was made up of a few shops, a post office, and two pubs. The houses were dark, with steep, grey roofs that reached up to the sky. Cars lined the road, the pavements full of young couples and families. Children screeched as they ran down the street. Some of them awkwardly greeted their headmaster. Their parents wished him good morning and commented on the fine, bright but cool April morning. The village was bustling with activity, yet one could not shake off the feeling of emptiness that lingered in the air.

Donal walked through the open doorway of the church. The altar was up at the front with aisles on either side leading to the pews of dark mahogany. The stained-glass windows cast off colours and shadows that made the room look cold and gloomy, the only light coming from the candles. The wooden floor was polished daily but looked dull and tired. The congregation had assembled, their clothes conservative, especially the men whose suits were dark, either black or grey – except for the ones who got the Yanky parcel of bright, gaudy clothes that made them stand out like a sore thumb.

These were the people who strolled down the street every day, the kids who played in the parks, the men who gathered in the pubs, the women who slept with candles in the cupboard under the stairs; they were the ones who paid their taxes, who answered their doors to the postman, to the priests and to the law.

There was coughing and chatter as people whispered to one another. Donal could hear the organ playing in the background. It was playing a Latin hymn, "Ave Maria". The smell of the church on a Sunday was of incense, floor polish, cheap perfume and mothballs. It was a smell Donal associated with faith and devotion.

At two minutes past eleven, Father O'Grady came out on to the altar, followed by two altar boys. It was showtime. The altar boys wore immaculate long white cassocks and both had floppy fringes and flushed red faces. Father O'Grady had hair you could land a plane on. His face was long and haggard, his eyes sunken and his complexion deathly pale, with a nose like a pick handle. He had a belly like a bag of water with a large salmon inside. He walked like he was wearing a back brace and was in constant pain but hid it well. He was a charming man, and all the middle-aged women fancied him. He often visited Donal at school, especially coming up to communion and confirmation time. He always smelled of ham and onions.

The priest's monotone drawl vibrated throughout the church as he spoke, his mouth opening and closed like a fish's gullet. The words released lacked conviction as if there was something else that he'd rather be saying.

He spoke like one of those old-fashioned tape-recorders that had started to work but not yet reached the end of their spool. The urge to shout at him to hurry up was almost overpowering.

The wooden pews were hard and uncomfortable, and the kneelers hurt after a while. The sound of the congregation praying aloud filled the warm and stuffy air, their voices overlapping to form one collective sound, like the buzz of a motorway.

As Donal was almost losing the will to live, he got an elbow in the ribs.

"Move in, McCabe, you big ball of shite," Sean Breslin said as he arrived fashionably late for mass as usual and pushed his way into the pew.

"The stink of porter of you Breslin, have you no toothpaste in that shack of yours," Donal remarked with a smirk.

"Toothpaste, what the feck is toothpaste?" Sean asked.

"Donal snorted in disbelief. "This priest would drive you to drink," he said with a sarcastic laugh.

"He's a feckin pure dose, that's what he is," Sean replied between clenched teeth.

“Are you thinking of going for one after mass?" Donal asked, raising an eyebrow inquisitively.

Sean grinned back wickedly as if it was already decided. “Is the Pope a catholic?"

As the mass reached communion time, Sean and Donal were delighted that the show was nearing a conclusion. The congregation quietly and respectfully queued up down the main aisle. The sound of a hundred people, shuffling and rustling their clothes, the odd cough and nose being blown, the shuffling of feet, the creaking of the pews and the organ. The taste of wine, the taste of bread, the taste of body odour, the taste of sweat. The communion wafer was bland, the wine thin and vinegary.

The two lads tried as usual to pick out the talent, the good-looking women in their Sunday best as they watched them receive communion. Donal's gaze was fixed on an attractive blonde woman, his curiosity getting the better of him. "Who is your one?" he asked, leaning in to get a closer look.

She was tall and willowy, her figure accentuated by the close-fitted cream dress that clung to her curves like a second skin. Her waist seemed impossibly high, and her skirt flowed into gentle folds around her frame, tracing the outline of toned flat stomach she hid beneath the fabric.

"Who?" Sean queried.

"That good-looking tall blonde."

"Oh, she is a fine thing all right, she is the new district nurse, I think. She started last week."

"What is her name?"

"I think she is Donnelly, I'm not sure of her first name," Sean said.

"Do you know if she's married?" Donal asked.

"I'm not sure, but even if she is, that shouldn't be an obstacle for you. It never stopped you before." Sean grinned.

As the mass ended, the parishioners filed out of the church. Seeing the congregation leave, the parish priest raised his hands in benediction and said, "Go in peace, the Lord be with you."

As the parishioners talked and laughed their way out of the church, a soft shaft of afternoon light filtered through the windows and cast a kaleidoscope of colours around the interior. The sound of the last few pews being vacated echoed in sharp staccato bursts against the walls, leaving an empty silence in its wake. A faint smell of incense and wax candles lingered in the air, while outside birdsong trilled cheerfully.

Sean and Donal stood in silence outside, taking in their surroundings as they searched for any clues about the mysterious blonde. The dried communion wafer still lingered on Donal's tongue, a chalky taste that he could not rid himself of. He tried to stifle a cough as he scanned the area for the girl in the creamy white dress, but she seemed to have melted into thin air like a ghost.

Old men stood under a tree in the graveyard and talked about their glory days, playing football and making hay. The April sun shone through the branches of the ash tree they were sheltering under, casting dappled shade like a patchwork quilt. They spoke and laughed with weak voices, their voices cracked and broken by age. Their hands were coarse, their skin wrinkled and folding over their thin arms, their faces seamed with years of sun and hard work, their eyes watery with evidence of cataracts and glaucoma.

Middle aged women stood around in small circles, exchanged the local gossip and cut poor misfortunates to ribbons with their tongues as they tightly clenched their handbags. The women's tongues were sharp and cut with the precision of a surgeon's scalpel. Their words rose and fell like the tide, their voices a wave of feminine anger and resentment as they glared at each other, like cats in a fight. As they spoke, their mouths were hidden behind a hard line of red lipstick. The colour was too bright for everyday wear and its evidence of application was blotchy and uneven. They were mainly women in their forties and fifties, dressed in floral print dresses. Some wore tight white blouses that drew attention to the beads of sweat on their necks and upper lips. Their large bosoms were pushed to the front of their chests and strained against their blouses' buttons. Their brown skirts were pleated and voluminous, to hide the roundness of their hips and the swelling of their posteriors. They wore flesh-coloured tights and sturdy black shoes that were good for chasing cattle that broke out frequently from their bottoms. Their hair was carefully curled under with tongs and curlers. The coven of women smelled of hairspray, with the odd whiff of cheap perfume, but they mainly smelt like cabbage and boiled bacon, the scent coming in waves from all of them.

Children chased each other around the gravestones as their mothers dished the dirt. Their noses ran and streams of green snot dribbled down their chins onto their jumpers as they ran. The children cheered with laughter over something one of them had done, their voices mingling with the shrill gossip of the women.

Sean groaned audibly, a sense of exasperation and disbelief combining to form a single expression. "Holy mother of Christ," he exclaimed in despair, "that was truly a long and painful mass."

Donal agreed wholeheartedly, shaking his head as he sighed. "If it wasn't for my Catholic guilt keeping me rooted to the spot," he lamented wearily, "I would have found some way to make a hasty exit ages ago."

"Oh, look who is coming now, this nosey bastard, Flynn," Sean said as he stamped out his fag on the steps outside the church.

The man approaching Sean and Donal was Tommy Flynn, a cattle dealer, farmer and a general pain in the ass. Tommy Flynn was a small man, not really a dwarf, but not tall either. He had a razor-sharp mind and a weak constitution. He had plenty of money, but his trousers were old and stained with what looked like cow shite and his jumper had a few patches on the elbows. He wore a flat cap, the peak was tattered with age. His homemade walking stick was made of ash taken from the tree that had fallen and knocked his hayshed last November. Despite his appearance, Flynn had a cocksure swagger.

He sauntered over to Sean and Donal and tapped the ash off his fag end to the floor and said amiably, "How are the boys?" Tommy's voice sounded like hard core gravel, his accent thick and demanding. His lips were pursed in a thin line of petulance beyond which they seldom ventured; they stretched tight and thin across his cheeks as if he had bit into an overly ripe lemon. His breath was sour like thick buttermilk, he was a man who people avoided at the bar. He was a bully with pale, soft hands. He was rarely invited to parties.

"Oh hello, Tommy, how's things," Sean muttered as he avoided making eye contact and stared at the ground.

"Sure, I'm only mighty, sure why wouldn't you be on a lovely spring Sunday like we have today?" He glanced up at the sky as a flock of birds flew by and shit down upon the cars in the car park. "It's a great day to be alive," he said with a hint of optimism in his voice. "I think we should make the most of it while we can!"

"You're right, Tommy," Sean agreed, still refusing to meet Tommy's gaze.

"Have ye lads any plans for today?" Tommy enquired.

"No, nothing," Sean said, giving nothing away to the nosey huar.

"And what about you, Donal, my learned friend, our local professor, what are you doing, are you still on Easter holidays? Ye teachers have it feckin handy." Tommy laughed as he slapped Donal on the back.

"You're a gas man, Tommy," Donal said sarcastically. "I could listen to you all day."

Tommy grinned. "A gas man, am I?" He winked playfully at Donal. "Ah sure I'm only having a bit of craic," he said cheerfully, nudging Donal in the side.

"Aye, I know," Donal retorted with a playful eyeroll. "Your humour is second to none."

"Are ye coming down to Gallagher's for a drink, I'll buy the first round," Tommy asked with an expectant smile.

"That will be a first, you tight bastard," Sean whispered to Donal while flashing him a knowing look.

"What was that, Breslin?" Tommy snapped with a furrowed brow.

"Oh, I said that would be grand," Sean muttered sheepishly.

"Come on then, let's make a move. No point standing around here talking shite all day," Tommy said impatiently as he led the way.

"Right, I'll follow you down, Tommy," Sean called after him. "Are you coming, Donal? I don't want to be stuck on my own with that clown," Sean said after Tommy had drifted off.

"I'll give it a miss, I might call in later this evening, I have a few things to do. Will you be out later?" Donal asked.

"I probably will. I'll see you later so, if I don't murder Flynn first and end up in jail." Sean laughed.

Donal smiled wryly and waved as Sean followed Tommy down the street. The last of the parishioners were leaving the churchyard as Donal made his way down the main street of the village. He stopped off in Doherty's shop to grab a paper.

The small interior was packed with locals picking up groceries for their Sunday. Past the rows of food and hardware was a long glass display with various sweets and confectionary. A boy of about ten was standing on a stool and reaching for a packet of biscuits. Sounds of noisy chatter, the rustling of crisp packets and the shifting of shopping bags filled the air. The cashier's fingers tapped loudly against the keyboard of the till, and it rang as it opened before being slammed shut again.

Donal picked up a copy each of the *Sunday Independent* and the *Sunday World* newspapers from the counter. The front page of the *Sunday Independent* was taken up with a black and white photograph of a man in his sixties, standing in front of a large sign and clutching a microphone, circled by the headline 'Jack Lynch opens new hospital ward'. The front page of the *Sunday World* was taken up with a photograph of a young couple, both in their early twenties, their faces blurred and the headline 'Missing Couple Found Dead in Boyfriend's Car'. The *Sunday Independent* was a broadsheet like all broadsheets the world over, it had a serious black and white masthead. Its pages were a little thicker than its competitors. The ink was darker, the paper felt thicker, and more expensive. It has an old-time feel to it, more like it should be read at home on a sofa than sat on a park bench. The *Sunday World* was a tabloid – a small, thin paper, its ink was lighter but more colourful, and the paper had a modern feel, trying to compete with the UK tabloids. More large colour photos of scantily clad young women straddled across the bonnet of shiny new cars peppered its pages. Donal bought the *Sunday World* for the back pages, the sports pages – well that was what he told people, anyway.

Donal took his place in the queue to the till and tried to keep his patience as the shopkeeper, Eddie Doherty, was in deep conversation with a man at the counter. He sighed heavily as he watched the conversation drag on. His gaze shifted to his wristwatch, desperately hoping that the man at the counter would soon be done with whatever it was that was taking up all his time. While waiting he glanced around the store and took in its rather eclectic vibe. The walls were lined with shelves stocked with a variety of goods ranging from antiques to kitchenware, each item carefully chosen and given pride of place in this small, family run shop.

At last the shopkeeper finished with the man, and he moved away from the counter. Donal stepped forward expectantly, only to hear Eddie Doherty start up another conversation with a woman just behind him. She was complaining about her husband's lack of enthusiasm in helping with housework and how difficult it had become to do everything on her own. Donal sighed loudly, trying to catch the shopkeeper's attention, but he seemed oblivious to him standing there.

Eddie Doherty smiled wearily at Donal as he placed his items on the counter; he seemed relieved that his discussion was done for now and gave a slight shake of his head in amusement over how seriously his customer had taken everything they had talked about. He handed Donal his change with an apologetic look before turning to help out another customer who had just entered the shop.

As Donal turned with his papers under his arm, he was surprised to see the blonde lady in the cream dress he had spotted earlier at communion at mass, the woman who according to Sean was a nurse called Donnelly, standing right in front of him.

They both nervously caught each other's eyes.

"Good afternoon, Miss Donnelly, you are very welcome to the area," Donal said, offering her a polite nod. "I'm Donal McCabe."

He waited for her to offer her name in return, the awkwardness of the situation palpable between them.

"Fiona Donnelly," she finally offered after an uncomfortable pause, giving him a slight smile.

"I heard you are our new district nurse," Donal replied.

"That's right, news travels fast."

Donal knew he should say something witty in response. His mind was racing as he tried to think of something appropriately funny or interesting to say but nothing came to him. He finally managed an awkward laugh and gestured towards the papers under his arm before saying, "I'm just off to read up on current events," pointing towards the newspaper under his arm. "So that I can be well informed when discussing them around town."

"Good idea, it's important to know what's going on." Fiona's face lit up with a smile.

"Well, I better get going so, nice to meet you, Fiona. I might see you around."

"Nice to meet you too, Donal."

Donal took a few steps towards the door and then paused for a moment to glance back at Fiona. She was still standing there with her hands clasped in front of her, looking after him. He gave her one last shy smile before quickly turning away and heading out of the shop. As he stepped outside into the bright sunlight, he felt a pang of regret at how inept the conversation had been and cursed himself silently for not being able to think of anything more interesting to talk about. He wished he could've been more charming, witty and engaging, but instead he had stumbled over his words. He kicked a pebble on the ground in frustration as he walked away from the shop, determined to do better next time around.

Chapter 3: Name of the Game

Monday April 24th

Donal returned to the predictable routine of teaching as the days grew longer and brighter and spring gradually gave way to summer. The much-anticipated holidays were drawing near, and he struck off another week on the calendar next to the pot-belly stove in his school classroom. The worn-out, antiquated apparatus was his only hope for warmth on cold, dark winter mornings, but it could be a temperamental beast at times. The ancient contraption was harsh and unforgiving in its illumination, but with enough pleading, it would eventually ignite a feeble flame. It took an eternity to fill the classroom with any warmth, and on a particularly blustery day the weak heat would often be accompanied by a plume of acrid smoke that surged through the room, obscuring sight and making it difficult to breathe. Thankfully, the stove was not needed at present as the days grew warmer.

The classroom was flat and mundane in its décor. Every wall was painted a plain, lifeless green, the only element of visual interest being the handful of bulletin boards, schedules, posters and maps dotted around the room. A clock hung from an exposed wire on the far wall, tocking away steadily as it counted down to break time. The desks were all arranged in neat rows facing a blackboard at one end of the room.

The classroom smelled of old books, glue, paint, chalk dust, smoke, stale socks and soggy sandwiches of butter and red jam and warm milk in badly washed-out brown sauce bottles, in PVC football bags with Man United, Liverpool, or Celtic emblems on the front.

The sounds were myriad and varied, the low and steady hum of children reciting the days of the week and the months of the year in Irish, the shuffle of feet and chairs moving about on the squeaky wooden floor, some sporadic whispering and giggling when the teacher's back was turned. Overall, a cacophony of children all muttering at once, some happy, some sad, some bored, some excited. All watching and listening to the tock of the clock and scrape of the chalk on the board, all waiting for the bell to ring at 3 o'clock, so they were free to kick a football or feed the calves at home.

Donal looked forward to the summer break as it gave him the opportunity to travel abroad and devote some time to his writing. He was still chipping away at his novel, the one he had been working on for the past four years and it was still no nearer to completion. But this summer he vowed that he would finally finish it. He had made the same promise to himself before the Easter holidays and the Christmas holidays, but none had come to fruition.

Ballygorman primary school was a four-teacher school. Donal, the principal, taught the senior classes, 5th and 6th. Anne Cox had her hands full with the infants, Maureen Murray with 1st and 2nd class, and Ciaran Tiernan taking on 3rd and 4th class. At break times they met for tea in Anne's classroom because it was a new, warm and surprisingly well-insulated prefab. Ciaran was rarely there at break time because he was a young, enthusiastic, ambitious teacher and a star county footballer, a mad GAA head who took the boys out football training any spare minute he could get in warm dry weather or in the pissing rain. He said it made men of them.

Anne Cox was reliable, she had the heating turned up and the pot of tea made with the biscuits out on a plate, generally Kerry cream or Mariettas bought with kitty money that the four teachers paid into twice a year, including Ciaran who never ate biscuits.

Anne was a charming woman in her twenties, nothing extraordinary about her though. Her hair had a gentle, auburn sheen that cascaded down to her shoulders in strands, surrounding an angelic face with soft freckles splattered across its surface. She always wore too much perfume which only added to the already pungent odour of Kerry creams and chalk dust that hung heavy in the air. When it came time for tea, she would always drink hers with far too much sugar and milk, giving it a pale and watery colour. She would nervously fiddle as she spoke, her slender fingers brushing her hair away from her face, or absentmindedly playing with a button on the blazer she wore. Her hands were small and soft and delicate like porcelain, yet they seemed devoted only to holding mugs of tea, stroking through her hair, or adjusting her clothing; she never seemed to use them to touch anyone. She had a slender, willowy figure that seemed almost fragile in its construction; delicate sinews and sharp angles concealed beneath her clothes. When she moved, her body shifted seamlessly like a marionette made of twine and plastic bags, the air around her wafting with ethereal grace. Her small frame seemed to contain an insurmountable strength, belying the fragility that seemed so apparent upon first glance.

On the other extreme, Maureen Murray was a short, stocky woman with grey hair and a stern face. Maureen was a formidable figure, her small stature and stocky frame giving her an imposing presence. Her stern face matched her grey hair, which was twisted into a bun atop her head, while brown-framed glasses dangled off her neck. She seemed to be supported solely by the strength of her substantial backside, which pushed against the fabric of the skirt and demanded attention. Her hazel eyes examined everything they encountered with a steady gaze, while the wrinkles around them hinted at years' worth of wisdom.

Maureen was in her mid-fifties and appeared to have seen it all. Her sharp eye for detail and cutting sarcasm could be felt by all in the classroom. In fact, it was often said that she possessed a bottomless pit of sarcasm. Maureen taught with an iron fist, demanding respect from her students. Though strict, she was always fair – requiring hard work and dedication from everyone, but offering praise and encouragement whenever it was deserved.

She openly loathed Donal and continuously attempted to erode his credibility since he had arrived from Monaghan and taken the leading role that she felt she deserved. After all, she had been teaching in Ballygorman national school for three decades and considered herself to be highly qualified for the position. Unfortunately, it was not meant to be, but this did not stop her from trying to undermine him at every turn. The previous principal, Francie Higgins, had promised her that the job was as good as hers and that he would put in a glowing recommendation for her with the board of management before his retirement. Before he could fulfil his promise, however, tragedy struck – Francie had dropped dead of a heart attack in his garden while planting a tree during the summer after he finished teaching. His unexpected death left an empty space to fill, and it wasn't long before Donal McCabe seized the opportunity and swooped into the post. He must have had some serious pull, some powerful connections, Maureen thought to herself; it's not what you know but who you know that matters in this game, that is the name of the game, she constantly reminded herself. Donal was keenly aware of the animosity Maureen felt towards him, he could almost sense the tiny daggers being thrown into his back every time he turned away from her. Though at first she may have masked her disdain with a polite facade, it didn't take long for Donal to realize that the coldness between them was very real.

The chat at the breaktime was generally safe and mundane, occasionally punctuated with some interesting exchanges.

"Ciaran is fantastic when it comes to football training, the boys love him," Maureen said as she took a satisfied bite of her Kerry cream biscuit, clearly aiming a jab at Donal who rarely took the senior boys for football training.

"He is," Donal replied bluntly.

"Look at him out there, such a hardy young lad." Maureen sighed in admiration. "He truly is a credit to the school," she added as she stole a glance over at Anne, whose gaze remained fixed on Ciaran who stood tall and strong, oblivious to the pouring rain. Anne stared out the window in a trance, she clearly had the hots for Ciaran.

"He has the boys in the final this Thursday, fair play to him," Donal said before Maureen could, stealing her thunder.

"What were you doing at the weekend, Anne?" Maureen asked, trying to pull her into the conversation so that she wouldn't have to talk to Donal as much.

"Oh, I had to go home to Tubbercurry for a funeral on Saturday." Anne sighed sadly. "One of my neighbours died, he was old, around seventy-five, I believe. May he rest in peace," Anne said as she made the sign of the cross and offered a brief prayer.

"Was that truly the highlight of your weekend? Attending a funeral?" Maureen shook her head in disbelief.

"I went out Saturday night with some friends in Sligo town. It was a good craic," Anne enthused with a twinkle in her eye.

"Did you go dancing?" Maureen asked as she leaned in eagerly, wanting to hear more.

"Yes, we went to see Gina, Dale Haze and the Champions in the Blue Lagoon. I love them, they are brilliant, they play all the latest pop stuff." Anne smiled.

"Well, don't keep me in suspense," Maureen prodded. "What else happened?"

Anne hesitated for a moment, her brows knitting together as she tried to process Maureen's question. She opened her mouth to reply but no words came out; instead, a confused expression was all that remained on her face. "What do you mean?" she finally managed to say.

Maureen let out a boisterous laugh and said, "Ah, child, did you find yourself a man?"

Anne's cheeks turned an almost luminous shade of beetroot as she coyly retorted, "Now, that would be telling."

"Leave the girl alone, Maureen, what Anne does at the weekend is her own business," Donal chipped in.

"Ah, you be quiet, I'm only having a bit of a laugh, sure I've no excitement in my life, I have to try and live through Anne," Maureen said with a sigh.

"I hear that we have a new district nurse in the area, just started last week," Donal said, changing the subject and fishing for information.

"Yes, that's Fiona all right – she just moved into the house down the road from me in Annaghcarraig. She's a real sweetheart. I had the pleasure of meeting her last Thursday evening when she was out for a stroll," Anne said.

"Did she buy the house?" Donal inquired with a hint of curiosity in his voice.

Anne nodded. "Yes, I think she said she bought it."

Donal thought for a moment before musing aloud, "She must be intending to stay a while so."

"Yes, I suppose so," Anne said as she shrugged her shoulders.

"Has she any kids? Is she married?" Donal inquired as he swallowed the last mouthful of his mug of tea.

"Why are you so interested in her, Donal?" Anne responded with a mischievous grin, her eyes twinkling in the low light of the room. Her tone was playful as if trying to tease out some secret from him.

Donal shifted nervously in his seat, and as he was about to answer the bell to sound the end of small break rang. He breathed a sigh of relief as it sounded, signalling him to escape this embarrassing moment.

Taking one final glance around the room, he muttered, "Best get back to class, I suppose," and quickly made his way towards the door.

Chapter 4: Supernature

Friday April 28th

Donal eagerly anticipated his favourite hour of the week: 3 pm on a Friday afternoon. As his school week wound to an end, he gathered some copies from his desk to correct over the long bank holiday weekend and placed them in his well-worn brown leather satchel. He greeted Mrs. McGuinness, who had just arrived to tidy up the classrooms, with a hearty smile, talked about the great stretch in the evening, and then made his way out the school gate to his car with a wide smile across his face as he felt the warm sun on his back.

Taking the keys out of his brown corduroy trousers, he unlocked the driver's door and flung his jacket and satchel on the front passenger seat of his sky-blue Fiat Mirafiori, complete with 1.6 litre, twin cam engine, and five-speed gearbox. The car was his pride and joy, he only bought it new in January and he was still like a kid with a new toy.

He drove his short half-mile journey home to the quiet outskirts of town. The Fiat, its engine noisily rumbling, crept up the brown gravel driveway to his house, a large 19th-century manse that had previously been owned by a Presbyterian minister, a ruddy-faced, whisky-drinking figure of authority who had long since passed away. The house was imposing and suitably aged with white stone walls and an ivy-strewn facade that commanded respect.

The manse towered majestically, its roof capped in black slate tiles. It had four tall chimneys, gothic arches and large windows with shutters that when opened let daylight pour in. A wide white door with a brass knocker welcomed visitors onto the large porch, which was ensconced by two grand grey Romanesque pillars on either side; it spoke of character and timeless elegance. Inside, the manse was a sight to behold. Ornate cornices lined the ceiling and stained-glass windows adorned the walls, letting in colourful beams of light. Antique furniture filled the room, with velvet-covered chairs providing comfort and luxurious carpets giving it an air of opulence. In the centre of this grandeur stood a large stone fireplace with striking religious iconography on its mantle – a testament to the previous owner's faith in his Lord.

The grounds surrounding the manse were meticulously tended to, with a sweeping expanse of an emerald green lawn and neat flower beds interspersed here and there. The gardens themselves were filled with lush vegetation of all shapes and colours, from brilliant blooms to rich foliage. Scattered throughout the garden stood proud oak trees, their gnarled roots running deep into the earth, giving the property a sense of grandeur and charm. Donal had paid an exorbitant price for the house four years ago which he covered with a hefty mortgage, but he believed that it was worth it.

After making himself some dinner in the large kitchen, Donal made his way up the mahogany staircase to his bedroom, where he removed his school clothes and put on a blue O'Neill's tracksuit and a pair of trainers. He decided to make the best of the long bright sunny evening and go for a run on the beach to get some fresh air and exercise.

Fifteen minutes later he had arrived at the small car park next to Tullan strand in County Donegal. Surprisingly in that short time, the weather had changed dramatically, and heavy rain-filled clouds were sailing in from the West.

"Bloody typical April weather, four seasons in one day, ah well, best get moving before the rain comes." Donal sighed to himself as he locked his car and made his way down the steps to the long sandy beach. The strand was deserted and he had the place to himself, just what he wanted. After doing a few stretches, Donal began to jog slowly, running parallel to the sea.

After five minutes he gradually increased his pace to a full sprint, pushing himself to stay at that intensity for another five minutes. Donal was in excellent shape for his age, but even so, he could feel the fatigue beginning to set in as he neared forty years of age. His lungs were burning and he came to a stop, turning around towards the sea to allow some cool ocean air to rush inside him as he stood gazing out towards the horizon. He watched the dark stratus clouds hover ominously overhead, forming a grey blanket across the sky. The clouds were in an angry tumble, a turbulent pattern that threatened to blot out the sun. With every passing second they appeared to grow darker and more agitated, forming profound shapes that were both menacing and beautiful in equal measure. The sky was laced with tension, he felt the storm's power hover over him like an unwanted omen of events to come. The muddled haze of the sun and sky created a silhouette against the bright sandy beach, the clouds cast an eerie blanket of dark shadows across the sandy shore, and the menacing and eerie shadows stretched out like a web, intertwining and merging with one another.

The air was thick with the smell of rain and briny moist sea air, a light drizzle of rain already beginning to fall, and he could feel the cool drops on his warm face – they felt good. The wind was picking up, carrying with it a low rumble of thunder in the distance as the storm clouds crept closer to the headland. The dull roar of the sea could be heard in the distance as the crashing waves reached the shore with white foam crested atop them. The close arms of looming clouds and rain seemed to emanate an ancient and fathomless loathing, as if Mother Nature herself were vengefully unleashing her ancient fury upon the world below. A loathing that stretched outward and shrouded everything beneath its maladroit shadow.

Donal became aware of the dwindling amount of time he had before being drenched in the rain, so he was determined to go for one final jog before calling it a day. As he spun around, with his back facing the endless expanse of ocean stretching out towards the horizon and beyond, something caught his eyes in the distance. Hanging under a brooding sky was a figure walking along an isolated stretch by the shoreline. He scrunched up his face and squinted, carefully studying the figure in front of him, trying to distinguish whether it was a man or a woman. Suddenly it dawned on him that it was none other than Jane Donnelly.

"Of all the chances," Donal whispered to himself as he made his way towards her.

"Hi, Jane, remember me from the shop last Sunday, I'm Donal McCabe."

Jane smiled and replied warmly, "Oh, hi Donal, how are you, out for a run I see."

He nodded and pointed to the sky. "Sure, but it looks like it's going to pelt it down with rain very shortly."

"Yes, it got very dark all of a sudden, such a pity, it was a lovely day," Fiona said with regret in her voice.

"It's always gorgeous when you are stuck inside at work." Donal sighed.

"That is always the way. Do you come for a run here regularly?" Fiona inquired.

"A couple of times a week, if the weather allows me," Donal said as he gazed up at the sky.

"This is only my second time here myself, it's a beautiful beach, isn't it," Fiona said as she scanned the shoreline.

"It is, I love this place," Donal agreed. "By the way, how are you settling into your new job and the area, Ballygorman is a quiet spot."

"Oh, I love it here, a big change from Dublin, where I was based for nearly ten years." Fiona nodded with enthusiasm in reply.

"What part of Dublin did you live in? I'm going to take a guess, was it Rathmines or Drumcondra?" Donal inquisitively asked.

"Yes, Rathmines, how did you know?" Fiona responded with a smile.

"Well, because everybody from the country lives in Rathmines or Drumcondra, and you haven't a Dublin accent, sounds to be from the West, Galway, or Mayo, maybe."

"Actually, it's Clare, close to County Galway. Well done, Sherlock!" Fiona playfully laughed as Donal smiled proudly at his deduction.

"When you have it, you have it," he replied. Changing the topic, he asked, "Any plans for the weekend? Are you heading home to Clare anytime soon?"

Fiona shook her head and said, "Oh no, I'm staying here for the weekend. I'm already planning a trip to Kilkenny for next weekend, so I will take it easy this weekend and relax, recharge the batteries."

Donal paused for a moment, considering his next words carefully. "I was wondering," he finally said, voice soft and hesitant, "if you had no other plans, would you like to go and see a film tonight at the Cinema in Sligo?" His cheeks grew hot and pink as he awaited her response.

Fiona was slow to reply as Donal glanced downwards, his feet toying with the wet sand that had collected around his trainers. He felt the weight of her gaze but kept his head bowed, avoiding eye contact. Suddenly her voice pierced through the silence like a ray of light. "Oh, okay," she said softly, "that sounds good – what film is on?"

Donal looked up hesitantly and caught her gaze before quickly looking away again. "I'm not sure, I think *Saturday Night Fever* is still running. Have you gone to see it already?" Donal was relieved that Fiona hadn't rejected his offer.

"No, I'd love to see it, John Travolta is easy on the eye, and I love the Bee Gees music. I have the soundtrack album at home. I have it nearly worn out playing it," Fiona said.

"Travolta doesn't do much for me, but he is a hell of a dancer. I'll admit that," Donal said with a slight smirk on his lips. "So do you want me to pick you up around seven?"

"Do you know where I live?" Fiona asked.

Donal didn't want to admit that he did, because it might sound creepy. "If you give me directions I'm sure I can find it, Ballygorman is a small place."

"Let's meet outside the church at seven, is that okay, does that suit you?" Fiona suggested.

"Sounds good to me, okay, I better get home and get out of this tracksuit. Have you a car? Be careful you don't get wet, the rain isn't too far away."

"Yes, my car is just up in the car park, I'll have a quick walk and head back in a few minutes. See you later, Donal," Fiona said as she smiled and turned to walk on down the beach.

Donal strutted back to his car with a spring in his step and anticipation in his heart. He got into the car, revved up the engine, and headed off on the winding roads that led home to Ballygorman. As he drove along, Donal kept replaying Fiona's smile in his mind over and over again. All of a sudden, the sky opened up and a rainstorm started to pour. The roads were slick and visibility was low, causing Donal to slow down his driving.

He finally arrived back at his home. It was just gone 5.30 so he went to the airing cupboard, switched on the immersion, and waited for the water to heat up for a bath. While he waited, he cleaned up the kitchen. Donal liked everything neat and well-ordered. The yellow walls were adorned with colourful plates, each containing a picture from various countries around the world. In one corner there was an enormous refrigerator humming cheerfully like it held some secret that only it knew about. A bowl of ripe fruit sat on the counter and copper pots lined the windowsill in orderly rows. It seemed like everything here had its place and purpose.

After a soak in the bath and a shave, he changed into a crisp white shirt, black trousers and his best leather shoes. He sprayed on cologne and went downstairs and grabbed an umbrella from the hallstand. As Donal opened the front door, he could smell the rain coming in from outside. He sighed and stepped out into the wet evening air that was warm and muggy.

With an umbrella offering some protection from the rain, Donal trudged through puddles on his way to his Fiat car. The engine rumbled to life and with wipers dancing erratically against the driving rain, he pulled off. He arrived at the church car park at two minutes to seven. A red car was parked at the gates which Donal presumed was Fiona's.

She stepped out of her car the moment she saw his vehicle pull up. Without a pause, he quickly opened his door and raced towards her with an umbrella in hand. His heart skipped a beat as she smiled at him warmly and he proudly tucked the umbrella above them both before escorting her back to his car.

Climbing into the car, they set off towards the cinema in Sligo as the rain continued to pour down heavily, flooding the streets with water. Donal drove cautiously, his gaze cast ahead of him – always on alert for any deep floods that could cause them to become stuck or risk losing control of the vehicle. Ahead of them lay a washed-out landscape, streetlights reflecting off slick pavements as they forged their path through.

By the time twenty minutes had passed, they had reached Sligo and parked along the street outside the Ritz cinema. A long line of people had formed outside, in eager anticipation to get a seat inside for one of the most popular films of the year so far. Fortunately, the rain had eased up so Donal could leave the umbrella behind in the car. It took ten minutes to get to the top of the queue and reach the ticket office. Donal paid and they made their way inside to the small one-screen cinema.

The Ritz had an outdated feel to it with its "classic" decor from the 1940s, the decade it was built in. It had clearly never been upgraded since. The walls were adorned with yellowing and torn wallpaper that displayed faded images of classic Hollywood stars and vintage movie posters. The floors were covered in worn-out and sticky carpets, soaked from a multitude of spilled cokes and orange minerals. The seats lined up in neat rows with worn, threadbare and uncomfortable cushions, destroyed by the arses of punters for the last thirty years.

As soon as they stepped in, the unmistakable stench of musty carpet, damp, mildew, popcorn and puffs of cigarette smoke hung in the air and filled their nostrils. You could almost smell the many years that had gone by within its hallowed walls.

As Donal and Fiona took their seats, the air crackled with anticipation as they waited for the lights to dim and the trailers to roll onto the screen. The sound of shuffling feet could be heard as stragglers made their way to their seats, along with the constant opening and banging of the main door. When the door opened there was a loud sound of laughter and chatter from the lobby area, with the rustling of popcorn and crisp bags accompanied by the clinking of glass Coca-Cola bottles.

The theatre was enveloped in darkness and the atmosphere grew expectant as a reverential hush descended upon the patrons. On the screen, the trailers started to play, their harsh colours and dazzling visuals popping up against the black backdrop, enticing the audience to visit again in the near future. The projection booth was nestled away at the back of the theatre. It had a single projector that, with its whirring and clicking, cast an ever-shifting mass of flickering images onto the screen.

As the main feature of *Saturday Night Fever* began, Fiona was instantly entranced by John Travolta on screen. Her face lit up with an endearing smile as she watched the movie for the next two hours. For Donal, his battle to keep his eyes open was real but he found joy in seeing Fiona wholly absorbed in the show. He marvelled at her engagement and allowed himself to take part in her enthusiasm for a few moments before drifting back into a state of contented relaxation.

When the movie had finally finished, they made their way outside onto the street. The sky had turned dark, and a light breeze blew through, carrying with it the musky aroma of damp earth and petrichor.

"I love your car, Donal; by the way, it's new, is it?"

"Yes, I've have it only a few months," Donal said with pride as he held the passenger door open for Fiona. "I try to give it a wash and clean out every weekend."

"You keep it well."

"You enjoyed the film, you were glued to it," Donal said as he started up the car and turned up the heater to defog the window.

"Oh, it was brilliant, wasn't it, John Travolta is fabulous."

"Yes, it was good, I liked it," Donal replied with feigned enthusiasm.

"Thank you so much for bringing me, Donal, I really enjoyed myself, hope my singing along to the Bee Gee songs wasn't too annoying, I know all the words off by heart."

"You have a beautiful voice," Donal said.

"Do you think so? I'm sure you're just teasing me," Fiona responded, blushing as she averted her gaze.

"I'm being serious," Donal replied with a genuine smile, still gazing at her fondly. He could tell that Fiona was somewhat embarrassed by the compliment and he admired her for it.

"Look, I had a great time, do you fancy meeting up again, maybe tomorrow night if that suits you, we could go for a drink," Donal suggested eagerly.

"Sorry, I can't do tomorrow night, some of the girls from work have asked me out to go to a dance with them."

"Oh, that's okay, no problem," Donal replied, feeling somewhat deflated.

Fiona hesitated for a moment before responding. "But I could meet you maybe on Sunday evening for a while if you want to go for a drink or two."

"That sounds good! I'll look forward to it," Donal replied with enthusiasm.

Twenty minutes later, Donal brought his car to a halt beside the looming iron gates of the church in Ballygorman, where Fiona's vehicle was parked. He waited until she got inside her car and drove away into the night. As her taillights faded off into the distance, his mind raced with possibilities about what Sunday night would bring.

Chapter 5: Hit me with your Rhythm Stick

Later that night

Trying to make love in the back seat of a Morris Minor took some doing, but Sean Breslin was doing fine. In fact, he was going hammer and tongs at it. The woman fortunate or unfortunate to be underneath him was Lizzy O'Dowd, a lady in her early forties who had a fine reputation for being amiable, bendable and generally all-around accommodating. Sean was just in his full stride and was approaching the finishing line, like Lester Piggott on Nijinsky.

"Go easy, will you, slow down for fuck sake," Lizzy groaned.

"It's full speed ahead now, Lizzy, I'm in top gear and I have a bad hand brake," Sean replied, trying to keep focused on the job in hand.

"Take it handy, it will be over before you know it."

"Oh, Jasus." Sean let out a long, slow exhale as he pulled himself back and tried to pull up his sagging white Y fronts.

"Is that it, have you finished already? That didn't take long," Lizzy inquired with a hint of annoyance in her voice. Her words hung in the air as he sat upright on the seat.

"That would be that," Sean said with a satisfied smirk and a sniff as he reached down and tucked his shirt into his pants before he zipped up his fly.

"Charming as ever, Sean," Lizzy said with a wry smile as she watched her partner with amusement in her eyes.

"Thanks, Lizzy, would you like a fag?" Sean said, extending his hand towards her with an open palm containing a single cigarette.

"Hold on a minute," Lizzy said as she began to cover herself up.

The pair sat quietly for five minutes in the back of Lizzy's Morris Minor and savoured their smoke. Sean and Lizzy had maintained a causal relationship for the last few years that seemed to suit them both. Neither of them appeared to take it seriously and got together whenever they felt like it. They never discussed their relationship or discussed if they wanted to change the arrangement. They were content to go with the flow.

Sean broke the silence. "It turned out a grand dry night after all that rain earlier this evening." He reached out and rubbed the condensation on the window next to him, staring out at the dark landscape.

"Aye, it did," Lizzy said as she blew out a ring of smoke.

Sean had met Lizzy earlier in Gallagher's pub and one thing led to another and they ended up driving out to the car park next to Lough Melvin. The car park was a quiet and secluded spot and a popular place for courting couples at weekends. Lizzy knew it well.

Lizzy had long, dark hair that cascaded over her shoulders, a round face and wide hazel eyes that sparkled with life. She was an older woman, but that only added to her graceful beauty. Her skin was smooth and creamy, and her lips were full and inviting. She wore a pale blue dress that hugged her curves in all the right places and accentuated her milky white skin. Despite her petite frame, she was strong and supple. She had an inviting presence that would draw people in with her charm, good humour and warmth. Lizzy O'Dowd smelled of jasmine and honeysuckle, with a hint of warm vanilla, but mostly she smelled of gin and fags.

Lizzy had been married for ten years but her husband, John, was killed in a farm accident five years ago. There were lots of rumours circulating at the time that he had been rough with Lizzy at times and that she was glad to see the back of him. John was a possessive and jealous type, and always thought that his wife was too flirty with other men whenever he brought her dancing. This jealousy would often boil over into bitter rows. Rumours circulated in Ballygorman when John passed away that he had stumbled home from the pub one night and found his wife in bed with another man. Although these whispers may have been unfounded, it caused consternation within the community at the time.

"How about we go grab a bag of chips? If we hurry, I think we can just make it to McDonagh's chipper before they close." Sean posed the suggestion to his companion as he glanced at his wristwatch; the enthusiasm was palpable in his voice as he anticipated their upcoming treat.

"Sean, you must have been reading my mind!" Lizzy exclaimed with a hearty laugh. "You know exactly how to show a girl a good time," she said sarcastically.

"I do my best," he assured her with a wink and a smile, feeling his chest swell with pride.

"Come on, let's go then," Lizzy said as she climbed into the driver's seat, her backside hitting Sean in the face as she manoeuvred.

After gorging on two bags of soggy chips doused in salt and drenched in vinegar, Lizzy and Sean made their separate ways home. However, before parting ways they arranged to meet up for a drink again the following night.

Sean drove his canary yellow Ford Escort car out of Ballygorman and travelled the two miles to his home. He drove into the yard at the side of the house. The car was battered and badly dinged. Its exhaust was blown and one of the front headlights was gone. Something else that Sean couldn't afford to get fixed. He finished eating the last of his chips, rolled the bag into a ball and flung it behind him onto the back seat along with all of the other rubbish that was on it.

He shared a farmhouse with his younger brother Derek and his mother Eileen. The two storey farmhouse had a sturdy, old-fashioned charm, typical of one built in the 1920s. A small overgrown garden hugged the house like an embrace. A path lined with rusty iron railings lay like a sacred river around its circumference. The dwelling had whitewashed walls and a red tiled sloping roof long weathered by the elements, by years of wind and rain. The windows were all framed in black, and the doorway was inviting with a small porch leading into the house. Inside the house, the main living area was rustic but homely. It was spacious but sparsely decorated. It had a large parlour with a tall marble-topped fireplace; this was the good room that nobody ever sat in. It had a kitchen which was bright and airy, with an old-fashioned Stanley range. Eileen showed off her best delph and china in the dresser on the wall next to the door. The floor of the hallway was wooden, and the staircase was wide and sturdy.

Upstairs there were four bedrooms, one each for Sean and Derek, and one for their mother. A spare room was kept clean, tidy and prepared for any relatives that came to stay from America. However, none had stayed in twenty years or more. Overall, everything about the house seemed to speak to another time long since forgotten.

Sean's father, Michael, had passed away when Sean was only sixteen. It left Sean as the man of the house and he had worked in vain ever since to make a decent living from the thin stony soil of the land. A land that was hard and unforgiving. It appeared to be purposefully defying his life itself. He had kept twenty-five head of cattle up until last summer, but his flock had been decimated by TB. He was literally hanging on now by his fingernails to pay the bills. He frequently thought about emigrating, but he was plagued by guilt at the thought of giving up on the sixty acre farm that his father and worked so hard to build up.

Life had been a never ending challenge for Sean and his spirit was often tested, but he remained unyielding, never putting his grievances on display and plodding along every day with an unwavering relentless work ethic as if nothing else mattered in the world. He could be found in the fields working tirelessly from sunup to sundown – a true testament to his strength of will.

He tip-toed in through the back door of the house, his feet barely making a sound as he crept up the stairs. The wooden steps groaned ever so slightly under his weight. He moved stealthily, careful to not disturb his mother who was sleeping in her room. Eventually he reached his bedroom and opened the door carefully, letting it close slowly behind him and allowing himself to relax a bit as he stepped inside and pulled the door shut gently. His bed welcomed him, and he snored away until eight the next morning.

Derek, who toiled away in the fish factory of Killybegs during the week, returned home for the weekends. Without fail, each Saturday he'd offer his brother a helping hand tending to the various chores and repairs on their family farm. On this particular Saturday, both Sean and Derek were out in the field right next to the house, fixing up some broken fencing that had been neglected for far too long. It was almost May. Soon what was left of their herd would be grazing on the summer grass. As they worked diligently throughout the day, they could feel the approach of the longer and warmer days ahead and the hope of better days to come.

"Well, that's it done," Sean exclaimed as he picked up his claw hammer from the damp grass and stretched his aching back, sore from hours of bending over the fence.

"Thank God for that and thankfully the rain kept off," Derek remarked in relief.

"It would be a bitch of a job if it was raining," Sean said as he surveyed the field.

"There was some feckin rain last night. I thought I wouldn't get home with the floods on the road."

"You have a brutal drive from Killybegs," Sean said solemnly as he started on his way towards the house.

"Tell me about it. I was on the road for ages last night, it must have taken me close to two and a half hours to get here." Derek moaned.

"Any craic in Killybegs?" Sean asked, the words tumbling out of his mouth as if he was desperate to get an answer. "Were you and Sharon out much during the week?"

"I was out a few nights!" Derek replied, a hint of excitement in his voice as he recalled the events of recent days.

"How long are you going out with her now?" Sean inquired.

"Two years last Christmas," Derek replied after some thought.

"Really, you must bring her up for a weekend; I'd like to meet her."

"I'm not sure about that, it might be a bad idea," Derek warned.

"Why do you think that?" Sean asked, his lips pursing in confusion as he marched up the sprawling hill towards the house, his breathing becoming heavier with each step. He glanced over at Derek with an inquisitive expression, waiting for a response.

"You know why," Derek spoke up, halting his older brother in his tracks.

Sean stopped walking and turned to face Derek. "No, I don't know, what are you on about?"

"Her religion," Derek replied simply.

"What about her religion?" Sean said, raising his eyebrows.

"She is a Protestant."

"So what?" Sean replied in a dismissive tone.

Derek let out a heavy sigh as he looked up at the house, taking in the area surrounding it. "Well, you know how some people are around here," he said softly, his brows furrowing with worry. "Mammy might not take too kindly to it." His gaze shifted from the house to the field and back again.

"Ah, fuck them," came the response of his confidant. "You do what you want, fuck all of them. If you like Sharon and you get on well together, what does Religion matter, what does it matter what religion you are or Sharon is, it doesn't matter. The people around here are all feckin hypocrites; they would smile in your face as they stab you in the back."

“What about Mother, how would she take it?” Derek inquired tentatively.

“She would be fine; she’d be more understanding than you give her credit for,” Sean replied confidently. “Our mother is not as conservative as you might think, she has a mind of her own. As Dylan said, the times are a changing, forget about all that nonsense about Catholics and Protestants not going out together. It’s all-out dated rubbish, it belongs in the past, and it’s time we moved on.”

"Maybe you are right," Derek muttered.

"I am right, Derek," Sean replied, patting his younger brother's shoulder. He had taken up the mantle of a parental figure since their father had passed away all those years ago. It had been a difficult transition for both of them, as there was still an emptiness that consumed them all these years later. Sean vowed to always be by his little brother's side and offer as much help and guidance as he could.

“Thanks, Sean.”

“Don’t waste your life like I did. If Sharon is a nice girl and you get on well, try and make a go of it, make a good and happy life for yourself.”

After eating a feed of bacon and cabbage that Eileen had prepared for the two lads, Sean took a look up at the clock on the kitchen wall.

“Well, it’s gone five, I think I’ll have a wash.”

“The water is boiling, I can hear the pipes rattling behind the range,” Eileen said.

“Great,” Sean said with enthusiasm as he rose from the kitchen table. “I'm going to take a nice hot bath and then head into town.”

"You're off to town awfully early, Sean." He could feel his mother's eyes on him as she replied.

"It's never too early for a pint, Derek. Are you coming in for one?" Sean asked with a mischievous grin.

Derek shook his head slowly, feeling exhausted. "Nah, I'm good," he replied wearily.

"Lightweight!" Sean laughed as he patted Derek on the back playfully.

“I left a clean and ironed shirt, trousers, socks and underwear on your bed,” Eileen said.

“Thanks, Ma,” Sean said as he kissed her on the cheek.

Chapter 6: Is she really going out with him.

Saturday April 29th

It was just gone seven and Sean was taking a large mouthful of his third pint of stout in Gallagher's pub. Next to him sat Paddy Farrell, a former classmate of Sean's when they both went to Ballygorman School together back in the fifties. Paddy was now a road sweeper for the council.

Paddy Farrell was a short, stocky man with a round, fat face. His eyes were warm and kind, with a twinkle of mischief in them when he chuckled. On top of his balding head he wore a scruffy-looking tweed cap which he rarely took off; he probably wore it in bed. His attire was completed by a sweat-stained white shirt, a brown cardigan covered in oil, grease and general dust and dirt, loose-fitting grey trousers and a pair of Wellingtons. His hands were calloused, his shoulders broad and sturdy from years of manual labour.

Paddy smelled of the outdoors, the damp earth, the exhaust from passing cars, farts and cigarette smoke. There was something comforting about him that spoke of an honest life. Everybody liked Paddy Farrell, most especially the publicans of Ballygorman.

"You are letting them down fast tonight, Sean, you have a right thirst on you," Paddy said as he lit a fag.

"I'm going at them easy enough," Sean replied as he took another swig of his pint.

"It's early yet lad, it's a long night yet," Paddy said.

Sean shrugged, finished the pint in one large gulp and signalled towards Joe Gallagher for another. Joe, the landlord of Gallagher's pub was fond of Sean and Derek. They were his best customers. He kept them in free pints whenever he could. "Here you are, Sean, same again, I had two settling for you," Joe said as he served up pints of stout for the two lads. Sean nodded and raised the fresh pint to his lips. He looked around the pub. Most of the regulars had settled in and it was beginning to fill up. He caught sight of another familiar face near the back of the pub. His cousin Jim Kelly had come in with a few other friends.

Sean waved to him and raised his pint in greeting. "Jim! Great to see you," he shouted over the noise of the crowd, but Jim didn't hear him or pretended that he didn't and continued on with whatever conversation he had been having. "Stuck up bastard." Sean shrugged and turned back to his pint.

"That cousin of yours has done well for himself. I heard that he has twenty men working for him now. He just got some big contract to build a new extension to a school in Sligo I heard," Paddy remarked with a sense of awe in his voice.

"He is a big-headed fucker, that is what he is, he is a Kelly, they think their shite is chocolate. They always thought that they were better than us. His father always said that my mother could have done much better for herself than marrying a Breslin," Sean replied with disdain.

"Ah, forget about them, they are a bunch of eejits," Paddy said, trying to console his friend. “Your father was a pure gentleman and a hard worker, he built that farm of yours up from nothing, God rest his soul.”

Sean nodded and took a swig from his porter, feeling a mix of sadness and admiration when remembering his father’s achievements; his father had worked hard all his life and died young due to a heart attack.

Paddy knew that he was thinking about him and tried to change the subject. “You should come with me and Liam tomorrow, to the horse races in Galway. It will be a good day’s craic,” he said with enthusiasm.

After some consideration Sean responded. “I suppose I could come, I haven’t been to the races in a while. We could make a day of it.”

Paddy smiled and slapped his friend on the back. “That's settled then! You can drive us there in your lovely yellow Escort car!”

"Where is your car?" Sean inquired.

"Oh, it's in for a service," Paddy replied. "I think the brakes weren't working properly, so it was best to get them looked at."

"And what about Liam's car?"

Paddy uttered a sigh of disgust and shook his head. "He went and wrapped the bloody car around a tree on the way home from the pub last Wednesday night. Can you believe it? It’s a pure right off.”

Sean sighed and shook his head. “So what you really want is a driver.”

Paddy laughed heartily and said, “Aye, that’s about it. Now what do you say?”

Sean smiled and said, “Okay.”

“Great stuff.” Paddy grinned. “We have to leave early in the morning, around ten, so go easy on the pints so.”

Sean nodded and said, “No problem.”

“Lovely, I’ll just go to the jacks so,” Paddy said as he got up from his seat and headed towards the gent’s toilets.

Sean watched him go then looked down at his pint. He smiled to himself.

“Well, Sean how are you keeping?” A man’s voice sounded next to him.

Sean slowly turned around; it was his cousin, Jim Kelly.

Jim was a tall, broad-shouldered man with dark hair and a moustache. His face was tanned and handsome. He modelled himself on the Hollywood actor, Burt Reynolds. He had an air of authority around him, and his bearing spoke of a confidence that couldn't be faked. His clothing, a denim shirt and flared jeans were neat, if a little outdated, and his deep blue eyes were full of life and keen and watchful. He has a slightly sardonic smile that hinted at a hidden sense of humour.

"Jim, how's things?" Sean asked.

"Things are going great," Jim said. "I'm flat out with the building work," he added, a look of pride etched into his face.

"That's fantastic, I'm delighted for you. Not too many men could say that at the moment," Sean exclaimed.

"You get what you work for in this life, Sean, as my father always says."

"Oh yes, of course." Sean nodded in agreement. "How is Uncle Peter getting on now?"

"He's flying it, like a young fella," Jim said, admiration infusing his voice.

"That's fantastic, he must be pushing sixty now," Sean responded with a small smile tugging at the corners of his mouth.

"He will turn fifty-eight in August. He has his hands full with the farm, milking one hundred cows and adding another seventy acres of land to his holdings just last month," Jim stated.

"Say hello for me," Sean suggested.

"I will! I must remind him that he needs to come down and pay a visit to your mother at some point soon," Jim replied.

"She would love that," Sean said sarcastically but it went over Jim's head, he was too busy admiring himself in the mirror across the bar.

"Is your mother keeping well?" Jim asked.

"Yes, not too bad, getting a bit stiff with rheumatism," Sean replied.

"Is she getting treatment for it?"

"Yes, she is on tablets."

"Are you just farming now, Sean, or have you a part-time job as well. That farm of yours would hardly support you and Aunty Eileen," Jim said, getting the dig in.

Sean knew it was only a matter of time. "We are doing fine Jim, thanks."

"There is no money in farming unless you are in it in a big way, it's a waste of time otherwise," Jim asserted with certainty.

"You would be surprised."

"Really, what would your turnover be in the year?"

"Enough," Sean said as he took a large swallow of his pint.

"You could be as well to sell it, Sean, there is no money in it, only hardship. If you ever wanted a job, don't be afraid to give me a phone call," Jim said as he placed a business card on the counter that said Kelly Building Services on its heading.

Sean looked down at it. His instincts told him to rip it up and tell Jim to stick it up his arse, but for the sake of his mother he just muttered, "Thanks."

"Right, I'll head back over to the lads, can I get you a pint?" Jim queried.

"I'm fine, I'm heading off soon," Sean said, shaking his head.

"Okay, good luck, Sean," Jim said as he turned and crossed the floor to the group of men he had been previously talking to.

"Well did I miss anything? I got talking to James Murray in the toilet, he is a complete and utter bollocks, but fierce craic, he told me that he is doing a line now with, yer one, Lizzy O'Dowd. He said that she is a fierce one to go, he calls over to her a few times a week," Paddy Farrell said as he took his seat again on the stool next to Sean.

"Really," Sean replied as he remembered he was supposed to meet Lizzy later. Thinking of her with James Murray was turning him off the idea.

"James must be fucking over sixty," Sean said as he lifted his pint to empty it.

"He would be," Paddy affirmed.

"He is a married man with grown-up children," Sean added.

"And what's more, he's a bloody granddad." Paddy chuckled, shaking his head in amusement.

"Jesus Christ, I need another pint," Sean said as he looked towards Joe

Gallagher behind the bar.

"You look agitated, Sean, what's up, are you jealous of James?" Paddy joked.

"I don't give a fuck," Sean said, but in truth, he did feel let down, he actually liked Lizzy and he half hoped that they might make a go of things. "Ah, that cousin of mine, Jim, came over when you went to the toilet, he was blowing as usual, he would make your blood boil."

"Don't worry about him, come on, we will have two half ones," Paddy said before he asked Joe Gallagher for two shots of Power's whiskey.

Sean and Paddy continued to drink on and the clock that tocked on the wall was soon pointing towards 10 o'clock. A three-piece band had set up in the corner of the bar, a typical Irish pub band, playing the "best of Country and Irish", plenty of Larry Cunningham covers and watered-down American country hits. Most of the punters in Gallagher's enjoyed them.

The bar door opened, and the pretty face of Lizzy O'Dowd walked in. Paddy turned around. "Speak of the devil, look, the woman we were talking about earlier, the bold Lizzy has just walked in, and doesn't she look well. I didn't realise that you could buy a skirt that short," he said, a cheeky grin on his face.

Sean didn't raise his head to look at her.

"I wonder will she have the neck to go over to sit beside James Murray." Paddy kept a close eye on her, as did almost every other man in the bar.

"Jesus, she is coming this way," Paddy said, his eyes widening as he spoke.

Lizzy made her way across the bar and ignored all the eyes that were watching her. She stopped, lit a fag, looked around and then continued to walk towards Sean and Paddy.

"Well boys, are ye in town long?" Lizzy asked.

"A while," Paddy said, not giving much away.

"There is a good crowd in here tonight, all the seats are gone."

Paddy took the hint and got up from his stool. "Would you like a seat, Lizzy?"

"Thanks, Paddy, you are a gentleman," Lizzy said as she got up on the barstool and blew a ring of cigarette smoke across the bar.

For a moment Paddy was transfixed, staring at Lizzy's legs in the short grey skirt that was practically stuck to her. She caught him looking and he turned quickly away, red-faced.

"Can you see enough, Paddy?" Lizzy said with a cheeky laugh.

"Will you have a drink, Lizzy?" Paddy asked trying to repair the damage.

"Thanks, Paddy, I'll have a Gordon's gin and tonic, please."

"Right, no problem," Paddy replied as he turned towards the bar to order the drink.

Sean kept staring down at his pint.

"You are very quiet, Sean Breslin, it's not like you. What's up?" Lizzy asked.

"Oh, hi Lizzy," Sean said pretending that he hadn't noticed her coming in.

"Nice to see you too," Lizzy said sarcastically.

"How were you after last night, did you get up to much today?" Lizzy asked, trying to ignite a conversation.

"Grand, did a bit of tidying up around home."

"Jesus, this is like pulling hens' teeth, what's up with you, I usually can't get you to shut up," Lizzy said with a frown.

"Nothing is up, can a man not be quiet, once in a while," Sean said, still avoiding making eye contact.

Paddy returned with the Gin and tonic and placed it in front of Lizzy. "Here you are, Lizzy, get that into you."

"Thanks, Paddy, you are a real pet," Lizzy said as she gave him a kiss on the cheek.

Paddy felt embarrassed, he felt awkward around women and looked around him for another stool, but they were all taken. He spotted a few lads standing next to the fireplace and decided to go over and join them for a while. Lizzy turned back to Sean; he was still staring at the pint of stout and still hadn't looked up. She knew something was wrong but decided to leave it at that, she wouldn't pressure him.

"So, let's talk about something else, what do you think of the music in here?" she asked.

Sean sighed before finally looking up and making eye contact for the first time since Lizzy entered the pub. "It's okay I suppose, not really my thing but it draws a crowd," he said shrugging slightly. Lizzy smiled, glad that she had finally got Sean to speak, but he looked away again, feeling uncomfortable.

"Oh, for God's sake, you are a barrel of laughs tonight." Lizzy sighed.

"I suppose."

"You suppose what?" Lizzy asked, losing patience with Sean.

"I suppose I'm just preoccupied with some things in my life right now."

"Like what?" Lizzy asked, prodding him for an answer.

Sean took a moment to consider how much he wanted to tell her. "The farm, to be honest, I'm struggling to keep my head above water."

"You never told me that before," Lizzy said, sounding concerned.

"I feel like I'm chasing my tail, working myself to the bone but getting nowhere, I just can't seem to make ends meet," Sean said his voice laden with exhaustion.

"Do you need help?" Lizzy asked.

Sean shook his head before draining the remainder of his pint. "No, I can figure it out on my own."

Lizzy nodded, understanding. She knew Sean was a proud man who would never accept financial help. The insurance pay out on her husband's death and the sale of most of the farmland had left Lizzy very comfortable financially. However, she would never offer money to Sean unless he asked for it.

"To be honest with you, Lizzy, there is something else bothering me, it's not just the farm." Sean turned to face Lizzy, deciding to bite the bullet.

"What is it, Sean?" Lizzy asked, furrowing her eyebrows in confusion.

"What do you think?" Sean asked, leaning in closer.

"I haven't a clue," Lizzy said as she took a mouthful of her gin and tonic.

"Is it not obvious?" Sean asked, attempting to hint at what he was trying to say.

Lizzy shook her head, her frustration boiling over. "No Sean, do I have to guess? Stop talking in riddles and just spit it out," she demanded.

Taking a deep breath in an effort to gather his thoughts, Sean finally said what he had wanted to say for so long. "Me and you," he said softly.

“What about us?” Lizzy said, her voice quavering slightly. She was avoiding Sean's gaze as she lit another cigarette. She seemed to understand the situation more than he let on, which made it even harder for her to meet his eyes.

Sean exhaled a long breath before finally asking, “What is the story with you and James Murray?”

“James is my neighbour, I’ve known him for the last twenty years since I moved here,” Lizzy said flicking ash into the ashtray on the counter. “Why are you asking, anyway?”

It was obvious to Sean that Lizzy was hiding something, and he had touched a nerve. “Well, there is talk around the town...”

“What talk?” Lizzy cut in. “This fucking town is full of fucking gossipers, what the hell are they saying now?” Her face was going bright red.

“Well... I heard that you and James had a fling?” Sean asked cautiously.

“Who told you that shite?” Lizzy asked, her eyes widening in surprise and anger.

“I just heard it somewhere,” Sean said sheepishly and stared into his beer.

Lizzy sighed and took a pull of her cigarette. “It was just a one-off, nothing more; it was a long time ago,” she said in a low voice. “I'm not like that. That's all it was.”

Sean nodded but he still wasn't sure he completely believed her.

“Anyway, why do you care, all you want is to meet up when it suits you and have a quick shag in the back of a car every now and then, you are like all the rest of them,” Lizzy said, her temper rising.

Sean was taken aback by her reaction; he had thought that maybe there was more between them. He hadn't expected to be dismissed so outright. He stood up and ran his hand through his blond hair. “Yeah, I guess you're right.”

Sean wanted to say more, he wanted to tell Lizzy that he cared for her, and he wanted to make their arrangement a bit more serious. But he knew that she was angry with him and it would be best to just leave it as it was.

Lizzy took the last mouthful of her drink, she was hoping that Sean would apologise or say something to make her feel better, but the words didn't come. She sighed and then grabbed her handbag and got up off the barstool.

"Well, I'm going. I can't listen to any more of your shite. Don't bother me again, Sean," Lizzy said as she made her way to the door.

Sean just nodded and watched her walk out. The bar seemed to enclose all around him, and he felt very alone. Like he did when his father died.

"Breslin, you bollix," he whispered to himself as he ordered another pint and half one. "You fucked it up again." He knew that he felt more for Lizzy than what he had let on and losing her made him angrier with himself than anything else.

Seeing the empty space at the bar next to Sean, Paddy came back over.

"Well, where did Lizzy go?" Paddy asked. "She has some body on her, well James Murray told me, anyway."

Paddy chuckled a little as Sean didn't react to his joke. He could tell that something had been bothering him and decided to drop it. Paddy didn't know that Sean had a casual relationship with Lizzy for the last few years; the pair had kept it quiet. Sean was perhaps too embarrassed or afraid to tell people that he was going out with Lizzy because of her reputation. He was never brave enough to stand up to the sharp tongues of the people in the town who had nothing else to do but mind everybody else's business. Sean sighed heavily and looked up at Paddy. "I think I'm done tonight, I'm headin home."

"Ah, Sean, it's early yet, it's only coming up to eleven, we will have a few more yet," Paddy said trying to convince Sean to stay.

"Okay, get me another whiskey; I have a pint in front of me. I'm off to the Jacks, I'll be back in a few minutes."

When Sean returned to his stool it was taken, Tommy Flynn was perched on it. He reached in by Tommy to grab his pint, trying to give the hint to Tommy to get up.

"Ah Sean, it's yourself, am I on your stool?" Tommy laughed.

"Yes," Sean grunted, still feeling sore from the run-in with Lizzy earlier and the chat with his cousin before that.

"Sure, you are grand standing, you are probably sitting all day, or maybe you were in the bed," Tommy said, slapping Sean on the back, causing him to spill half of his pint on the floor.

"Go easy, Tommy, for fuck sake," Sean said, trying to control his temper that was boiling up inside him.

"I'll get you another pint, Sean," Paddy said, noticing that Sean was agitated.

"No, I'm fine, Paddy," Sean replied.

"Who rattled your cage, Breslin?" Tommy said. "It was only an accident."

Sean didn't reply and took a swallow of the remainder of his pint.

"I suppose you two wasters were doing fuck all day, probably propping up the bar," Tommy said as he sipped his brandy. "I was busy, sold ten good cattle at the mart, and made a tidy profit, a nice few pound."

"Good for you, Tommy," Paddy said.

Sean was sick of Tommy blowing about all the money he was making.

"You should have been at the mart today, Sean, instead of wasting your time in here talking to Paddy. You need to restock that farm of yours, you have fuck all cattle left," Tommy said mockingly.

"Fuck you, Flynn," Sean snarled in response.

"No need to get all upset, Sean, and spit out the dummy." Tommy took pleasure in slagging Sean, he'd been doing it for years and Sean took it, up until now.

"Shut the fuck up, Tommy, I'm in no mood for your shite talking tonight, go and annoy the head of some other poor bastard," Sean demanded – he had heard enough.

"As the saying goes, if you can't take the heat, get out of the kitchen,

Breslin. Sell up that farm of yours, it's obvious that you haven't a clue what you are doing. You are no farmer, like your father before you, a fucking idiot." Tommy laughed loudly.

"That's it," Sean said as he smashed his pint glass on the floor, reached over and grabbed Tommy by the lapels of his jacket, lifted his sixteen-stone frame off the bar stool, and began to drag him quickly across the floor of the packed bar towards the front door, pushing customers out of his way as he walked backwards.

"What the fuck are you at, Breslin, let me go," Tommy demanded as he waved his arms in the air.

"I'm going to do something I should have done a long time ago," Sean said as he opened the front door with a kick. He reached the footpath outside Gallagher's pub and pushed Tommy against the wall.

"Don't you ever insult me or my father again," Sean said before he pounded Tommy in the face four times in quick succession with his right fist. He was reaching back for a fifth blow when Joe Gallagher grabbed Sean's arm and pulled him back.

"Sean, Sean, for fuck's sake stop it, you have the face battered off him," Joe Gallagher ordered.

Paddy Farrell held Sean back as Joe went over to examine Tommy who had now slumped to the ground and was pumping blood from his nose. A woman standing on the footpath handed Joe a handkerchief and he placed it on Tommy's nose, putting pressure on to try and stop the bleeding.

"Paddy, get Sean out of here before the Guards come," Joe shouted." Some busybody will have them rang already."

"Right," Paddy agreed. "Come on, Sean, let's get out of here."

Sean complied and followed Paddy down the street.

"Fair play to you, Sean, Flynn had that coming a long time, the big-mouthed fucker." Paddy laughed. "I wish I had the balls to do it."

Chapter 7: Comes a Time

Sunday April 30th.

It was a fine Sunday evening as Donal McCabe stood at the gates of the church and waited for Fiona Donnelly to turn up. He watched a single old woman walk down the church steps slowly, fearful that she might fall. The slender old woman was dressed in a buttoned-up coat with a shawl draped around her hunched shoulders. Her skin was wrinkled and sprinkled with brown age spots, her grey hair pulled into a neat bun, and she walked cautiously as if she was fragile like glass, one foot warily in front of the other as she nervously gripped the handrail with her long, thin and bony hands. She took steady steps, gripping the handrail tightly, her eyes wide with fear of losing her footing and her gaze fixed just in front of her as she descended one step at a time, as if any movement was a great effort. She knew that a bad fall could result in a long stay, perhaps a permanent one, in an old folk's facility because she had nobody to look after her at home. Donal recognised her and ran up the steps towards her to link arms with her as she came down.

“Mrs Collins, how are you, careful on those steps, they are still a bit wet from that heavy shower earlier.”

“Oh, Master McCabe, always the gentleman,” the old lady said.

"There we are now, safe and sound," Donal said as they reached level ground and came off the final step.

"Thank you, Master McCabe.”

"Donal is fine, Mrs Collins. Do you want me to walk you over to your house?"

"No, there is no need, I’m just calling down to see Bridie Mulhern down the street. I don't mind the flat ground, it’s the steps I don't like.”

"You are right to be careful, you could get a nasty fall, Mrs Collins."

"It’s Helen, if I call you Donal, you will have to call me Helen so." She laughed.

"Okay so, if you insist. How are you keeping these times, Helen?"

"Not so bad, I was just in lighting a candle for Eugene, today would be his birthday."

"Ahh, would it, Helen, poor Eugene, how long is he gone now, god rest him."

"Eugene is gone three years on February 14th last. He would be 82 today if he was still with us."

"Is it three years, I didn't think it was that long." Donal sighed.

"I will be eighty myself next month, what do you think of that, Donal?" Helen said in a weak voice as she smiled and waved her fingers through her grey hair. “You wouldn't think it, would you.”

"Wow, eighty, I would never have thought that, Helen. I thought you were only in your sixties yet," Donal lied.

"You will have to send me a birthday card," Helen said, delighted to be getting some attention from a younger, handsome man.

"I sure will, Helen, what date is your birthday on?"

"May 17th."

"Well, I will have a card and a cake, how about that?" Donal said with a large smile.

"I'll hold you to that, don't forget," Helen said as she poked him gently on the arm.

"Don't worry, I have a great memory," Donal said and patted her on the shoulder.

"Okay, I better be off now, the tea will be gone cold in Mulhern's," Helen said as she waddled off down the street.

"Bye, Helen," Donal said after her as she walked down the street.

"Have I competition now?" a younger female voice said next to him. "You are chatting up other women."

Donal turned and was delighted to see the tall, blonde figure of Fiona standing next to him.

"It's nice to see you again, Fiona," Donal said with a smile. "How have you been since last Friday?"

"I'm doing great," Fiona said. "And you, what did you get up to?"

"Nothing much, trying to do some writing."

Fiona's eyes lit up as she responded with enthusiasm, "Writing, really? What sort of writing?" She couldn't contain her curiosity. Donal flashed one of his signature grins and replied casually, "I'll fill you in later. It's all quite dull and not worth talking about now." He extended his arm with a gallant gesture. "Let's go for a drink first."

She gladly took it and they walked down the street.

"Who was that old lady you were talking to, she looks familiar," Fiona asked.

"That sweetheart is Helen Collins, a lovely woman. She told me that she will be eighty soon."

Fiona furrowed her brow as the realisation dawned on her. "Oh, that is right, Helen Collins. I called to see her with the doctor last week," she said, looking at the ground, regretting now that she had mentioned it.

"Is Helen all right?" Donal asked, his concern evident in his voice as he studied Fiona's posture.

She let out a long sigh and with a sorrowful shake of her head replied,

"Not so good, not so good." Fiona closed her eyes for a moment before continuing, "It's so unfair."

"Oh, right," Donal responded, not wanting to pry too much into something confidential. He hoped that Helen would be around to see her eightieth birthday and many others.

The main street of Ballygorman was quiet as they crossed over the street and went into McDaid's pub. The village only had two pubs, McDaid's and Gallagher's. McDaid's was the larger and cleaner of the two and attracted a different clientele than Gallagher's. For a good night of craic and boozing, Gallagher's was the place to go and in truth, it was the place that Donal usually went to. However, if you were trying to impress a lady, McDaid's was the best choice. The language inside would be quieter and more "toned" down. For a start, it was much, much cleaner and smelled a hell of a lot better.

The outside of McDaid's pub was painted in a warm cream hue, the windows flanked by thick green curtains. Inside, it was well-lit by large windows that let in a lot of natural light. It had a long polished bar counter that ran the length of the room, behind which sat a shining collection of glasses and liquors. The pub was lined with wooden tables and cushioned chairs that were all finished to a high level and the gleaming tiled floor had been freshly scrubbed. The walls, a comforting beige colour, were adorned with old Irish photographs and framed mirrors, giving a sense of history and class to the place. The place was clearly designed for tourists who stopped off in the village during the summer months.

The conversation inside the bar was muted, small groups of people sitting in corners and talking quietly. The bar smelled of wood polish and pine cleaner, a gentle aroma of peat burning in the open fire. Unlike Gallagher's, it didn't stink of stale beer and dirty toilets. Instead, there was a fresh smell of detergent. A sweet air of piped tobacco wafted across the bar. It came from the landlord, Johnny McDaid, who was sitting up at the bar reading a Sunday newspaper whilst enjoying a smoke on his pipe. Behind the bar, his eldest daughter, Pauline, was polishing glasses with a cloth. Overall, the place felt inviting, and Donal wondered why he didn't come in more often.

Donal and Fiona chose a table next to the window. It was still bright outside and they could watch the comings and goings on the street. Pauline McDaid, the barmaid, was quick to notice them and came over.

"Hello, folks, would you like a drink?" she asked pleasantly.

"What would you like, Fiona?" Donal inquired.

She considered her options for a moment before replying. "Could I have a Harp lager shandy please, with plenty of lemonade?"

"And I will have a pint of Guinness please," Donal said as he smiled up at Pauline.

"Sure, I'll drop them down to you," Pauline said cheerfully as she made her way back to the bar.

"So, I'm intrigued, tell me about your writing. What are you working on?" Fiona said as she leaned across the table and rested her chin on her hand.

"Well, not much really. I've got a book that I'm trying to finish for the last number of years," Donal started off with a deep breath and a slight apprehension in his voice.

"Do you write books, I mean professionally?" Fiona asked.

"No, not at all," Donal replied with an uncertain shrug.

At this, Fiona smiled encouragingly at him and suggested, "Why don't you give it a try? I'm sure you are talented enough."

"Thanks for the advice, Fiona, but I only ever wrote poetry and short stories before, and I wasn't very good at it," Donal replied with a sigh.

"I'm sure that's not true, you just need to believe in yourself, " Fiona said earnestly, studying his face intently.

"I guess it never hurts to try," Donal said with a smile.

"Well, in that case, let's make a deal. If you write your book I'll buy you dinner when it's done," Fiona said with an air of determination.

Donal was taken aback by her offer, and he couldn't help but feel a warm blush creep into his cheeks. He nodded slowly, almost disbelievingly. "It's a deal then." Donal extended his hand towards Fiona and she shook it. Fiona smiled back at him, her eyes twinkling in the soft light of the bar. "I look forward to it! So, what is the book about anyway, I'm curious."

"I am only about three-quarters way through the first draft. It's historical fiction, set at the time of the 1798 rebellion. The main character is an ex-British soldier who turns sides and becomes a rebel when he witnesses the ways the civilian population were being mistreated."

"Sounds interesting," Fiona said, her eyes lit up with excitement. "I read a lot of books about history."

"Really?" Donal replied, intrigued by Fiona's enthusiasm.

She nodded in response enthusiastically and continued explaining her thoughts further. "I think it's important to have knowledge and understanding about the past in order to make sense of the present. Plus, I just can't help but love a good story."

Donal smiled at her enthusiasm, he liked her already and maybe having someone to be accountable to would help him finally finish his book. He didn't expect to make such a connection so quickly with Fiona. He wanted to learn more about her and what she liked and disliked.

Pauline the barmaid came back with the drinks they had requested and set them down on the table. "Here you are, sir," she said in a cheerful manner, placing Donal's pint of stout in front of him. He smiled warmly at her and said, "Thank you, Pauline, great service as always, I really appreciate it."

"No problem, Mr McCabe."

Pauline wore a white blouse and dark slacks, exuding professionalism in her job. She stood around five feet four in her work shoes. Her warm and wide smile conveyed friendliness. Her hair was cut short in a bob that framed a round face. Overall, her enthusiastic nature and cheerfulness were one of the reasons why tourists enjoyed spending time at McDaid's. Her father had trained her well.

"I'll leave a bit extra for you here," Donal said as he handed her some money for their drinks.

"Well thank you so much!" she exclaimed gratefully.

"It's a big year for you this year, Pauline. Leaving Cert exams coming up in June," Donal said with a hint of concern in his voice.

"It's coming up fast, only six weeks away now." Pauline sighed heavily, feeling overwhelmed by the task ahead of her.

"You will be fine, Pauline; you were always an excellent student and you have worked so hard for this. Your hard work will pay off in the end and I'm sure you'll do extremely well," Donal reassured her.

"I hope so," Pauline replied.

"What do you want to study in college?" Fiona asked Pauline.

The barmaid took a deep breath. "Well, I would like to study to become a vet, but if I don't get enough points I will go for nursing." Pauline pushed a strand of cinnamon coloured hair out of her eyes as she responded.

Fiona beamed and said, "Nursing is such a fulfilling profession!"

Pauline looked at her in admiration and asked, "You're the new district nurse, aren't you?"

"I am, my name is Fiona, pleased to meet you, Pauline," she said warmly, shaking the girl's hand.

"Nice to meet you too. I'd better keep moving, give me a wave if you want another drink," Pauline said as she turned and sauntered away.

Fiona watched her go with admiration in her eyes and remarked, "What a lovely young woman."

Donal nodded in agreement and added, "Yes, she is."

"Anyway, cheers," Fiona said as she clinked her glass off Donal's.

"Slainte."

"I'd better not have too many this evening, busy day tomorrow – Mondays are always crazy. So many people calling the clinic asking for help and attention," Fiona said, shaking her head as she took another sip of her drink, conscious of the fact that she shouldn't stay out too late.

"But tomorrow is a bank holiday," Donal said with a hint of disappointment.

"I know, but I still have to work, people still need care on a bank holiday." Fiona sighed.

"Of course," Donal said and took a sip of his pint. "Where is your clinic anyway?" he asked, curious about the location.

"I am based in Carrowmore, just next to the bus station."

"Oh, I know it," Donal replied. "I have been there a few times to see Dr. Casey."

"Oh yes, Oliver," Fiona said with a hint of disdain.

"What is he like, he always seems a bit aloof, a bit full of himself."

"He is all that for sure, I can't figure him out. He is not very friendly at present, maybe he might improve after a while."

"I'm sure he will, give him time, use your charm on him." Donal laughed.

The conversation then shifted to other topics, and soon three hours had passed in a blink of an eye.

"Look at the time, it is gone ten, I'd better go," Fiona said, as she looked up at the clock on the wall.

"Stay for another?" Donal suggested.

"I'd love to, but I will be wrecked tomorrow morning if I do," Fiona said as she stood up and put on her coat.

"Okay, I'll walk you back to your house."

"There is no need, it's only a few minutes away," Fiona said.

"I will walk with you, the least I can do," Donal said as he offered her his arm and they walked out into a calm night outside.

They walked in a comfortable silence, the streetlamps lighting their path and the stars shining above. After turning right up the street at the side of the church they reached a small housing development of new houses called Annaghcarraig, where Fiona lived.

"Thank you for walking me home, Donal," Fiona said with a smile, as she turned to him before unlocking her door.

"It was my pleasure, Fiona, thank you for a wonderful night, you are great company," Donal replied as he leaned in and kissed her on the cheek.

"Thanks, I really enjoyed talking to you." Fiona smiled. "Do you want to meet during the week, I could cook us something, if you like." She paused, her expression hopeful and expectant.

"That sounds lovely, how about Tuesday?" Donal suggested.

"Perfect, call around 7:30. I hope you are not too fussy about your food."

Fiona added, "My cooking is nothing special, I'm afraid."

"I'm sure it will be delicious."

"Great, good night, Donal," she said. She moved closer and kissed him gently on the lips and then turned and went inside.

Donal stood there for a moment, the warmth of her kiss lingering on his lips. He smiled to himself and turned to walk back to his car, feeling better than he had done in a long time. As Donal approached his car, he noticed Paddy Farrel stumbling across the street.

"How are you, Donal?" he mumbled.

"I'm doing well, Paddy," Donal replied with a smile. "Are you in town for a while?" He knew what the answer would be before it left Paddy's mouth by the cut of him and the bottle of whiskey half-hidden by his coat.

"I am in a while all right." His words were almost incomprehensible.

"Have you a way home, can I drop you out? I'm going past your house," Donal said, afraid that Paddy might stagger out in front of a car on his walk home.

"I have the car down the street, Donal, I'm fine."

"Hop in here with me, I'll drop you out, it's no bother."

"Okay so," Paddy said and got into Donal's Fiat.

"Good man, let's get going," Donal said as he started up the car and headed out the road.

"Were there many over in Gallagher's tonight, Paddy?"

"No, it was very quiet, very few in there tonight, he had a busy night last night. Saturday night is always a busy night. He had a fantastic band last night. The place was jam-packed."

"Sounds like I missed a good night," Donal said steering along the narrow road.

"Oh, it was eventful, anyway." Paddy nodded.

"Why, what happened?" Donal asked.

Paddy hesitated for a moment before responding. "I shouldn't be telling tales, but your mate Sean Breslin got into a bit of a row."

"Really, Sean fighting, that doesn't sound like him, are you sure?" Donal said in a concerned tone, truly taken aback.

"Oh yes, sure I had to step in to separate them and pull them apart," Paddy said with a touch of pride. "He would have killed him if I hadn't stepped in."

"Killed who, exactly who was Sean fighting with?" Donal asked curiously.

"Tommy Flynn," Paddy answered curtly.

"Oh, that toe rag, he is one annoying bastard, he is always winding Sean up," Donal said.

"Well, he didn't take it last night, he hit him three or four good solid punches in the face. I think he bust Tommy's nose. He was pissing blood anyway when we left him. Joe Gallaher cleaned him up."

"Is Sean okay?" Donal enquired, an expression of genuine concern on his face.

"Oh, he was fine, not a loss on him. He came back to my house and we drank a bottle of whiskey I had left over from Christmas. He slept on the couch in the kitchen, and he must have drove home this morning because he was gone when I got up."

A few minutes brought Donal's car to Paddy's house.

"Right, well here you are, Paddy," Donal said pulling up at the gate.

"Thanks, Donal, you are a gentleman, will you come in for a cup of tea or something?"

"No, I'm fine Paddy, I'm tired. I'll get to my bed."

"Right so." Paddy nodded in agreement as he slowly got out of the car, closed the door, and banged the roof to signal he was good to go.

On the short journey to his home, Donal thought about Sean and hoped that he was okay. He made up his mind to call out to see him the next day.

CHAPTER 8: YOU CAN TUNE A PIANO, BUT YOU CAN'T TUNA FISH

Monday May 1st.

Donal drove the narrow laneway that wound its way up to the Breslin farm on an overcast Monday afternoon. The sky was an ominous shade of grey, the low clouds looming over the landscape, the air still and humid. The laneway was little more than a cattle track and the ground soft and wet from recent rainfall, making the surface muddy and uneven. Bushes and trees loomed over the lane from the unkept ditches on either side, forming a canopy of dark shadows, their branches creaking under the weight of the wet leaves and tearing against the side of Donal's car as he drove. The damp long grass growing on the verges gave off a musty smell.

The farmyard was visible at the end of the narrow path, with Sean leaning against a Massey 135 tractor, smoke rising from his cigarette. He appeared to be deep in thought and didn't notice the car pulling up at the front of the house.

"Hiya Sean, how are you?" Donal said as he got out of his Fiat and approached the farmyard.

Sean's trance was broken, and he squinted as Donal came into focus. "Another short day over in the classroom Mr. McCabe, and me breaking my heart all day trying to get this feckin tractor to start. You have it handy. Look at the lovely clean hands on you."

Donal looked at Sean's hands as he took a pull of his fag; they were as black as pitch from oil and grease. "It's a bank holiday, May 1st, no school today," Donal said with a sly grin.

His words seemed to animate Sean as he took a large pull of his fag. "No bank holidays for farmers."

"Let me help you get that tractor going," Donal said, bending towards the engine.

"What the hell would you know about a tractor engine," Sean responded sceptically.

"We have tractors in Monaghan too, you know. I was raised on a farm, we had the very same make like probably ninety percent of farmers," Donal said.

"I appreciate your offer, but before you go any further you need to change out of those good clothes or else you'll be covered in shite," Sean said with a smirk.

"No problem!" Donal replied cheerfully as he went over to his car and opened the boot. He pulled out an old pair of overalls and some well-worn boots before changing into them.

"Christ, you came prepared," Sean said in awe.

Donal's hearty laugh rang through the air as he responded nonchalantly, "I always am."

They worked together for over an hour, focused and committed to getting the tractor going again. Tinkering endlessly and trying different techniques, their only goal was to make it function. And finally, they succeeded in their efforts.

Sean was able to breathe a huge sigh, relieved beyond measure. "Fair fecks to you Donal, you weren't bullshitting. You know a bit about tractors, that's for sure," he said. "You're an absolute lifesaver. What do I owe you?"

"You can buy me a pint at the weekend," Donal said with a chuckle. "I used to help my father fix the tractor at home. He knew his stuff and showed me a few things."

"He taught you well," Sean said, a hint of admiration in his voice. "If you ever want to move away from teaching, you could turn your hand to tractor repair."

"Might not be a bad idea." Donal chuckled and nodded in acknowledgment. He had always prided himself on his skill with machines and vehicles, especially tractors which he quite enjoyed tinkering with from time to time.

"Come into the kitchen and wash up, I'll make you a mug of tea and a cut of bread. It's the least I can do," Sean offered with a warm smile.

"Sounds good, lead the way," Donal said and followed Sean into the kitchen.

Inside the kitchen, Sean and Donal began by scrubbing their hands at the sink, vigorously washing them with fairy liquid in an attempt to rid their skin of the stubborn, ground in grease. While they didn't get it all off, they were satisfied enough with the result and moved on. Next up was taking out a fresh loaf of soda bread from which Sean sliced four generous wedges, liberally spreading a layer of golden butter atop each one. There was still some grease left on his skin as he handled the bread.

Donal took his place at the kitchen table and waited for the tea, steeping in the pot, to be strong enough. Thirst somewhat taking over, Donal started pouring himself a mug.

"Ah now, McCabe, will you just leave it be for a moment more? Have you no patience? If you don't let it sit longer, it'll still be as weak as dishwater!" Sean demanded in exasperation.

Despite his demands, Donal couldn't quite resist and decided to ignore

Sean, drinking the tea as soon as it was poured. With a tired sigh, Sean placed the plate of buttered bread on the table before sinking into his chair and pouring himself a mug of tea.

“If you want some, there's a pot of jam right there in front of you.” Sean motioned toward the Bo Peep blackcurrant jam. Donal eagerly dug the knife into it and spread a generous portion across his piece of bread. “Jasus! Go easy on that, we have to make it last us for the whole week!” Sean cackled merrily as he watched Donal go to work with the jam pot.

"I'll buy you a pot, you tight bastard," Donal replied, his mouth curling into a smirk. He marvelled at the delicious sight of the soda bread in front of him. "Lovely soda bread, is that your mother's?" he asked.

"It is." Sean nodded with a proud smile on his face. "She bakes us one loaf every day."

“Is she about, I haven’t seen your mother in a while.”

“She is gone visiting a friend of hers, I dropped her off after dinner. I have to pick her up again at six,” Sean said, checking at the clock on the wall and going over to a plastic bucket next to the door. In a single motion, Sean lifted two large sods of turf from the bucket. They looked like they were recently cut, as small bits of grass and dirt still clung to them. He carried them hastily across the floor, ignoring the small segments of peat falling at his feet, opened the front door of the range and placed them inside. He stirred the existing embers with a poker and the heat from the range quickly began to char the sods, releasing a smoky-sweet smell of earth into the air that clung to clothes, hair and everything. As the sods of turf began to burn, they licked the walls of the range with orange flames that radiated heat from the firebox.

"That’ll keep her going, she was nearly out," Sean said as he took his seat at the table again.

“Anything exciting happen over the weekend?” The corner of Donal's mouth quirked up in anticipation as he looked to his friend for an explanation of what happened with him and Tommy Flynn.

“Where were you all weekend, no sign of you in the pub, were you keeping a low profile or something?” Sean avoided the question by asking his own.

"You know me," Donal said with a satisfied grin, knowing that curiosity had taken control of the conversation.

"I do surely know you; it must have been a woman that was keeping you occupied, keeping you out of the pub all weekend, well not quite all weekend, you were spotted last night in McDaid's Pub."

"Was I indeed?" Donal replied, his expression a mix of surprise and confusion.

"Yes, and you had company," Sean affirmed with a nod. "Very good looking company, a fine blonde woman, fitting the description of the district nurse you spotted at mass last Sunday. McCabe you are some boy, it didn't take you long to snare her."

"News travels fast," Donal said.

"It sure does, there are eyes watching you everywhere in Ballygorman, you should know that by now." Sean's words carried the weight of a long-standing truth, one that all the inhabitants of Ballygorman knew well. It didn't matter where you were or what you were doing, there were always eyes on you, and whatever happened was sure to spread around faster than a telegram, it would be carried by the hotline of gossip.

"Anyway seriously good luck to you, you have done well for yourself there. She is a keeper, a teacher and a nurse, two good pensionable jobs," Sean said as he put up his right thumb.

Donal gave a half smile in reply, feeling slightly bashful about the praise. "I'll take that as a compliment, I suppose."

"I don't give compliments too lightly so take it," Sean said. "By the way, what about poor old Patricia O'Neill that you were with at the party the weekend before? She won't like it when she gets wind of your new romance."

Donal paused for a moment before he replied, an expression of resignation on his face. "Myself and Patricia broke up."

"When did that happen?" Sean asked in a curious tone.

"After you spotted us at the party on that Friday night," Donal replied.

"Christ, you guys seemed to be doing all right when I saw you," Sean said, a slight hint of disbelief in his voice.

"It just didn't work out and she told me that she wanted a break, so I agreed," Donal said in a very matter-a-fact way, he obviously wasn't very upset about the breakup.

"Oh right, it didn't take you long to get back on the saddle either," Sean said with a hearty laugh.

Donal finished off his mug of tea and decided to get to the reason why he called out to see Sean. "So, talking about news traveling fast around here, is the news around town about your fight on Saturday night with Tommy Flynn true?"

"Who told you?" Sean queried.

Donal's response was swift. "Paddy Farrell."

"Good man, Paddy, you can't hold your piss." Sean sighed exasperatedly as he banged his fist on the table. "What exactly did he tell you?" he enquired, his voice edged with apprehension.

"He told me that Paddy was winding you up and you pulled him outside and gave him a good beating," Donal replied.

"Flynn had it coming, he went too far this time," Sean stated angrily.

Donal shook his head, replying, "He is always winding you up, Sean, you shouldn't take the bait. He'll just keep doing it if he knows it rattles you." Donal knew all too well how easily Flynn could push Sean's buttons when they were together. But still, just because Flynn was trying to provoke him didn't mean that Sean should rise to it.

"He just went too far last Saturday night, too fucking far," Sean said with a shake of his head.

"Why, what did he say?" Donal asked, his brow furrowed with concern.

"It doesn't matter," Sean said looking away from his friend's gaze.

"What was it?" Donal persisted.

Sean took a deep breath before speaking. "He insulted me, he said that I hadn't a clue what I was at farming, like my father before me, implied that we were both stupid."

Donal was appalled by what he heard. "That was terrible, what a thing to say, but you shouldn't have hit him. A fucker like him might get the Guards involved and press charges."

"Well, if the Guards were gonna come, they would have called by now," Sean replied, his eyes shifting uneasily. His words seemed more like a question than an affirmation.

After a moment of silence, Donal replied with some resignation, "I suppose you are right."

Sean got up from his chair and paced the kitchen floor, like he was searching for something, until eventually stopping at the sink where he lifted his pack of twenty major and took a fag out and lit it with a match that he discarded into the sink.

"Look, Donal, things haven't been going too well for me on the farm lately," Sean said as he stared out the window. "You know it, the whole bloody Parish knows it. I'm barely keeping my head above water and the last thing I need is a smart arse like Tommy Flynn reminding me, rubbing salt into the wound."

"If you are stuck, Sean, I could definitely help you out," Donal offered. "I have a few pound in the bank, and I would be happy to lend you some cash if that's what you need. Just let me know – don't hesitate to ask."

Sean smiled at his friend's kind offer, but his demeanour was still one of worry. "Thanks, Donal, but unfortunately it would take big money to sort this place out. I appreciate your offer all the same."

"Well, the offer stands if you ever change your mind," Donal said staring at his friend who had his back to him as he continued to stare out the window, too embarrassed to make eye contact as he spoke about his problems.

"It wasn't just Tommy Flynn that annoyed me Saturday night. My cousin Jim Kelly was there as well, earlier in the night. He was blowing about how well he was doing with his building firm, hinting that I would be better off working with him rather than scraping a living on this bloody farm. It all just got to me," Sean said, running his fingers through his hair in frustration.

Donal knew there was something else bothering Sean, something that cut him deeper.

"Maybe your cousin has a point, I mean maybe you could work part time for him and still do your farmwork," Donal suggested.

"I couldn't take orders from that fella, no bloody way," Sean cut in with a resolute and firm tone. "It's okay for you, Donal, everything comes easy for you, nice cushy job and now a fine-looking woman – what have I got."

Donal took a deep breath before he spoke. "My job didn't come easy, I had to work for it. My father never had much, just a small farmer trying to make a living and raise five kids on boggy ground in Monaghan. Nobody had it easy."

"Yea, I suppose," Sean said with a shrug.

"Anyway, you get your fair share of women," Donal added with a smirk, trying to lighten the mood.

"Do I, like who?" Sean replied, giving Donal a sideways glance.

"Well, there is Lizzy O'Dowd for one," Donal pointed out.

"How the hell do you know that?" Sean queried with a hint of suspicion and surprise.

"Ah, come on Sean, as you said, everybody knows everybody's business around here," Donal responded with a faint smile.

"I thought I was keeping that quiet and nobody knew," Sean said after a deep exhale.

"Think again," Donal said with a grin. "Lizzy is a fine-looking woman by the way."

"She is, but the problem is that she is shagging somebody else." Sean sighed heavily and shook his head ruefully.

"Does that really bother you? I thought your relationship was fairly casual and easy going," Donal asked.

Sean thought for a while before answering, mulling over the question. "It was, I suppose but..."

Before he had a chance to finish, Donal interjected with another inquiry. "Who is she shagging, anyway?"

"Her neighbour, James Murray," Sean said with a solemn expression.

"Christ, are you sure, he must be sixty," Donal said with raised eyebrows.

"He told Paddy Farrell he was shagging her; he was bragging about it in the jacks in Gallaghers on Saturday night," Sean said as he stubbed out his fag in the ashtray.

"I can't believe it, James is married to Maureen who teaches with me in the school. He doesn't strike me as the type, seems as dull as dishwater to me," Donal replied, still trying to process the information. "Are you sure Paddy had his facts right? He could just be spinning a yarn." Donal asked with a sceptical tone.

"Well, I confronted Lizzy about it when she came into the pub, she denied it at first and eventually she said there was some truth to it, but that it only happened once, a few years after her husband John died," Sean replied.

"How did she take that?" Donal asked curiously, leaning in on the kitchen table. "I mean, was she angry that you questioned her about it?"

"She stormed off, that was the reason why I had no patience for Tommy Flynn later on," Sean said, turning from the window and returning to his seat.

"Maybe Lizzy was telling the truth, maybe it happened once, before she started going out with you," Donal suggested.

Sean remained silent for a few moments. His brow was furrowed as he thought about it and then he said quietly, "Maybe."

"Why don't you call over to Lizzy and talk to her, you might sort it out," Donal proposed.

"I might," Sean replied, looking up at the clock on the wall. "Anyway, I'll have to throw you out now, it's ten to six and the mother has to be collected."

"Right, well as I said, why don't you call up to see Lizzy sometime, there is nothing quite like makeup sex," Donal joked as got up from his chair and made his way out of the kitchen.

"Who made you a relationship counsellor, McCabe, all of a sudden?" Sean smiled, amused by his friend's advice, closing the kitchen door to keep in the heat.

"That's me, teacher, tractor repair man and counsellor all in one good-looking package," Donal said with a confident smile.

Sean was doubled over with laughter as he slapped Donal on the back. "Good luck, McCabe, and go easy on that nurse," he managed to get out between bursts of laughter.

Chapter 9: Just what I Needed

Tuesday May 2nd.

The silky voice of Stevie Nicks singing "Gold Dust Woman" drifted across the sitting room and into the kitchen from the silver Sanyo music centre, the needle of the stylus in the groove of Fleetwood Mac's *Rumours* album. Fiona Donnelly sang along as she stirred a pot of beef goulash on the electric cooker. She checked the time on her watch and ran upstairs to change her clothes.

She hastily fixed her makeup and brushed her long blonde hair before wriggling into a tight fitting skirt and a white blouse. Just as she was putting on her shoes the doorbell rang, and she quickly made her way down the stairs. She turned the latch and opened the door. Donal McCabe stood on the doorstep holding a bunch of flowers and a bottle of red wine. He was wearing a pair of black jeans and a navy cable knit jumper. His brown hair was neatly combed, and his face had the slightest hint of stubble.

"Hi Donal, ahh thanks, what beautiful flowers," Fiona said as she took the bunch of flowers, smelled them, and led the way along the hallway. "Come in and have a seat in the sitting room, dinner is almost ready."

Donal sat on a brown plush sofa next to a warm open fire. His gaze travelled around the room, taking in the high ceiling and large bay window that overlooked the road outside. The late evening sun lit up the table set for dinner at one end of the room. The walls were decorated with cream-coloured paper that gave the room a cosy feel and the floor was covered in an old, patterned rug. The room was illuminated by the soft glow of the fire that cast a yellow hue across the room. Four red candles burned brightly from the dinner table and threw shadows against the wall. The room smelled fresh, as if the windows had been opened all evening to air the place out. A faint smell of wood burning filled the air, merging with the scent of cooking coming from the kitchen.

"I hope you are hungry because I think I made far too much," Fiona said as she came out of the kitchen and handed Donal a glass of wine.

"I am, that smell is making me hungry anyway, it certainly smells good," he said taking a sip of the wine. He couldn't help being captivated by the aroma wafting out from the kitchen.

Five minutes later Fiona appeared in the sitting room and placed a large red casserole pot of goulash on the dining table, along with garlic potatoes, roast carrots, and onions.

"Come over and take a seat, it's ready. I didn't bother with a starter, I hope you are okay just diving into the main course." Fiona smiled.

Donal took a seat while Fiona placed two other dishes on the table before sitting down herself. After saying grace, she dished out generous portions of the meal and they both tucked in with hearty appetites.

The conversation flowed over dinner and after finishing, Fiona cleared the dishes away before bringing out a large bowl of trifle. Donal couldn't believe how good it was. "You are a great cook, this is delicious!" he said warmly, sampling the dessert.

"Thank you." Fiona beamed with pleasure. She had always taken pride in her cooking and Donal's words of approval meant a lot to her. "Do you want to take a seat back at the fire? I'll get you another glass of wine."

Fiona returned with a bottle and two glasses and placed them on the coffee table in front of the couch. She poured out two glasses and handed one to Donal as she sat next to him.

"Thank you so much," Donal replied. "Now tell me, how was work today?"

Fiona sighed heavily before responding. "It was hectic – I'm still getting used to this area and trying to figure out where all the patients live. I had to make so many calls to patients' homes today, and I got lost a few times. I probably called to the wrong house at least ten times." She paused for a moment to collect her thoughts. "It's like being caught in a maze sometimes, there are so many lanes and backroads around here."

Donal chuckled at her description of the area. "Ah, I know what you mean. It's taken me eight years to get a good feel for the place." He took a sip of his wine before continuing, "I think the thing to remember is that each small road and lane has its own character. I always try to get out of my car and take a walk around, just to get an idea of what's going on in each place and how it all fits together."

Fiona smiled, appreciating Donal's advice. She had always been an inquisitive person, wanting to learn more about her surroundings. "Thank you, I'll definitely take your advice."

Donal smiled warmly and nodded in agreement. "Well, I'm glad that I'm some use to you. I love it here in Ballygorman. It really is a special place – once you get over how nosey everybody is," he added with a laugh.

"Yes, I noticed that everybody wants to know every little thing about you, what you bloody had for breakfast when you meet them. Who you are, where you come from, so damn nosey," Fiona replied, pulling at her hair in frustration.

Donal laughed. "I suppose it's their way of making sure strangers aren't up to any mischief," he said as he refilled her wine glass. "I suppose I'm quite used to it by now."

Fiona smiled and raised her glass in admiration. "Eight years is a long time; you must know everybody here within an inch of their lives!" she said, intrigued.

Donal laughed and nodded in agreement. "Yea, I suppose that's true. You know, if you're ever looking for any more information about the area or its people just let me know, I think the nosiness is contagious."

Fiona nodded. "I'll keep that in mind, Donal."

The two talked for hours as they listened to music and finished off two bottles of wine, finding out more and more about each other.

"I Like your taste in music," Donal said. "I'm glad that it stretches beyond the Bee Gees." Simon and Garfunkel's *Bridge Over troubled water* album played on the stereo.

"Shut up, I love the Bee Gees," Fiona said and playfully poked Donal in the belly.

Donal laughed as he grabbed her hand to stop her. The feel of her skin sent a tingle up his spine. They looked at each other and their eyes locked as they eagerly anticipated the kiss; it was as if time stopped. Their cheeks were flushed with excitement and their lips moved in closer. Donal didn't hesitate as he gave in to his desire for those soft lips. He could smell the heady scent of Fiona's perfume and the sweet taste of wine that lingered in her mouth. The firelight danced across their faces as they kissed deeply. When the kiss ended, they held each other tightly. Their hold was passionate and intense as the room around them seemed to fade away.

"It's getting late, I should go back home," Donal said reluctantly as he got up from the sofa, hoping that Fiona would ask him to stay.

'It's early yet, there is no rush," Fiona said. "Anyway, you can stay if you want."

Donal looked into Fiona's eyes, seeing the desire there.

She grabbed his hand and stood up. "Let's go upstairs for a while," she said softly.

Donal nodded and followed her up the staircase, feeling an excitement he hadn't felt in a long time. As they reached the door to Fiona's bedroom,

Donal paused for a moment. He was ready to experience what had been building between them all night.

Fiona opened her bedroom door and stepped inside, allowing Donal to follow her in. The curtains of the window were open and Donal's eyes fell on Fiona's body, illuminated by the soft light from the full moon outside, giving her an otherworldly glow. He could see how perfect she was. Her curves were highlighted by the shadows in the room, her beauty captivating even in the half-darkness. She had an air of grace and confidence which made her even more attractive.

Donal brought his lips close to Fiona's as they moved towards her bed. He felt her body press against him as they kissed, her blonde hair cascading over his shoulder as she wrapped her arms around him. He could feel the softness of her skin and the gentle curves beneath his hands. The heat of her body radiated through her clothes and sent tingles through him. The two of them spent the night entangled in each other's embrace until finally, morning came.

Donal looked at the clock on the locker next to the bed, it was 6:45. He decided that he'd better get up and go home to get ready for work.

Fiona reached out and touched Donal's hand as he was getting dressed. Her eyes twinkled in the morning light. "I had a wonderful time," she whispered, her voice almost like a lullaby.

"So did I. I'm sorry I have to rush off, I have to get back home to collect a few things for work," Donal replied. "Can I see you again this evening?"

"Sure, call around whenever it suits you, I will be here all evening," Fiona said, sitting up in the bed.

Donal smiled back and nodded. He kissed her one last time before heading downstairs. He felt content, knowing he had finally found someone special in Fiona.

Chapter 10: Can't Stand Losing You

Wednesday May 3rd.
8.00 PM

Sean Breslin pulled his Ford Car to a stop in the car park overlooking Lough Melvin. He took out a cigarette from the pack on the dashboard and drew the smoke in deeply, letting it out slowly, watching the smoke drift up from between his fingers and out the opened window as he stared into the distance at the still lake below. The sun reflected off its glassy surface which mirrored the colour of the sky above, making it sparkle and shimmer in the evening light as if it was constructed of millions of tiny diamonds dancing across its skin. His eyes scanned the wide expanse of the lake. It was still, like a deep, dark abyss of secrets and mysteries. The shoreline was lined with tall reeds, wild grasses, and lush greenery, swaying gently in the breeze, all adding to the tranquil and peaceful atmosphere, that was only broken by the birds singing sweetly in the soft light of dusk and by distant splashes as other birds swooped and dived to catch their supper.

Sean took another large inhale, lost in thought, contemplating his next move. Should he take Donal's advice and go and visit Lizzy, try to make up with her, or should he just forget about it and move on. He had already had a bath and put on clean clothes earlier which his mother was totally confused about, a bath on a Wednesday night had her scratching her head because Sean religiously only had one bath a week and that was on a Saturday evening.

"Oh, what the hell, here goes nothing," Sean said as he turned on the ignition, swung the car around in the layby and drove off in the direction of Lizzy's house. A hundred thoughts on a hundred different possible outcomes spun around inside his head as he drove. He pushed the cassette tape into the car stereo to try to distract himself from his thoughts as he drove. The power chords of Brain Robertson and Scott Gorham playing the intro to "Jailbreak" blasted through the body of the Ford as Sean turned the steering wheel and gunned the car forward.

Two miles down the road brought Sean close to Killard crossroads where he would have to swing left to turn off for Lizzy's house. His thoughts were interrupted by the sight of a figure walking along the road. He squinted in the half-light to make out who it was and realized it was Lizzy O'Dowd. She walked slowly along the side of the road, her dark hair swaying in the breeze. She was wearing a light raincoat, jeans, and boots and carrying what looked like two shopping bags. They were seemingly heavy, as her shoulders slumped under the weight, and she was struggling to keep them balanced as she walked. Sean debated for a few seconds whether to stop and offer her a lift or just drive on, but he thought about what Donal said about trying to make things right with her, so he pulled over and stopped his car next to her. He smiled to himself and thought that this must be fate.

"Well, Lizzy, you look like you've a heavy load there. Can I give you a lift home?" Sean said as stretched over and rolled down the side window next to her.

Lizzy looked at him in surprise and was unusually lost for words. Sean got out of the car, walked around to the passenger side and opened the door for her. At first, she seemed unsure what to do.

"Get in, Lizzy, I just want to give you a lift home. Those bags look heavy," Sean said.

"Okay so," Lizzy said and hesitantly got into the passenger seat. Sean took the two bags from her and placed them on the back seat. Lizzy shifted slightly in her seat as she still felt uncomfortable and unsure if she had made the right decision in accepting the lift.

"Where is your car?" Sean asked as he got back behind the wheel and drove off, pretending to be oblivious to her unease.

"I don't know what is wrong with it. I couldn't get it going yesterday morning and I had to get John McGinley to come out and tow it to his garage to take a look at it. I got a lift into Ballygorman earlier and had to get groceries for myself and Mrs Boyle and carry them out. Aine Curran said that she would give me a lift back out home. I waited and waited for her outside the shop, and I haven't a clue where she went, so I decided to walk it."

"You walked a good three mile," Sean said, taken aback.

"Don't I know it. I wouldn't mind, but the bags weigh a ton, especially the shopping for Mrs Boyle – ten tins of feckin cat food, they would rip the arms off you." Lizzy sighed in exhaustion.

"How is Mrs Boyle, she must be a good age now?" Sean asked.

"She must be near eighty," Lizzy said. "She is all alone in that house all day, God love her, she sees no one. I do the shopping for her, it's no problem when I have the car. I don't mind doing it at all."

"Her son Brendan is in England, he hasn't been home in years," Sean said. "I went to school with Brendan, he was a bit of a gobshite."

"Was he, I never met him. She is always talking about him though, she thinks the sun shines out of his behind."

"He was always a useless bastard, about as useful as tits on a bull," Sean said biting back a smirk.

"A lovely phrase, Sean, you have a lovely way with words. You should be a poet." Lizzy couldn't help but laugh in response to his remark and it broke the tension between them. She loved how well Sean conveyed his point with just the right amount of sarcasm and humour. It was clear that he could easily craft effective phrases that got right to the heart of any issue, even so those words were sometimes harsh.

Sean was happy to hear Lizzy laughing, they always had good craic together. He didn't want that to end, she was good company. Sean said nothing and drove on in silence for a few moments, trying to think of the right words to say and how best to approach the topic he wanted to discuss with her. He took a deep breath and then with determination turned the conversation around to what he really wanted to talk about. "Listen, Lizzy, I know that things haven't been going the way they used to and I know it's my fault. I just want you to know that I'm sorry. I'm sorry about last Saturday night in Gallagher's. I was out of line. I shouldn't have accused you about going out with James Murray. If you did go out with him in the past, well that was your business and I would really like us to try and patch things up and try to get back together again."

"Why?" Lizzy asked, surprised by the apology.

"What do you mean, why," Sean replied.

"Why do you want to get back together with me, is it just for a quick shag whenever you feel like it?" Lizzy responded.

"No." Sean's expression was one of confusion mixed with something resembling hurt.

"Then why do you want to get back with me?" Lizzy was wondering if Sean just wanted someone to scratch an itch, or did he want something more.

"Because... I like being with you, Lizzy. I just... like you. Let's start again and act like a normal couple, not always skulking about. We have nothing to be ashamed of, you are a single woman, I'm a single man; let's just put Saturday night behind us and start again."

Lizzy gazed at him with a surprised expression, not fully believing what he had just said. It was an assertion she hadn't really considered before. She cracked a smile and said, "I was thinking the same thing myself earlier today when I was walking along the road."

Sean smiled back in relief. "Listen, Lizzy, I was wondering if you would like to go for a drive with me tomorrow night. There is supposed to be a good folk band called Jargon playing down at the Blackbird Bar in Kinlough, and Horslips are playing in the hall in Glenfarne afterwards. I thought it might be a bit of craic. A change from the same old scene around Ballygorman," he said nervously.

Lizzy paused for a moment before responding. "Okay, sure," she said quietly. "That sounds nice."

"Terrific," Sean said as he drove the car up into Lizzy's driveway and turned off the ignition. "Thanks, Lizzy, for not taking the head off me after the way I spoke to you last Saturday night."

"It's okay, Sean, come here to me," Lizzy crooned softly as she reached over and tenderly brushed his cheek before drawing closer and pressing her lips against his. Though she could feel the uncertainty in him through their embrace, she knew that if she just held him close for a moment then it would all be all right. Sean put his arm around Lizzy and pulled her closer, tenderly running his fingers through her dark hair, and as he did Lizzy could feel one of her earrings fall down, hitting her on her leg.

"Oh shite," Lizzy exclaimed, her eyes widening as she frantically searched the floor beneath her seat.

"What's wrong?" Sean asked, feigning concern.

"One of my earrings just fell off." Lizzy laughed.

"Don't worry about it, I'll buy you a new pair for your birthday," Sean said, wanting to carry on with what they had started.

"What time is it?"

"I haven't a clue, who cares, it must be around half eight," Sean responded with a nonchalant shrug of his shoulders.

"I have to bring the groceries over to Mrs Boyle before she goes to bed," Lizzy said as he moved away from Sean.

"Ill drop you over and we can come back here then," Sean suggested, the wheels of his mind turning with plans for what could happen later in Lizzy's bedroom.

"Okay, but I will have to bring mine in first and stick the milk in the fridge. Come into the house for a minute."

"Right," Sean said reaching behind him to grab the two bags of shopping off the back seat, and got out of the car.

He followed Lizzy up the short path to the front door and she bent down and lifted a key from under a flowerpot next to the porch, then straightened herself up with a light groan and opened the back door to her home. The house that Lizzy called home was a four-bedroom bungalow, straight out of the pages of "Bungalow Bliss". Mature ash trees surrounded the dwelling, and the garden was ablaze with the colour of spring flowers and lush greenery. The bungalow had a pitched roof with a white fascia, the outside walls painted a soft yellow. It had two small porches and tall, arched windows that let in plenty of sunshine. The front porch featured a rocking chair and a small bench. The outside door was wooden and painted a bold blue. Overall, the bungalow was a welcoming home with a peaceful and cosy atmosphere. Lizzy took great pride in keeping herself and her house looking well.

Sean walked through the front hallway, it was decorated with photos of Lizzy and her husband, John on their wedding day. Lizzy opened the door to the kitchen, and Sean placed the two shopping bags on the table. Lizzy immediately began to unpack one of the bags and placed the items into cupboards and the fridge. The kitchen was equipped with modern appliances and fitted kitchen units.

"Go and have a seat in the living room, will you have a cup of tea?" Lizzy asked.

"No, I'm fine," Sean said as he walked into the adjoining room and took a seat. Inside, the living room was warm and inviting, with cream-painted walls, couches upholstered in bright floral fabric, and colourful patterned carpets.

"Here have a quick shot of this, pour me one while you are at it," Lizzy said, placing a bottle of Powers whiskey and two crystal glasses on the coffee table in front of Sean. Her voice exuded a sense of authority.

"Right so, I thought you said you were in a hurry to go to see Mrs Boyle?" Sean reminded Lizzy.

"Ahh, she will be grand for ten minutes or so."

Sean poured the whiskey into the glasses and handed one to Lizzy. "Slàinte!" he said as they clinked their glasses together and took a sip of the whiskey.

It was warming on their tongues as it made its way down their throats. They chatted away, talking about anything and everything until their glasses were almost empty.

"Well, I suppose we should be getting going if we want to get Mrs Boyle's groceries over before she goes to bed," Lizzy said and stood up from her chair, grabbing her handbag off the armchair.

"Thanks for the drink," Sean said as he stood up and lifted the glasses to carry them out to the kitchen.

"No problem, leave the glasses there, I'll wash them when I get back."

"Right, I'll get the shopping bag," Sean said and headed out the living room door. Lizzy picked up her coat off the back of the chair and put it on.

"Right, all set!" she said with a smile as they locked up the house and walked out to the car.

Sean followed Lizzy out, opened the car door for her as she got in and went around to the driver's side. As they pulled away from Lizzy's house Sean looked out at the stars twinkling in the sky and felt a sense of peace wash over him. The night was still and calm, it was a beautiful evening, and he couldn't help but feel content. He was happy to have Lizzy by his side. On the other hand, Lizzy was more engrossed in trying to find the earing she had lost in the car earlier.

"What are you doing?" Sean asked as he watched Lizzy doing contortions trying to look under the car seat.

"I'm trying to find that damn earring that fell on the floor a while ago. I can't find it," Lizzy said in a muffled tone.

"Do you want me to pull over and help you find it?" Sean asked.

"No don't bother, they were only a cheap pair anyway," Lizzy said and sat back up in her seat.

"What did it look like?" Sean asked. "I will look for it in the morning when it's bright."

"It's silver with a red love heart hanging off the end of it," Lizzy said.

"Okay, I will find it tomorrow," Sean said and looked ahead on the road, his gaze fixing on a distinctive red Opel Record car approaching them. "Oh, look who this is."

"Who is it?" Lizzy inquired.

"Tommy Flynn, the feckin asshole, and he had a good look to see who was in the car, he doesn't miss much," Sean replied with evident annoyance as he shook his head.

"I heard you and Tommy had a bit of a disagreement after I left last Saturday night," Lizzy said as she looked intently over at Sean.

"That's right," Sean said bluntly, not wanting to be reminded of it. His expression didn't give anything away. He remained focused on the road ahead, avoiding eye contact.

"Well, here we are," Lizzy said as they reached the gate to Mrs Boyle's house.

Sean almost drove past it, still mulling over the events of the previous Saturday night. "Oh, right," he said, putting the car into reverse and rolling back to the gate. Lizzy got out of the car and took the bag of shopping from the back seat.

"I'll wait for you here," Sean said as he watched Lizzy get out of the car.

"Look, there is no need, I'll have to sit with the poor old dear for an hour or so. I'm the only person she gets to chat to, so you go ahead. I can walk back," Lizzy said leaning in the opened passenger window. Out of empathy and compassion, Lizzy was willing to put her own plans on hold in order to provide some company for her elderly neighbour.

"It's a good walk back and it's dark," Sean said in a concerned tone.

"It's less than a mile, it's a lovely warm night and I need the exercise. I'll be grand, this body doesn't keep in such good shape without a bit of exercise."

Lizzy laughed.

"Are you sure, it's no problem for me to wait," Sean offered, assurance in his voice. He was content to wait however long it took. He had no other pressing engagements.

"Yes, I'm sure. Thank you Sean, for giving me a lift and rescuing me earlier with my heavy bags, and I'm looking forward already to meeting you tomorrow night."

"Okay, well, I'll call out for you tomorrow evening around seven, does that suit?"

"Perfect, see you then," Lizzy said and blew Sean a kiss.

As he watched her walk away Sean smiled, happy that he had been able to help Lizzy out tonight and happy that they were back together. He put the car in gear, beeped the horn and drove off.

Chapter 11: Cold as Ice

3 hours earlier.

James and Maureen Murray sat across from each other at the kitchen table, hunched over their dinners. The scent of cooked lamb, fried onions, and potatoes wafted through the air, a reminder that this was a routine they'd been doing for decades. It was the smell of domesticity, of a life shared and experienced together, but now a heavy atmosphere of silence hung over them. They hadn't much to say to each other after thirty-three years of marriage, the passage of time making conversation harder. The only sound was the screeching noise of James scraping the last of his food off the plate with his knife.

James always ate his dinner quickly, as if somebody was going to steal it, wolfing it down in a few minutes. He dropped the cutlery on the plate, took a swallow from his glass of milk, and burped loudly. He then sat back on his chair with his hands clasped together, his eyes focused on the oilskin tablecloth that had illustrations of teapots on it. His face was expressionless, with no hint of emotion. He made no eye contact with his wife who was pushing the food around her plate, barely eating, only picking at her food without enthusiasm.

Maureen was wearing the same dress she'd had for years, her grey hair pulled back in a bun. Their home was too quiet now, their two sons had grown up and moved away and they rarely saw them or their wives and children. Maureen lived for her job, for her teaching position in Ballygorman national school where she worked alongside Donal McCabe.

James Murray was fifty-nine years old, but he didn't look it. He could have passed for a man ten years younger, still a good-looking man despite his years. His thick wavy hair had greyed slightly at the temples but he had a youthful face, with a strong jawline and strong brows with deep-set blue eyes. His body was still lean and muscular, and he carried himself with a confident air and commanding presence, being tall and broad-shouldered. A lifetime of hard manual labour working on his land had kept him strong and fit, alongside twenty years playing football for club and county. James still had an eye for the ladies and the ladies still had an eye for him, much to Maureen's annoyance. She had forgiven his affairs too many times but now she was at breaking point.

She had heard rumours about a fling he was having with their neighbour, Lizzy O'Dowd, but she wasn't sure if she wanted to believe the talk or not, afraid to confront James and risk breaking up their marriage. Afraid to have to start again, a life without him. She felt that she was too old for that now.

After a few moments of awkward silence, James broke the tension. "So, how was work today at school?"

Maureen looked up from her plate, astonished that James was actually taking an interest in her work for once. She paused to take a moment to gather her thoughts before answering, "It was a bit chaotic if I'm being honest. Donal McCabe was away on some sort of training course so I had to fill in for him as well as keep up with my own classes. To put it lightly, I feel like I've been run off my feet." Her voice wavered slightly with the last word, conveying the exhaustion in her voice.

James feigned a sympathetic expression as he absentmindedly picked pieces of meat from between his teeth with a matchstick. "I can only imagine how difficult that must be," he said, before continuing, "Things have been busy on the farm lately for me too, preparing to bring out the cattle next week." He spoke with deliberate ease as his eyes drifted off in thought, reflecting on all the work it would take to ready the land for grazing.

A thick, oppressive silence descended upon the room again, broken only by the gentle hum of the electric fridge that sat in the corner. Its monotonous buzz provided a strange comfort and familiarity in this otherwise uncomfortable atmosphere.

Maureen leaned forward with a worried expression. "Have you heard of the bomb that went off last night in Belfast?" she asked, her voice quivering slightly.

"No, I haven't had the chance to check the news yet. I was so busy all day," James replied.

Maureen shook her head sadly and continued, "It was the UVF. They planted the bomb in a pub. It's just awful. So many innocent people were hurt and killed."

James sighed in disbelief. "That's terrible. Where will it all end?"

"I know. It's been weighing heavily on my mind all day. It's hard to imagine why someone would do something so senseless," Maureen replied as she made the sign of the cross.

"I hope they catch the people responsible and bring them to justice," James said, his jaw clenched in anger.

"Me too. It's just so sad. I don't know what this world is coming to," Maureen said, her voice thick with emotion.

They continued to make awkward small talk, but the heavy silence lingered in the background. Maureen couldn't shake the feeling that something was off, that James was hiding something from her. As Maureen finished clearing the dinner plates off the table, James suddenly stood up from the table, causing Maureen to jump in surprise. "Christ, I've just remembered, I've got to go. Tom Burke's cattle have broken out again and he needs my help to put them back in," he said hastily, grabbing his coat from the hook by the door.

"Right, will you be long?" Maureen asked.

"Oh, I could be hours, god knows where the feckin cattle are," James said placing his fedora hat on his head.

"But it will be dark by half eight, sure it's nearly seven now." Maureen voiced her concern.

"Oh, I have a flashlamp in the car, I'll be fine. Don't wait up, you look tired. I'll see you later on," James assured her.

Maureen's heart sank as she watched him leave. She knew that Tom Burke's farm was on the way to Gallagher's pub in Ballygorman, where James had been spending more and more of his time lately. She couldn't help but wonder if he was really going to help with the cattle or if he was just using it as an excuse to go to the pub and drink away his problems.

As she cleared the cutlery from the table and washed them in the sink, Maureen couldn't shake the feeling of loneliness and betrayal that had settled over her. She felt like a stranger in her own home, with a husband who seemed more interested in the pub than in her. Her mind was racing with thoughts and worries. She speculated if James was cheating on her and the thought made her sick to her stomach.

James Murray pushed open the door to Gallagher's pub, a faint smile on his face as he greeted the familiar surroundings. He stepped up to the bar where Joe Gallagher, the owner, was cleaning glasses with a rag.

"Evening, Joe," James said, nodding.

"Ah, James, good to see you," Joe replied, setting down the glass he was polishing. "What'll it be tonight?"

"A pint of Harp, Joe," James said as he placed money on the counter.

"Just the one, mind you."

"Right you are," Joe said, reaching under the counter to grab a pint glass.

"It's quiet in here tonight," James said as he looked around and saw that the only other patrons were Paddy Farrell and Tommy Flynn, both sitting at a small table in the corner.

"Aye, it's a bit quiet, but sure Wednesdays are always quiet. But that's no bad thing. Gives you a chance to chat without having to shout over a racket," Joe said as he handed James his pint of Harp.

"True." James laughed. "How's business been?"

"It's been steady enough, can't complain. Any news around your neck of the woods?" Joe enquired.

"Nothing much, just the usual. A few cattle broke out from Tom Burke's farm, so I'm off to lend a hand."

"Aye, sure the life of a farmer is never done," Joe acknowledged.

"How's the family?" James asked, taking a sip from his pint.

"Ah, they're grand, the missus is still on my back about fixing up the house though." Joe sighed.

"Ha, tell me about it. You can never win with them." James empathized.

"So true. But sure, we do what we can to keep them happy." Joe agreed.

"Any news or gossip around the pub lately?" James asked.

"Not much, just the usuals coming in for a pint or two. Although Tommy Flynn did have a bit of trouble with Sean Breslin last Saturday night," Joe whispered as he moved closer to James so that Tommy wouldn't hear.

"Oh really? What happened?" James leaned in to get more information.

Joe explained, "Well, I'm not too sure of the background details, but Sean gave him a bit of a beating outside the pub."

James expressed concern. "Jesus, I hope he's all right."

"Ah, he'll be grand. Tommy's a tough one," Joe reassured him. "But speaking of gossip, I heard a few whispers about you and Lizzy O'Dowd."

"What? That's bullshit." James was taken aback.

"I don't know if it is bullshit, I heard she's been seeing Sean Breslin as well. You better watch yourself, James. Sean might give you a beating like he did to Tommy," Joe said with a grin, delighted to be stirring up James.

"You are fucking unbelievable, Gallagher. There's nothing going on between me and Lizzy, and as for Sean Breslin, he can go and jump in the lake for all I care," James responded angrily.

"Calm down, James, I'm only having a bit of craic with you, no need to get so upset," Joe said as he went back to polishing a glass.

James grew, unsurprisingly, tired of his chat with Joe and decided to join Paddy and Tommy at their table. He slid into an empty chair, nodding a greeting to both of them.

"Evening, lads," he said. "How's things?"

"Not bad, not bad," Paddy replied, taking a sip of his pint. "Just glad to be out of the house for a bit, you know how it is."

"Aye, I know the feeling," James said. "Well, the weather has been a bit all over the place lately. Can't seem to get a break from it."

"Aye, it's been a rough season for farming. You can't get any work done when it's always raining," Paddy agreed.

Tommy chimed in. "Tell me about it. My fields are soaked through, and the cattle are restless. They are mad to get out and I'm nearly out of hay."

James nodded in sympathy. "Cattle can be a right pain in the arse sometimes."

Their conversation was interrupted by Paddy's sombre tone. "And speaking of trouble, did you hear about the bomb that went off in Belfast last night? Terrible news."

"Aye, I did hear about that. It's a sad state of affairs when people resort to violence like that," James replied, his expression reflecting his concern.

Tommy nodded in agreement, adding, "I agree. It's a scary world we live in these days. It's just senseless," he said. "All this fighting, all this killing. What's it all for?"

"The British could sort it all out in a day if they wanted to," James said, confidently gesturing with his hands as he spoke.

Tommy, however, shook his head and argued back. "It's not that simple," he said. "If it were that easy the problem wouldn't even exist in the first place – why would they have allowed such a situation to persist for so long?" He crossed his arms as if emphasizing this point.

"I just hope it doesn't spill over into our little town here. We're not that far away from it, you never know," Paddy said, his eyes flickering with worry.

Tommy tried to lift their spirits. "Let's hope for the best, lads. But we can't let all that violence get us down. We still have to carry on with our lives and work."

James leaned in, his tone lowering, "Speaking of violence, Tommy, I heard about your run-in with Sean Breslin the other night. Is everything all right?"

Tommy tensed slightly but tried to shrug it off. "Aye, I'm fine. It was just a little disagreement. Nothing to worry about." Tommy was clearly embarrassed that Sean got the better of him. James noticed that Tommy had a bruise on his cheek. "What happened there?" James prodded, gesturing towards the bruise. Tommy winced as he touched his cheek. "I heard he gave you a good beating. Are you sure that you're okay?"

"I can handle myself, don't you worry about that, James Murray," Tommy replied firmly.

James raised his eyebrows. "Sean Breslin? That lad's a troublemaker if ever there was one."

"Aye, he is," Tommy said. "But he's got Lizzy O'Dowd on his arm now, so he's feeling pretty confident and cock sure of himself."

James's heart sank at the mention of Lizzy's name.

"But speaking of rumours, what's all this I hear about Lizzy O'Dowd going out with Sean Breslin and you James as well," Tommy said launching a swift counterattack. "She is a busy girl."

"There's nothing going on between me and Lizzy." James's jaw clenched as he shot Tommy a withering look.

Paddy interjected, sensing the tension. "Tommy, that's enough. Let's not stir up any trouble here."

Tommy leaned back, holding up his hands in mock surrender. "I'm just having a bit of fun, Paddy. But seriously, James, you need to get your house in order before someone else does it for you."

"Fuck you, Flynn. I hope Sean Breslin beats you twice as hard the next time, because if one man deserves it, you fucking do," James said as he slammed down his empty pint glass on the table and stood up. "I'm going to McDaid's for a few, I'm not listening to your bullshit all night."

"Did I touch a nerve, Murray?" Tommy laughed loudly as he watched James walk out of the pub with haste.

"You are an awful man, Tommy, scaring off my customer," Joe Gallagher shouted from behind the bar.

"Ahh, he'll be back," Tommy replied as he stood up, finished his pint and placed the empty glass on the counter. "Now I'm off too, I haven't time to sit around talking bullshit to you fellas."

Chapter 12: You're the One That I Want

Wednesday May 3rd.
10.15 PM

Lizzy had just got back to her house after her walk from Mrs. Boyle's house. She felt tired and slouched down on the couch to watch some TV. It was gone 10 pm and she was struggling to keep her eyes open as she watched an episode of Trom agus Éadrom, presented by Liam O'Murchu. She drifted off into a snooze, feeling content that she had rekindled her relationship with Sean earlier. Just as quickly as she dropped off to sleep, a loud knock at the door woke her up.

She jolted upwards in surprise, quickly wracking her brain to try to figure out who it could be at such a late hour. Hope blossomed within her that it could be Sean and that maybe he had decided to call back. Adrenaline coursed through her veins as she got up from the couch, turning off the TV before rushing to the back door. She opened it with no trepidation, expecting to see Sean standing there, but instead was met only with darkness and a tall figure standing in the shadows with a hat pulled down covering their face.

She fumbled for the switch, flicking on the outside light with a click. The sudden rush of brightness made her squint, and she rubbed her eyes until they adjusted to the harsh illumination. Her vision cleared and there was James Murray, standing before her. His face was twisted into a look of contempt.

Lizzy felt apprehensive and unsure. "James, what are you doing here?" she queried uneasily. He stepped closer and briefly paused before answering, his gaze intense as if willing her to read between the lines of his unspoken words. "I just came to see you, Lizzy," he finally replied as he attempted to make his way into her back porch.

Lizzy tried to bar the door with her body, but James forced her out of the way and stomped into the kitchen. She knew she was no match for him in terms of strength. He slammed his wide-brimmed black fedora onto the table like a gesture of authority before turning his attention towards Lizzy. His eyes were glacial, cold, and calculating. His sneer seemed to mock her as he stood tall, his body stiff and unyielding, his posture was aggressive, hands curled into fists at his side, ready to take action if necessary.

“You must have been expecting me, you have the drinks ready,” James said as he looked over at the bottle of Powers whiskey and two crystal glasses on the worktop next to the sink, the glasses that Sean and Lizzy had drank from earlier and Lizzy hadn’t gotten around to washing yet.

"Let’s go into the living room, where it is cosier and we can have a nice little chat beside the fire and have our little drinks," James said as he made his way to sit down on the couch in the living room, making himself at home. "I heard that you and Sean Breslin had a row last Saturday night, and I thought maybe you could use some company. I could protect you if that animal, Breslin, dares to come around. He's a brute, Lizzy, you need to be careful. Have you heard about what he did to poor Tommy Flynn? All those broken bones and that awful wound on his forehead—it's a miracle the poor man survived after such a brutal attack."

"What do you think you're doing here, James?" Lizzy thundered, her voice reverberating off the walls.

"I'm not here to cause trouble," he replied calmly as his eyes travelled around the room, taking in every detail. "I just thought I'd drop in and say 'hello'. A friendly social call." His gaze shifted back to Lizzy, and he offered her a conciliatory smile.

"I heard that you were bragging to Paddy Farrell in Gallagher's the other night that you were with me, whenever you felt like it, at your beck and call. The gall of you. Our dirty little fling was years ago. Get over it, James, I moved on, and you should too." Lizzy spat out the words with anger as she remained standing in the middle of the living room floor, her eyes fixed on James.

"Don't listen to Paddy, he is a useless bollox," James scoffed, disdain in his voice. He shifted on the couch.

Lizzy felt her stomach twist into knots with dread. "James, I really don't feel comfortable having you here, I want you to leave now," she demanded.

"Come on, Lizzy, don't be like that, don't be so stubborn." James smiled as he stood up, moving closer to her. "I know you like me. I can tell by the way you look at me," he said softly. His eyes sparkled with intensity, his eyes locked on Lizzy's eyes, searching for some form of agreement, scanning her face, looking for signs that she liked him.

There was a slight smirk on his lips and the air between them was charged with tension. James looked determined to get his own way. His posture was rigid as he leaned in, towering over her, trying to intimidate his host. His expression was confident with a hint of menace. His voice was low and persuasive, almost threatening in its quiet intensity.

Lizzy felt her stomach churn with nerves as she stepped backward, trying to put some distance between them. She felt scared and unsure of what to do. Her heart pounded in her chest, fear coursing through her veins as she realised that she was in danger. All she wanted was for him to leave, but he seemed determined to stay.

"James, please, I think you should leave," Lizzy said, backing even further away from him.

But James just laughed and grabbed her arm, pulling her towards him. Lizzy struggled to break free, but he was too strong. She felt his hot drunken breath as he whispered in her ear, "Come on, Lizzy, let's have some fun like we used to." James's face was close to Lizzy's, his lips forming the words as he spoke. His grip on her upper arm was tight and unrelenting, while an intense heat radiated from his body. His bloodshot eyes were aflame with desire and raw carnal rage, eager for the possibility of pleasure within his grasp.

Lizzy pushed him away with all the conviction she had in her. "No, James, I don't want this and I'm telling you to go," she said firmly. All the softness that had been previously in his eyes disappeared and anger flashed across his face. "You're a tease, Lizzy," James hissed between gritted teeth. "You think you can play games with me? Lead me on and then reject me? Well, I won't stand for it any longer."

Lizzy tried to run, but James caught her and threw her to the ground. She screamed and kicked at him, but he was too strong. He held her down with one hand. Lizzy struggled against him, she screamed and kicked, her fingernails digging into the skin on his face, flesh and bone against flesh and bone. She was in a whirlwind of motion, thrashing and flailing and trying to turn on her back so she could use her legs to break his grip and push him away. She felt like she was going to be crushed under his weight. James's large, hulking body overpowered her. Trying to fight back, her feeble punches and kicks did nothing to him. She felt like a child fighting a grown man, impotent and useless.

Lizzy felt a wave of panic wash over her as she desperately tried to break free from his grasp. James snarled as she tried to push him away, his eyes narrow and his expression twisted in anger, the way a wolf scowls at its prey. She screamed for help, hoping someone would hear her cries, but there was no one around to help her. She felt helpless and terrified as James continued his assault. Lizzy tasted fear, she tasted the coppery taste of James's blood on her lips from her nails drawing blood from his cheeks. She could feel the weight of his body pressing against her, the pressure on her chest, feeling her rib cage would crack as he pushed her face into the carpet. The sound of his heavy, laboured breathing rang in her ear.

She tried to struggle, to break free before it was too late. In a desperate attempt to escape Lizzy frantically scanned the floor, her gaze darting back and forth, searching for something she could use as a weapon, something to defend herself against James. As his grip tightened, she noticed a glint of metal and with a burst of courage and strength, she grabbed it with her trembling fingers, a brass poker beside the fireplace. In one quick movement, she swung it hard at James's head with all her strength, feeling a ripple of satisfaction run through her as it made contact with his skull, leaving angry red welts on his face. James yelled in pain and released her from his grip and she scrambled away from him. Lizzy got up off the floor and tried to run out of the living room, her face streaked with blood and tears.

"Come back here," James roared as he sprang to his feet and chased after her, his arms outstretched as he moved with determination, his face twisted in rage, quickly grabbing her around the waist. She struggled again against his grip, her eyes wide, her face contorted with fear and desperation, her pleading screams of terror and despair piercing the air.

"Let me go, please James, let me go," Lizzy pleaded.

In response, James wrapped his large hand across her mouth and her screams were muffled. She desperately kicked out at James's shins, her arms flailing against his chest, trying to break free from his clutches.

James's raw strength was undeniable as he used his arms to effortlessly pick Lizzy up from the ground. In a single, powerful effort, he hoisted her body into the air, her limbs dangling limp like a ragdoll. For a moment it seemed as if time had stopped as he held her suspended in mid-air before flinging her back into the centre of the room with an unceremonious thud. She collapsed onto the coffee table, her head hitting the wood with a dull crack that reverberated off the walls. The only sound now was James's heavy, ragged breathing as he stared down at Lizzy, who lay motionless. He closed his eyes and felt an overwhelming sense of dread fill him as he realized what had happened. He opened them again and all he could do was stand there in solemn silence, unable to comprehend or accept what had happened.

His face went pale, his expression a mix of guilt, horror and shock, unable to register what he had just done. His brows were furrowed, his jaw slack in disbelief. Tears welled up in his eyes, his lips quivered as he kneeled beside her, his hands trembling as he reached out to touch Lizzy's lifeless body. His fingers gently traced her face, as if he wanted to capture her memory forever. No breath was coming from her lips, her body was still, and no signs of life were present.

James looked around the room, his mind racing with thoughts of what he should do. Should he call the Gardai and immediately confess to what he had done? Should he just run away and try to forget about this horrible incident? He felt paralyzed by fear and uncertainty, unsure of what his next move should be. Cold sweat ran down the back of his neck.

James made his choice, he slowly got to his feet, and without another glance at Lizzy's body he quickly walked out of the living room and into the kitchen, He grabbed a tea towel from the worktop and used it to wipe his handprints off all the door handles that he touched as he exited the house. He got into his Hilman Hunter car and drove away, not looking back, not knowing what the future held for him.

Chapter 13: Darkness on the Edge of town

Thursday May 4th

Nestled on the edge of the small village of Ballygorman, the garage stood like a relic of a bygone era, a place that time seemed to have forgotten but a place where hard work and perseverance were the norm. Its dilapidated exterior was covered in rotting sheets of corrugated iron, and the faded wooden sign above the door proclaimed it to be the workshop of John McGinley, the village mechanic. As you approached the garage, the pungent smell of oil and petrol would hit you like a wave, and the sound of metal clanking against metal drowned out any other noise in the vicinity.

Outside the garage lay a graveyard of old, rusted cars. The sight was a mix of sadness and nostalgia, an odd combination of beauty and decay. The cars were all different shapes and sizes, some so old that their make and model were unrecognisable, just rusty carcasses left out in the rain and sun to deteriorate. They were like the bones of dinosaurs, a reminder of another time. Each car had its own story, its own journey, but now they were all just a part of this graveyard of cars.

The cars were parked haphazardly, some on top of each other, the ground around them covered in oil stains and bits of broken car parts. The grass and weeds grew tall around the cars, entwining themselves around the rusted metal, and the wind whistled through their broken windows. The birds perched on the roofs left white shite stains all over them.

Close to the front entrance was a battered blue and white Ford Anglia, which had seen better days. The paint was peeling and the body was corroded through in several places. The headlights were missing, and the windscreen was cracked. The wheels were flat and the car was sitting on blocks. Next to the Ford Anglia was a 1950s white Volkswagen Beetle with a rusted roof and doors that barely opened. The car was so old that it didn't have seat belts or a radio. The windows were shattered, the tyres flat. The car's white paint had faded and it was covered in dirt and grime. Further down the row, a brown Austin A40 looked like it had been parked there for decades. The car's bonnet was open and the engine missing. The seats were torn, the floorboards rusted through. Despite the decay and the rust, there was something beautiful about the cars. Each one had a unique design, a work of art in its own right. They were like sculptures, frozen in time, a reminder of a bygone era.

Stepping inside into McGinley's garage was like entering a different world altogether. The brightness of the outside world was replaced by the dim light of a few flickering bulbs hanging precariously from the ceiling. The walls were lined with tools of every kind, most of them old and tarnished from being left out in the rain. The floor was slick with grease and oil, and it felt like walking on ice as you made your way through the cluttered space.

In one corner of the garage sat a pile of old tyres, some with rims still attached and others lying haphazardly in a heap. The air was thick with dust and cobwebs, and it was clear that no one had bothered to clean the place in years. The only sign of life in the garage was the occasional grunt or muttered curse from John McGinley, who was buried deep beneath the bonnet of a battered old car.

The cars in the garage were just as neglected as the building itself. Some were carelessly half-dismantled, their parts scattered around the garage like a jigsaw puzzle waiting to be pieced together. There was an air of hopelessness about the place, as if the cars were doomed to remain in this state of disrepair forever.

John McGinley himself was a sight to behold. His face was creased with lines from years of squinting at engines and etched with deep furrows around his brow and mouth, the furrows black from oil stains. John's upper lip was adorned with a thick, black, bushy moustache that matched the colour of his hair, which was slicked back with sweat and grease. His eyes were deep-set and piercing, their colour a shade of blue grey that seemed to change depending on his mood. There was a sense of intensity to his gaze, a hint of danger that suggested he was not a man to be trifled with. His hands were rough, calloused and dark from handling tools day in and day out, a testament to the countless hours he had spent tinkering with engines and repairing vehicles. His clothing matched his rough-and-tumble demeanour. He typically wore a pair of oil-stained overalls which hung loosely over his muscular frame. His shirt, which was usually unbuttoned at the collar, was a faded plaid pattern that looked like it had seen better days.

Overall, McGinley was a weathered man like the rusted cars scattered around his garage, with a rugged and tough exterior that suggested a life of hard work and perseverance. At fifty-one years old, he still had a strong, muscular build, with broad shoulders and powerful arms, evidence of years spent working on cars and hauling heavy machinery. Despite his rough exterior, however, there was a kindness in his eyes that belied his tough exterior. It was clear that John

McGinley loved his job. He took pride in his achievements, regardless of the mess the place was in, and every time he managed to fix a car that others had given up on his face would light up with a sense of satisfaction that was palpable. His passion for his work was infectious and it was clear that his customers respected and admired him for it. John had a certain charm that endeared him to many of his customers. He had a quick wit and a sharp sense of humour and was always ready with a joke or a quip to lighten the mood; the village mechanic with a heart of gold, who kept the cars of Ballygorman running despite the odds, and wasn't greedy for money and would never leave you stuck.

John wiped his hands on his overalls and stood back to admire his handiwork. The black Morris Minor that had been sitting in his garage for the past few days was finally ready to be returned to its owner. It had been a tricky fix, the starter motor had to be repaired. But John had persevered and now the car was purring like a kitten. He popped the bonnet one last time to make sure everything was in order, and then closed it with a satisfying thud. Turning to the interior of the car, he reached for a dirty rag and began to wipe down the steering wheel. It was an old wheel, worn smooth with years of use, but John took care to clean it as thoroughly as he could. He knew that his customers appreciated the small touches, and he took pride in making sure that their cars were not only fixed, but also cleaned and polished.

Next, he turned his attention to the seats. They were cracked and faded, but with a little elbow grease John managed to make them look presentable. He wiped down the leather with a damp cloth, being careful not to damage it, and then applied a coat of leather conditioner. The seats looked almost new by the time he was finished. Satisfied with his work, John stepped back and surveyed the car once more. It was an old car, to be sure, thirteen years old, but it had character. The paint was chipped in places, and there were dents and scratches all over the body, but it was clear that this car had been well-loved. John knew that his customer, Lizzy O'Dowd, would be pleased with the work he had done and he felt a sense of fulfilment that was hard to describe.

Checking his watch, it had gone six. It had been a long day, starting work at seven that morning, but he was content in the knowledge that he had done good work. He knew there would be more cars to fix tomorrow, but for now, he was happy to close up shop and head home and cook his dinner. It was a simple life, but it was a good one, and John was grateful for it. But he couldn't leave until Lizzy O'Neill came to collect her car.

John had tried calling earlier on her phone, to let her know that it was ready, but there was no reply. John sighed and leaned against the doorframe of the garage, watching the few remaining cars on the lot bathed in the evening light of the sun. He knew he could park the car outside the gate, leave the key on top of the front right tyre and she would collect it later. He had a feeling that she was on her way, but that she was just running late, maybe waiting for a neighbour to give her a lift into town.

With a resigned shrug, John decided to wait a little longer. He walked over to the phone box on the street next to his garage, pulling out a little black book from his pocket. It was filled with phone numbers, addresses, and other bits of information John needed to keep track of for his business. He flipped through the pages, searching for Lizzy's number. After a few moments of searching, he found it and dialled her phone. The phone rang and rang, but there was no answer. John frowned, wondering if Lizzy had forgotten to tell him she wouldn't be able to collect her car today. But then he remembered that she was a stickler for schedules, and she had always been prompt in the past. She had arranged to come by before the end of the day to collect it, she had called into the garage the day before to tell John.

John was getting impatient, pacing back and forth in front of the garage, muttering under his breath. He wouldn't be able to relax at home until he knew she had picked up the car. Finally, he made a decision. He would drive the Morris Minor out to Lizzy's house himself. It was only a few miles away and Lizzy could run him back into town, or he could walk back if he had to. It was a fine May evening. With a sense of determination he grabbed the keys to the Morris Minor and started up the engine. As he pulled out of the garage he spotted Paddy Farrell, one of his regular customers, walking down the street.

"Hey, Paddy!" John called out, pulling up next to him in the Morris Minor. "I need a favour. Can you follow me out to Lizzy's house in your car so I can drop off her car? I will only be five minutes."

Paddy grinned and nodded. "Sure thing, John, no problem. I'll follow you out there, you go ahead."

Paddy climbed into his black Ford Cortina, started up the engine and followed the Morris Minor out of the village. The evening sun painted the sky in vibrant oranges and pinks. The birds were singing, and the air was fresh and fragrant with the scent of grass and flowers. The countryside stretched out ahead of them as they drove.

After five minutes they arrived at Lizzy's house. John parked the Morris Minor in the driveway and Paddy pulled up behind him in his Ford Cortina. John got out of the car and rang the doorbell at the back door, but there was no answer. He tried knocking on the door, but still there was no response. "Damn it," John muttered under his breath. "Where is she?"

Paddy got out of the Cortina to see what was wrong, standing next to John at the back porch. They could see a light on in the kitchen through the window, but the silence inside the house made them uneasy. After knocking again with no response, John turned the handle on the back porch door and to his surprise, it opened. He looked at Paddy before he entered the porch, looking for approval. Paddy nodded. John cautiously stepped into the kitchen, calling Lizzy's name, but there was no answer. The room felt stuffy and oppressive, the fluorescent lights overhead buzzing incessantly.

He walked into the living room, still calling her name, and was horrified to find her lying lifeless on the ground. Lizzy's body lay limp, her eyes shut and her skin pale and lifeless. Her long dark hair fanned out around her head, splayed against the coffee table. The soft fabric of her blouse was torn and dishevelled and stained with dark, red blood that had streamed from the back of her head. Her arms were still outstretched, as if she had been trying to reach for something when the life left her body. The coffee table was partially overturned, the lamp next to it lying broken on the floor.

"Oh my God," John gasped. "Lizzy's dead."

Paddy looked at him in shock. "What? Are you sure?"

John nodded, unable to find any words.

Paddy walked over to the body and crouched down beside it, examining it. "She's not breathing, her skin is cold," he confirmed, his voice low.

John stood there, still in shock, unsure of what to do. "We need to call the Guards," he said finally, his voice trembling.

Paddy nodded, getting up from the floor. "Yes, we do," he agreed. "Come on, I'll help you find the phone."

They walked down the hallway and Paddy spotted a phone on a table next to the front door. He picked it up and dialled the emergency services. "Hello, we need an ambulance and the Guards to Lizzy O'Dowd's house. It's about three miles from Ballygorman village on the back road to Sligo, the townland is called Cloghan, near Killard crossroads. There's been a death." Paddy's voice was steady despite the gravity of the situation.

John watched as Paddy spoke to the operator, his mind reeling with shock and disbelief. He couldn't believe Lizzy was dead. She had always been such a lively and kind person, and the thought of her being gone was incomprehensible. Paddy hung up the phone and turned to face John. "We should wait for the Guards outside," he said, his voice low. "They'll want to talk to us."

John nodded, still in shock, and the two men walked out of the house. They stood on the doorstep, waiting for the authorities to arrive. The silence was oppressive, and John couldn't shake the feeling of anxiety that had settled in his stomach.

Twenty minutes later the sound of sirens cut through the stillness, and two Garda cars pulled up outside the house. The officers got out of their vehicles and approached John and Paddy as they placed their hats on their heads. The first officer was a sergeant, a tall, broad-shouldered man with a thick moustache and deep-set eyes. His name was Tom O'Donnell, and he had been with the Leitrim police force for over twenty years. The second officer was a younger man, with brown curly hair and bright green eyes. His name was Martin Kelly, and he was a relative newcomer to the force.

"What seems to be the problem?" Sergeant O'Donnell asked, his voice gruff and authoritative.

"It's Lizzy O'Dowd," John replied, his voice shaking. "I went to drop off her car, and I found her... I found her dead."

The sergeant's expression immediately grew serious. "Dead? Are you sure?"

John nodded. "I'm sure. She was lying in the living room. I didn't touch her."

"What is your name?" Sergeant O'Donnell asked as he took out a black notebook.

"I'm John McGinley, a mechanic from Ballygorman. I was just leaving back Lizzy's car," John answered as he pointed at the Morris Minor, his hand still trembling.

"Right, and your name?" the Sergeant asked as he turned his focus on Paddy.

"I'm Paddy Farrell, from Ballygorman, well from outside the village a bit."

"Why were you here?"

"I was following John out so as I could give him a lift back into town."

"I see," Sargeant O'Donnell said as he finished writing notes in his book. "All right, Mr McGinley and Mr Farrell, we need you to stay here while we investigate. Is there anyone else in the house?"

"No, just Lizzy," John replied, still looking shaken.

"All right. Garda Kelly, I want you to go in and take a look. Be careful, and don't touch anything," the sergeant said as he glanced over at the other officer. Garda Martin Kelly nodded and made his way into the house. The Sergeant turned back to John. "Can you tell us what happened? Did you notice anything unusual when you arrived?"

John shook his head. "Well, I noticed that the light was on in the kitchen. I knocked on the door, but there was no answer. Then I tried the handle on the back porch door and it was open. I went in, that's when I found her in the living room."

The sergeant nodded. "All right. Can you give us a list of anyone who might have had reason to harm Lizzy, can you think of anyone who might have had a grudge against Ms. O'Dowd? Anyone who might want to hurt her?"

John thought for a moment. "Nobody, I can't think of anyone, she was well liked, a lovely person. Lizzy was a kind woman; she never had an enemy in the world."

"Is she, or rather was she married, had she a husband?" Sergeant O'Donnell inquired.

"No, Lizzy was a widower, her husband, John is dead a good few years now," Paddy answered.

"What about any ex-boyfriends, or anyone she had a falling out with recently?" the sergeant asked.

Paddy paused for a few moments, unsure how to answer the question, knowing the recent rumours about Sean Breslin and James Murray. "No, not that I know of anyway," Paddy said as he looked down at his boots.

As the sergeant continued to question Paddy, he found himself growing increasingly uneasy. He wished he could just go home and forget everything that had happened, but he would never be able to get the image of Lizzy's dead body out of his head. It would stay with him now and in the future, until he had memories to rake over, until the day he would die.

"All right. We'll look into it. You two lads can head off now, but I might need to ask you a few questions in a day or two. I will be in contact," Sergeant O'Donnell said as he walked off and entered the back door to the house.

John nodded, his eyes still fixed on Lizzy's car. "Of course. Whatever you need to do."

John, still reeling from what had happened, felt sorrow for Lizzy. She was a good woman, and she deserved better than to be murdered in her living room. His mind kept wandering back to the image of Lizzy's lifeless body. *Who could have done this to her? Is anyone else in danger?* hc thought.

John and Paddy couldn't believe that something like this could happen in their quiet little village. They knew their lives would never be the same again.

Just as the two men were about to get into Paddy's Cortina, Sean Breslin pulled up outside Lizzy's house. He was expecting to collect her for their night out as arranged and was dumbstruck to see the Garda car parked in the driveway. Had Lizzy's house been burgled, had she failed to pay her car tax; various explanations for the presence of the Guards at the house were running through his head.

"What's going on?" Sean called out to Paddy.

Paddy turned around and looked at Sean with a grim expression. "Lizzy's dead, Sean," he said. "It looks like she might have been murdered."

Sean's mouth fell open in disbelief. "What? No, that can't be true," he said as he got out of his car and walked over to Paddy.

Paddy put a hand on Sean's shoulder. "I'm sorry, Sean. It's true. The Guards are still inside investigating, you can't go in."

Sean felt like he had been punched in the gut. He couldn't believe Lizzy was gone. He had just seen her the night before, and she had seemed fine. They had talked about going out for a drink, and now she was dead. "How did it happen?" Sean asked, his voice shaking.

John shrugged. "We don't know yet. We found her half an hour ago, it looks like her head crashed against the coffee table in the living room and the blow killed her."

Sean felt a sense of numbness wash over him as he tried to process the news. He had never experienced anything like this before. He had lost friends and family members before to illness and old age, but never lost someone as sudden as this, never to murder.

"What do we do now?" Sean asked, looking to John and Paddy for guidance.

"We wait for the Guards to do their investigation," John said.

"You look like you could do with a stiff brandy. Follow us back into Ballygorman, I think we all could do with one." Paddy sighed.

As Sean walked into Gallagher's he spotted John and Paddy sitting in a booth at the back of the pub and made his way over to them. They ordered brandies and sat in silence for a few moments, each lost in their own thoughts.

Finally, Paddy spoke up. "Lizzy didn't deserve to die like that, nobody deserves to die like that."

John nodded in agreement. "It's hard to believe that something so cruel could happen in our parish, at the edge of our town, such... darkness," he said. Sean took a sip of his brandy, the warmth of the alcohol spreading through his body. "Do you think the Guards will catch whoever did it?" he asked.

Paddy shrugged. "It's hard to say. But they'll do their best and we can help by giving them any information we have."

Sean nodded, feeling a sense of responsibility. He knew that he had to do everything he could to help bring Lizzy's killer to justice.

As they sat in the pub until midnight they shared stories and memories of Lizzy. They laughed and joked, trying to remember the good times and forget the pain of the present. But underneath it all, there was an undercurrent of sadness that couldn't be ignored. They were all struggling to come to terms with the loss of her. Especially Sean, he knew it would be a long time before he would be able to move on from Lizzy's death.

At seven o'clock in the following morning, John McGinley groaned and made his way back inside the garage, grabbing a rag and some tools. He had work to do, but his mind was still reeling from the events of the night before. He could hardly focus on the task at hand, his thoughts constantly drifting back to the sight of Lizzy lying dead, lifeless on her living room floor. As he worked, the minutes stretched into hours, until finally he finished repairing the last of the cars for that day. He stood back, wiping his brow with a dirty rag, and looked around the garage.

He made his way to his tiny office, collapsing into his chair, and ran his oily hands through his greasy hair. He needed to get some sleep, but he couldn't shake the feeling of shock, sadness and horror out of his head. He probably never would.

Chapter 14: Who Are You?

Friday May 5th

James Murray's Hillman Hunter car was parked on Main Street, Ballygorman, just down from the Garda station. The car sat still and silent; with its drab dark colour, fading paint and rust spots dotting its surface it was barely noticeable amongst the hustle and bustle of the activity around it. Inside the vehicle, James sat tensely in the driver's seat, watching the activity with wide and interested eyes. His hands clenched the steering wheel tightly. He watched in nervous awe as a flurry of commotion took place, squad cars whizzing by, officers bustling in and out of the station with an abundance of vigour. All around him seemed to be alive with energy and movement.

His eyes scanned the scene warily, as if he was expecting something major to happen at any moment. He was trying to remain still and act normal, but his breath came in short gasps and his forehead was covered with sweat, his face filled with worry and apprehension. His right cheek had three long scratch marks where Lizzy O'Dowd had dug her nails in deep. His wife Maureen had spotted the scratch marks early on Thursday morning and James explained that he got scraped by briars in a ditch when he was trying to round up Tom Burke's cattle the night before.

James was trying to act relaxed but inside he was a bundle of nerves, worrying that the Guards might be getting close to finding the killer of Lizzy O'Dowd, to finding out that it was him.

Onlookers stood outside Doherty's shop, attempting to make sense of the rumours swirling around them. Theories were offered and debated between them as to who had been responsible for the death of Lizzy, but no clear answer seemed to satisfy their curiosity. In hushed tones, they discussed and speculated amongst themselves as they tried to piece together what happened that night. Some suggested it was a jealous lover, some suggested that it was a robbery that had gone wrong, others even suggested that Lizzy was somehow connected to the IRA and there was paramilitary involvement.

Speculation ran rampant, leading to many wild conjectures and over the top explanations. All in all, no one could seem to make sense of what had happened. Other locals just minded their business and got on with their daily routines. Schoolchildren scurried off the school bus. Farmers drove through the village on their tractors. Willy O'Donnell wearing a bright yellow crash helmet rode through town on his Honda 50. Pauline McDaid brushed the fag butts off the footpath in front of her father's pub and tried to remember the chapter she had studied the night before about Charles Stewart Parnell in preparation for her upcoming Leaving Certificate history exam.

James Murray was so lost in his own thoughts that the sudden interruption of a loud voice coming from the footpath pulled him back down to reality.

"Well James, how's things, fierce sad about poor Lizzy," Tommy Flynn said as he stood looking up at the Garda station.

James sighed and looked out through the open driver's door window to see who had spoken.

“Some activity around the town, eh? The Guards are up and down the roads all day,” Tommy said. As Tommy spoke a heavy shower of rain began to suddenly pour down from the heavens and without an invite he got into James’s car and sat on the passenger’s seat.

“I tell you, the murder of Lizzy has put a real damper on the area,” Tommy said, taking a good look around the inside of James’s car. The interior was a worn shade of brown, the windows were slightly foggy with age and there was a large crack in the windscreen.

James didn’t respond and just nodded in agreement.

“It’s terrible altogether .... What do you think happened. Who do you think killed her?” Tommy inquired.

"How the hell do I know who killed her,” James replied, his tone noticeably terse as he kept looking out of the car's window.

Tommy squinted as he began to rub his hands together, seemingly in deep thought before speaking again. "Well, I noticed something interesting on Wednesday evening close to Lizzy O'Dowd's house," Tommy said with a certain level of intrigue in his voice.

James quickly shifted his gaze towards him, wondering what this mysterious revelation could be. "What did you notice?”

Tommy laughed and avoided the question, reminiscing instead about the Wednesday night they had spent in Gallagher’s pub. “God, you were sore!” he joked. “I left shortly after you made your dramatic exit.”

“Yeah, well you were spouting some bullshit,” James replied defensively. “So, what did you notice at Lizzy’s house on Wednesday night?”

“Anyway, when I left Gallagher’s and got into my car and drove out the road to Cloghan, I met Sean Breslin driving towards me and who was in the car with him, only Lizzy O’Dowd,” Tommy explained.

“Really,” James said with interest, leaning forward in his seat.

“Yes, and I heard that the Guards reckon Lizzy was killed on Wednesday evening,” Tommy responded.

James paused for a few moments, carefully weighing up the implications of what Tommy had just told him. Could this information be useful to him in some way? He decided it was worth prodding Tommy further. "Have you told the Guards what you saw?" he asked, his voice a low murmur.

Tommy stared back at James and replied, "No, I haven't."

"Well, I think that you should tell the Guards... it could help them with the investigation."

"Do you think that Sean Breslin could have killed Lizzy?" Tommy asked in a surprised tone.

James paused and gathered his thoughts before giving a response. "I don't know."

"I doubt it was him, Sean is many things, but he is not a killer." Tommy shook his head in disbelief.

"I know... but he is violent, he attacked you last Saturday night for no reason, didn't he."

"I was winding him up in fairness, and it was only a scrap. Killing somebody in cold blood is a totally different thing altogether." Tommy shrugged.

James looked concerned as he spoke, his voice holding a hint of urgency. "You need to go down to the Garda station and inform them of what you have seen. Tell them that Sean and Lizzy were together in Sean's car after nine o'clock on Wednesday evening," he said.

"Do you really think that I should?" Tommy replied, feeling hesitant at the thought of getting involved.

James nodded in response. "Yes, definitely. You have to tell them."

Tommy hesitated for a moment before deciding to agree with James. "All right, I'll go up now," he said.

"Good man, Tommy, you're doing the right thing," James encouraged him.

With a deep, shuddering breath, Tommy stepped out of James's car and began his slow ascent up the street to the Garda station. He paused for a moment, looking back at James's car, trying to steady his racing heart. He then gathered his scattered courage and walked on. James watched intently from the car as Tommy finally disappeared out of sight through the station's doors.

Chapter 15: Blue Valentines

Two hours later

The soft light of the evening sun cloaked the farmhouse in a warm hue as Sean Breslin sat at the kitchen table with his mother Eileen and his brother Mark. It was a fine Friday evening in May, and Mark had just returned home for the weekend. The kitchen was filled with the aroma of freshly cooked ham, mixed with the strong smell of hard-boiled eggs and scallions. The salty smell seeped into every corner, crack, and crevice of the room and beyond.

Sean sat at the head of the table, his hands resting on his lap, his eyes distant and unfocussed, his mind preoccupied with sorrow. He had lost his appetite and pushed his salad aside, barely touching it. A lone tear spilled down his cheek and he quickly wiped it away with the back of his hand, not wanting to show weakness in front of those around him. Mark, on the other hand, was animated and full of life, sharing stories of his week in Killybegs. Eileen sat opposite Mark, her kind face full of joy and interest as she listened to her sons' conversation. She was delighted to have them with her again for the weekend.

Sean leaned over the table, taking a deep breath before asking, "So how's everything going at the factory anyway? I bet it's been busy as ever."

Mark nodded in agreement, his mouth full as he replied, "It sure has been. But that isn't anything to complain about, it definitely keeps me on my toes!" He paused for a moment and then added, "You know what? I think you should come up to Killybegs and join us, we could do with taking on a few more men."

"Maybe one day, Mark, but right now I've got my own work to focus on," Sean said, forcing a smile.

Eileen listened intently, her brow furrowed with concern. "And you're working those long hours again, Mark?"

"Aye, Ma, it's the only way to make a living these days," Mark replied, his expression serious for a moment before breaking into a grin.

"I'm glad to hear it, son. You know your father would be so proud of you, working so hard, with a good job," Eileen said, her voice breaking as she spoke.

"Thanks, Ma. It means a lot to hear that," Mark said as looked up from his plate and smiled at her warmly.

As they finished their meal, there was a knock at the back door. Eileen rose from the table, her floral apron rustling across her hips as she went to see who was calling and found Sergeant O'Donnell standing there, his expression grim.

"Good evening, ma'am," Sergeant O'Donnell said, his voice a deep and resonant rumble. "Is Sean Breslin here?"

Sean and Mark heard her exchange a few words with someone. They couldn't make out what was being said, but both sensed that something was wrong.

Eileen turned and called out to Sean, who had risen from his chair and was now standing nervously behind her. "It's for you, Sean," she said, her voice trembling slightly, her face white with shock.

Sean felt a sudden sense of unease, and he could feel his palms beginning to sweat. He stepped forward. “Yes, Sergeant, are you looking for me?" he asked, trying to keep his voice steady.

"I'm afraid I need to take you in for questioning, Sean," the sergeant said. "There's been an incident involving a woman by the name of Lizzy O'Dowd, and we think you might be able to help us with the investigation." His tone was firm. "I'll need you to come with me to the station now."

Sean's mind raced as he tried to make sense of what was happening. He glanced at his mother and brother, who were both looking at him with concern. "I'll need to get my coat," he said, turning to head towards the hall.

"Make it quick," the sergeant barked, his hand resting on his baton.

Sean scrambled to the hall and frantically grabbed his coat, feeling a heavy sweat begin to form on his forehead. As he stepped back into the kitchen he saw the sergeant standing by the door, his arms folded across his chest.

"Let's go, Sean," the sergeant said, gesturing towards the door.

Sean took a deep breath and stepped out into the cool evening air. He could hear his mother calling out to him, but he didn't turn back. He knew he had to face whatever lay ahead. Sean nodded silently and followed the sergeant out to the Garda car parked in the driveway. As he got in the back seat, he glanced up hesitantly and could see the worry on his mother and brother's faces through the kitchen window.

The car ride to the Garda station was a quiet one. Sean was lost in thought, wondering what he was going to say to the Gardaí. He had nothing to do with Lizzy's murder, but he had been perhaps one of the last people to see her alive. He still couldn't believe that Lizzy was dead. She had been so full of life and energy, and now she was gone, and he was possibly a suspect in her murder.

As the squad car reached the familiar sight of Ballygorman lines of the town's residents stood on the streets. Sean could feel their eyes watching him.

He could sense them whispering about him and speculating on his guilt. He tried to ignore them but their looks stung him, nonetheless.

When they arrived at the Garda station Sean was fingerprinted and photographed, and then escorted to an interview room and left alone for a few minutes. He sat down at the wooden table that occupied the middle of the room, feeling nervous and unsure of what to do next, his legs trembling slightly underneath him. The small, claustrophobic room was cold, sterile and uninviting. White walls loomed ominously around the wooden table, their cold glare sneering in judgment, hard floor tiles reflecting his every movement back to him. Everything seem to amplify the feeling of dismay that was slowly creeping up his spine. The room was silent and empty, but the air was thick with tension, creating a looming sense of danger. Sean felt it wash over him. He needed to divulge all the information he knew to the Gardaí, but he didn't want to accidentally incriminate himself in any way. His mind was in turmoil, his thoughts darting around like a moth caught in a storm. He tried desperately to keep his attention on the task at hand, but no matter how hard he tried, he could not help but be pulled back into the memory of Wednesday night and his last kiss with Lizzy in the car. The warmth of her lips against his still ran through him like an electric current, but now her body was lying on a cold slab in a mortuary.

Sean's focus was suddenly returned to the here and now as the door to the room opened. A tall and lean man walked in and pulled out a chair from the table that Sean was sitting at and sat straight across from him. He was carrying a brown cardboard file and placed it on the table. Two other men in suits followed him in and leaned against the wall, staring directly down at Sean. The tall man who sat across the table opened the file and began to remove its contents. He slowly lifted out photographs and sheets of typed print, then paused to reach into his pocket and remove a small leather case. Opening it carefully, he drew out a pair of glasses which he diligently cleaned with an embroidered cloth before placing them upon his face. His every movement was precise and deliberate; his gaze focused solely on his task at hand.

Sean looked at the man, taking in his aged features. The man appeared to be in his early sixties, with hair that was closer to white than grey. It was thinning on the top, yet long enough to run down over the collar of his jacket at the back. His face was lined with years of experience and wisdom. His neck was long, like the graceful neck of a splendid turkey. There was silence apart from a cough from one of the men who leaned against the wall. The man at the table stared at the documents on the desk, he paused, took a breath, collected his thoughts, took off his glasses, placed them on the table and then introduced himself and the two other men.

"My name is Detective Inspector Pascal Harding, and the two men you see here are detectives Mick Dunne and Seamus Byrne." It was hard to identify exactly where Harding was from; he certainly had a West of Ireland lilt to his speech but there was no trace of Leitrim in his accent. His face bore expressionless features which gave nothing away – he cut an intimidating figure despite his somewhat frail stature.

It was obvious that the two men who leaned against the wall with their arms crossed were the muscle if it was required. They looked tall and firm, like two guard dogs prepared to defend their territory. Detectives Mick Dunne and Seamus Byrne were tall and stocky, with broad shoulders and a confident bearing. Mick was bald and clean-shaven. He had dark eyes and a determined expression. Seamus had a full head of curly brown hair, with a hint of grey at the temples. He had a square-jawed face and sported a thick moustache. They both looked alert and focused, with sharp eyes that darted around the room taking in their surroundings.

"Your name is Sean Breslin, correct?" Harding asked.

"Yes," Sean replied.

"All right Sean, if you cooperate and answer our questions truthfully then this process should be easy and over before you know it. Do you understand what I'm saying?"

Sean solemnly nodded. It was clear that he felt uneasy about the situation he found himself in – being questioned by a detective inspector about a murder wasn't something he was expecting to happen to him in his lifetime.

"You knew Lizzy O'Dowd, didn't you."

"I did," Sean replied.

"Can you explain to me how well you knew her. Was she a neighbour, a friend, or something more?"

Sean paused, considering his response before continuing. “She was a... friend," he said nervously.

"Lizzy was more than a friend to you, so I have been told. Can you please be more specific?" Harding stated.

Sean paused for a moment before gathering his thoughts. "We went out together a few times," he began slowly, "it was fairly... casual. We were never really committed to one another, and nothing ever became too serious.” He shrugged.

With a deep sigh, Harding reached into the interior pocket of his jacket and retrieved a short pen knife. Unfolding its blade with a crisp click, he placed it up on the table. He then reached back into his pocket and produced a classic Peterson pipe, lightly tapping its chamber before using the blade of the knife to carefully scrape away dry clumps of used tobacco.

He meticulously repeated this process as he began to speak again. "Casual or otherwise, whatever way you young fellas want to term it nowadays, you were romantically involved with Lizzy O’Dowd for a number of years, isn’t that right?” Harding kept his gaze focused on the task of cleaning out his pipe, not so much as glancing over at Sean. His hands moved in practiced movements as he worked, carefully scraping out the old ash and polishing the bowl.

"Yes...I suppose so," Sean replied with a slight hesitation in his voice. Despite the agreement he was showing, it was clear that there were still doubts lingering in his head.

"You suppose so, either you had an ongoing relationship with Lizzy or not? Please don't waste our time," Harding said with an edge of impatience in his voice, as he rigidly dug into the chamber with the pen knife to get it perfectly clean. His quick motions suggested a man running out of patience, and his brow furrowed in frustration as he worked. He seemed determined to get the job done quickly and efficiently, refusing to have his time wasted on such trivial inquiries.

"I was going out with Lizzy, yes," Sean said.

"That is better. All right then, is it also true that last Saturday night you and Lizzy were engaged in an altercation at a local public house called Gallagher's?" Harding asked as he gently tapped his pipe against the wooden table, releasing the final specks of ash from its depths. His inquisitive gaze now fixed upon Sean, as if willing him to answer in confirmation.

Sean sighed heavily, his shoulders sagging as he uttered the words. "We had a bit of a disagreement..." His voice was heavy with remorse and regret, the weight of the situation resting heavily on his mind. The room seemed to darken slightly as if a cloud had passed by outside and a sombre stillness settled around them.

Harding shot a questioning gaze, shook his head slightly and reached into the pocket of his shirt for a pouch of tobacco, fiddling with it for a moment before finding the small box of matches stashed away inside. His eyes trained on the ground as he took in a deep breath and let it out slowly. "A disagreement, altercation or argument... it's all the same," he said.

Sean tried to downplay the situation, as he often did when faced with a difficult situation. "It was nothing really serious," he said in a casual manner, though it was obvious that there was more to it than what he revealed. He sat there, barely making eye contact, looking down at his hands.

"It must have been about something crucial for Lizzy to march off in such a dramatic fashion according to the onlookers that night in the pub, leaving you alone at the bar," Harding declared in a thoughtful tone as he carefully filled the chamber of his pipe with rich, aromatic tobacco and packed it down tightly with his thumb. He struck a match and set the flame to the stem of the pipe, drawing long puffs until it was lit like a beacon in the dark room.

"It wasn't anything major," Sean said, his voice trailing off. He was trying to be nonchalant about it, but the regret in his tone betrayed him.

"Was Lizzy seeing someone else? Were you perhaps jealous? Is that what you were arguing about in the pub?" Harding questioned as pungent aromas filled his nostrils and he inhaled deeply, savouring the faintly sweet smell of smoke from his favourite pipe.

Sean paused, debating whether he should bring up the topic of Lizzy's fling with James Murray or not. His brows furrowed as his mind weighed the decision carefully. He sat in deep thought, torn between what he should do. He shut his eyes briefly before opening them again and drawing in a deep breath before finally opening his mouth to speak.

"She wasn't seeing anybody else."

Harding's face scrunched in suspicion as he posed his burning question. "Are you sure? You told me that you had a casual relationship with Lizzy so it wasn't very serious, was it? Is it not possible that she was seeing somebody else?" he queried, his eyes narrowing. He waited for an answer carefully, waiting for any sign of hesitancy in Sean's voice that might indicate he wasn't being entirely honest with him.

Sean's words faltered in his throat, unsure of how to proceed. Was it wise to mention Lizzy's relationship with James? That likely would give Harding enough reason to suggest that he had killed her out of jealousy. He let out a breath, stalling for time while he collected his thoughts. Eventually, he spoke up again, "Well if she was seeing somebody else, I didn't know about it..." His voice trailed off as the ramifications of his words sunk in.

"You seem very unsure, Sean," Harding said condescendingly, blowing smoke out from his pipe in a steady stream, directly into Sean's face. The wisps of smoke seemed to linger in the air around them as if Harding was trying to use it as a form of intimidation. The smell of the heated tobacco and burning wood from his pipe filled the room with an overwhelming aroma that made Sean's nostrils burn. His eyes began to water, and he started coughing uncontrollably.

"She wasn't seeing anyone, at least not to my knowledge, that is all I can tell you," Sean replied.

"So, you don't know for sure if Lizzy was seeing someone else behind your back?" Harding asked, leaning forward on the table. He watched intently as Sean gradually wiped his palms on his jeans pockets and replied in a grave tone, "I didn't say that." His voice betrayed deep-rooted suspicion and Harding felt sure there was more to the story than what Sean was letting slip.

“So just bear with me for a moment, Sean. Take a step back and imagine what it would be like if you discovered that Lizzy was seeing another man on the sly, deceiving you and playing you for a fool. How would it make you feel? Would your chest tighten with anguish as your heart shattered into pieces? Would an overwhelming sense of betrayal rip through your soul like an icy chill, leaving you feeling numb and helpless all at once?” Harding said as he waved his arms like a hammy actor on a stage.

“I don’t know,” Sean replied with a hint of uncertainty in his voice. He ran his fingers through his hair, a gesture of frustration that he often used when he was feeling overwhelmed. He exhaled slowly, trying to take in the magnitude of what was being asked of him before giving an answer. His gaze drifted around the room as if searching for an answer written on one of the walls before finally settling back on the speaker.

“Would you not be angry, feel betrayed? I know I would if I discovered that Mrs Harding made a fool out of me and had an affair with another man,” Harding said with a sinister smirk pulling at the corners of his mouth. His eyes flashed with malevolence as he mulled over the possibilities.

Sean shifted nervously, his gaze cast down and his thoughts a flurry of confusion. He bit his lip, trying to keep the floodgates of emotion from spilling out. "I don't know how I would feel," he said quietly, biting back the words that wanted to escape him despite himself. With clear determination and unwavering focus, Detective Harding continued to press on with his questioning. He glanced up from his notepad, piercing green eyes locked firmly on the suspect as he spoke. "All right then," he said. "Let's move on. Why was Lizzy in your car on Wednesday night at nine o'clock? Did you take her back to her house? Did you kill her?" His voice was firm and confident, conveying the gravity of the situation.

Sean's frustration was growing by the minute. His voice shook with emotion as he pleaded his innocence, desperation and panic palpable in every syllable. "I didn't kill her, I swear," he said fervently. "All I did was give her a lift home."

The detective leaned forward, his gaze filled with suspicion as he asked, "Did you go back to her house later that night and commit the unthinkable? Did you snuff out her life in a single moment of unbridled rage?"

Sean shook his head slowly and his lips pressed into a thin line as he uttered an emphatic, "No, I didn't." His eyes conveyed a hint of defiance as he continued, "After I safely dropped her off at Mrs Boyle's house, I made my way straight back home."

With a stern look, Harding leaned forward and asked, "Why was Lizzy in your car so late at night? Explain to me why she ended up dead in her own house later that night. I need an answer." He fixed his gaze on the man before him, awaiting an explanation he knew would not come... yet.

"I was driving close to her house. I was driving out to see her. She was carrying heavy bags of shopping and I stopped and gave her a lift the short distance back to her house. Her car was in for repairs in John McGinley's garage. She said that she had to call to see her neighbour, an old woman called Mrs Boyle. So I gave her a lift to Mrs Boyle's house. I said that I would drop her back home afterwards, but she told me that she wanted to spend some time with the old lady and that she would walk back home and that she would be fine," Sean recalled.

"So that is your story," Harding said with a solemn expression and a heavy sigh.

"It's not a story, it's the truth," Sean said, his voice firm as he responded.

"What time did you eventually make it home, after dropping Lizzy off at Mrs Boyle's house?" Harding inquired.

"I'd say it was around 9:20 pm," Sean replied thoughtfully, wracking his brain for the exact details of that evening. "Yes, about that time, I remember switching on the TV and the news was finishing up."

"Who was in your house when you got home?" Harding asked.

"My mother was at bingo, she always goes on a Wednesday night. She gets a lift with a neighbour. She came home about eleven, she usually gets back about eleven," Sean replied.

"So you have nothing to prove that you were actually at home between nine and eleven o'clock, you have no alibi, which means it is possible that you could have murdered Lizzy during that time." Harding looked intently at Sean, waiting for a response.

"I told you before that I didn't kill Lizzy," Sean said in frustration, his voice rising. "Why would I want to kill her, what reason would I have to kill her?"

"The motives for taking a human life are varied, be it money, land, revenge, insanity, the love of someone else, or in your case, jealousy. You were enraged that your girlfriend Lizzy had broken things off with you last Saturday night at Gallagher's pub because she was going out with another man. You were so consumed by resentment and envy that you decided to take matters into your own hands. On Wednesday night at her home, you killed her," Harding said decisively.

"That is not true, not true at all," Sean implored in anguish.

Harding observed Sean sceptically as he leaned back in his chair. He didn't have enough evidence to arrest him yet, but he wasn't entirely convinced of his innocence either. "Your story doesn't add up," Harding said sternly. "We're going to have to place you in a holding cell overnight so that we can gather more evidence before ruling you out as a suspect." His voice was authoritative, leaving no doubt that this was not a request but an order.

Sean shuffled his feet wearily as Detectives Byrne and Dunne led him away to the holding cell, his shoulders hunched in defeat. He was barely able to look up, feeling utterly dejected and helpless.

The holding cell was a small, dismal and grim box of a room. Its walls were made of cold, grey concrete and the only window was a small, barred hole near the ceiling. The walls felt rough and gritty to the touch, like cold stone. A single, dim light bulb hung from the ceiling and cast long shadows across the grim walls. The floor was covered in worn tiles which were heavily discoloured by stains, dirt and grime. The floor was damp with an icy chill that seeped through clothing and into the skin. The only furniture consisted of a wooden bench, a steel toilet and a bed with a thin stained mattress resting over steel bars. The mattress was bumpy and filled with lumps, its material thin enough to feel almost nonexistent when touched. Over it was cast a brown threadbare blanket.

The air inside the cell was stale and musty with a faint whiff of mould, stale body odour, sweat, urine and a thick muskiness that hung in the air like a fog. The atmosphere was oppressive and haunting, creating a feeling of fear and hopelessness.

As Sean lay in the musty confinement of his cell, all he could think about was who could have brutally taken the life of Lizzy and why. He dreaded having to stay confined in such a pitiful environment for any amount of time, yet at this point what options did he have?

Chapter 16: Stained Glass

Saturday May 6th

As Donal McCabe drove the laneway up to the Breslin farmhouse on that cloudless and luminous Saturday morning, he experienced a sense of outrage and bewilderment. The sunny day seemed to be mocking him with its brightness and merriment, contrasting starkly with his own feelings of shock and despair. How could his friend Sean be in Garda custody as a suspect, accused of committing the heinous crime of taking Lizzy O'Dowd's' life, when he knew Sean was incapable of such an act? He had to find out what was really going on.

Donal felt a tension knot twist in the pit of his stomach as he anxiously knocked on the hard door to the Breslin farmhouse. The door was an old one, made of solid oak and bolted with a heavy iron lock. Its deep grain ran in intricate swirls across the entire surface, creating a texture that seemed almost like flowing fabric. He was aware that behind the door, Eileen would be scared and distressed, and he had a desire to do what he could to give her ease in this tragic hour. The door creaked open slowly, revealing Eileen's troubled and drawn face peeking out. It was clear from the heavy bags under her eyes that she hadn't slept all night.

Her wrinkled hands shook slightly at the sight of Donal. She released a long sigh of relief and with tired eyes, she gratefully looked upon him and said with tenderness, "Thank goodness you're here."

"I came to see how you're doing, Eileen," Donal said, his mouth curling into a gentle smile as he spoke. "I know this must be a difficult time for you."

"Thank you, please come in," Eileen said as she opened the door fully and made way for Donal to enter the kitchen.

Eileen's body shook, tears welling up in her eyes. "It's a nightmare, Donal," she said, her voice barely above a whisper. "My son is innocent, and they're treating him like a criminal. I don't know what to do."

Donal stepped into the kitchen and placed a gentle hand on Eileen's shoulder in a gesture of sympathy, before grabbing one of the chairs at the kitchen table. He watched as Eileen shuffled over to the worktop, her movements slow and measured.

She looked up at him briefly with a sad expression before she started to scald the teapot. "You will have some tea?" she said softly, her voice barely audible.

"Don't put yourself to any trouble, Eileen," Donal said.

"It's no problem. I was just making some for Mark, he is outside looking at the cattle. He will have to take over now if Sean..." Eileen stopped mid sentence as the tears returned once more, her eyes clearly sore from crying all night.

Donal quickly rose to his feet and awkwardly embraced her, trying to offer what little comfort he could. "Don't you worry, Mrs Breslin. Sean will be out in no time. He's innocent, I promise you that. But we have to keep strong for him – we can't let him think that we don't have faith in him." His words were soothing and gentle, he wanted desperately to alleviate her pain by providing some form of assurance in such a difficult time.

Eileen nodded slowly, wiping away her tears with the back of her hand. "You're right, Donal," she said, finding a temporary strength in her voice. "I'm going to be strong for Sean." She knew it would take every ounce of courage and resilience within her to face the challenge that lay ahead. But if there was one thing she had learned over time it was that courage isn't just about being brave in moments of danger; it's about being brave enough to keep going no matter what.

Donal sat back down and took a deep breath, trying to figure out what to say next. "Do you know which Guard brought Sean to the Garda station?" he asked finally. "I might be able to talk to him, see if he can tell us anything."

Eileen carefully laid the china teapot on the polished wooden table and looked up with an inquisitive expression. "Sergeant Tom O'Donnell, do you know him?"

Donal considered the name for a short while, his mind rolling over memories of the man in question. "Yes, indeed I do know him," he recalled with a smile. "He is married to a woman from my parish back in Monaghan. I was at their wedding about ten years ago and have visited them at their home in Sligo a couple of times." A plan began to form in his head as he spoke. "I can try to contact him and see if he can tell us anything."

Eileen's face brightened a little. "Thank you, Donal," she said, a small smile tugging at the corners of her mouth. "That would be a great help." She spoke in an almost hushed whisper, the slight quiver of gratitude that laced her words unmistakable. "You were always a good friend to my Sean."

"I will do my utmost to get Sean out, Eileen," Donal reassured her, not completely sure if he was going to be able to keep his promise. His heart was aching for her, wanting nothing more than to somehow make sure she wouldn't have to suffer anymore. Yet in reality, he wasn't certain what the future held and if his plan would have any success. He wanted her to believe in him now, to give her something to believe in, to give her hope, even if things didn't turn out as they expected.

Eileen filled a large mug with steaming tea and set it down before Donal. She carefully carved up a large slice of baked apple tart, the sweet smell of cinnamon and apples rising as she did so. To finish it off, she added a dollop of fresh cream to the top and placed it next to his mug of tea. "Now drink your tea," Eileen said gently, her face softened with fondness as she watched him eagerly dig in.

Chapter 17: Right Down the Line

Two hours later

After bidding farewell to Eileen Breslin and departing her home, Donal wasted no time in making his journey towards Sligo town, where Sergeant Tom O'Donnell resided in Meadow Brook Park, close to the Rosses Point Road. Meadow Brook Park was a modern housing development with neat rows of two-story houses with well-maintained lush green lawns and vibrant flowerbeds. Its avenues were wide, clean and inviting and lined with streetlamps which illuminated the vibrant new housing development at night. The homes were surrounded by trees and shrubs, giving it a tranquil atmosphere despite its close proximity to the main road. Each house has its own driveway, leading up to the porch or front door. The overall atmosphere of the housing development was one of peace and calm, with the occasional sound of birds chirping in the distance. Further out, the landscape opened up to a wide open space with a pond, park benches, and a children's playground. The place was obviously purpose built for the upwardly mobile, those who could afford a hefty mortgage.

Donal's Fiat purred along the avenue until he found himself parking alongside a driveway at number 42. He stepped out of the car and onto the gravelled path that led him up to the front door of the O'Donnell's home. Taking a moment to collect himself, Donal breathed in deeply before pushing the button for the bell. After two rings, he could see movement in the hallway through the brown frosted glass on the right-hand side of the door. The door opened, and Sergeant Tom O'Donnell stood before him dressed in his weekend casuals. He was wearing a pair of navy trousers, a light blue checked shirt, and a brown Aran cardigan that struggled to button around his stomach. His feet were clad in a pair of brown leather loafers. His salt-and-pepper hair was combed neatly, and he stood tall with his broad shoulders back and his head held high. His expression was neutral but with a hint of surprise, his grey eyes bright and alert.

"Donal! How are you, long time no see," Tom said. “Come in.”

“I want to apologize for not letting you know before that I was coming over, and I’m sorry for disturbing you on a Saturday,” Donal said as he made his way into the hallway.

Tom smiled warmly in response and replied, “Don’t be silly Donal—you are always welcome here. You know that. Why don't you come into the sitting room and make yourself comfortable?” His invitation was kindly extended with an outstretched arm.

As he stepped into the living room, Donal's gaze drifted to Geraldine, Tom's wife. She was cozied up in an armchair next to a marble fireplace, her attention focused on the newspaper in her hands. Geraldine was a petite woman, with a slim figure and an air of elegance. Her auburn hair was draped across her shoulders. She had porcelain skin that was dusted with freckles, and she wore a dark green dress, adorned with intricate embroidery around the neckline. Her eyes were almond-shaped and a warm hazel colour, still visible despite being hidden behind small, round glasses. She had her feet tucked up in the armchair, with her hands placed comfortably in her lap. The marble fireplace was burning brightly, and she looked content to be sitting next to it with the pleasant warmth of the flames radiating around her.

“Look who it is, Geraldine, your old school friend Donal McCabe,” Tom said with a hearty laugh.

"Well, hello Donal, what a pleasant surprise!" Geraldine exclaimed, putting her newspaper down and smiling at him. "What brings you here?" Her eyes lit up with joy and anticipation as she removed her reading glasses.

Ever since their childhood spent in the town of Clones, Monaghan, Geraldine had always harboured a fondness for Donal. Despite her attempts to take things further between them, they stayed as good friends and nothing more. Their relationship was characterised by deep conversations and intense laughter that filled up the long summer days; they were best of friends who could tell each other anything. Geraldine thought she could detect a hint of anxiety, a subtle tremor in her old friend’s stance as he tensed his muscles and shifted over and back on his feet while he stood in the middle of the sitting room.

She looked at him with a raised eyebrow and said firmly, "Will you please sit down for the love of God."

Startled, Donal quickly replied, "Oh right, of course, thank you." He moved to the couch behind him and sat down.

“Will you have a cup of tea or coffee?” Geraldine inquired.

“No, I’m grand, I just had some before coming here,” Donal replied.

There was a difficult silence as Donal hesitated, unsure how to approach Tom about his knowledge about Sean Breslin and how the investigation was going. He took a breath and spoke. “How... are your boys?”

“Oh, they're off soccer training, one of our neighbours took them over. We take turns bringing them every other Saturday. They’re usually back by now, so they should be home any minute," Tom responded in a cheerful voice.

“So, Donal, will you be giving us a big day soon?” Geraldine asked with a curious expression.

“A big day, what sort of big day?” Donal scratched his head in confusion and looked at her blankly.

"A wedding, you daft yoke." Geraldine laughed. "It's about time you were getting hitched, you don't want to be left on the shelf."

Donal smiled, his lips curving upwards into a mischievous grin. "No, I'm afraid not," he replied in response to Geraldine's question.

She was quick and didn't hesitate to ask her follow up. "Any romance on the go?"

His eyes sparkled with amusement as he teased her with his answer. "There might be, I'm not sure yet," he replied with a wink.

"Well, that is as clear as mud," Geraldine said, her face twisted in confusion.

"Leave the man alone, it's like the Spanish Inquisition in here." Tom laughed and continued, "Now go out to the kitchen and put the kettle on like a good woman, Donal wants a cup of tea."

"He just said that he doesn't want tea," Geraldine mock protested.

"Come on, go out and put the kettle on and get some of that Swiss roll too," Tom suggested.

"You're supposed to be on a diet, Tom O'Donnell – you know what the doctor said," Geraldine reminded him sternly, waving her finger to emphasize her point.

"Never mind the doctor, go on," Tom said.

"Okay," Geraldine said reluctantly as she walked out into the hallway.

With Geraldine out of the room, Donal decided that it was now or never to get to the reason why he called.

" Look, Tom, I won't beat around the bush any longer, you are obviously curious as to why I called. So I will get to it. Sean Breslin is a friend of mine. I just called to his mother Eileen, and she is devastated. She told me that it was you who called to her house last night and brought Sean to the Garda station in Ballygorman. I need to know what's going on with Sean. I'm worried about him."

Tom was taken aback, this request was unexpected. "Donal," he began, "you know I can't discuss that with you. It doesn't matter that you are an old friend of Geraldine's, the law has strict rules and regulations and I need to abide by them. This isn't something I'm allowed to go into, even with a friend."

Donal put his hands up in supplication as he spoke. "I understand that Tom, I really do. But what I'd like to know is why was he taken in for questioning?" he pleaded. "Do you have any more information on it? Is there anything you can tell me?" His brow furrowed with worry and his voice cracked slightly, unsure of what answer he would get.

"No way, I said that I can't tell you, do you want me to lose my job?" Tom said sternly, his voice full of determined conviction.

"I just need to let his mother know, she's going out of her mind with worry," Donal implored, desperation in his tone. He urgently needed answers for a woman who had already been through so much hardship in her life and was now clinging onto any hope at all.

Tom looked around the room as if searching for some sort of guidance. He cleared his throat and spoke. "Look, if I tell you this, you didn't hear it from me, right, do you understand?" he said with an air of uncertainty and caution in his voice.

"Yes, absolutely, you have my word," Donal replied.

"On Friday afternoon, we received intelligence from a man in the Ballygorman area that Lizzy O'Dowd had been spotted in Sean Breslin's car around 9 o'clock on Wednesday evening, which we believe was only an hour or two before Lizzy's murder. According to Sean, he had provided her with a lift to her house and then gone home after dropping her off, yet he has no corroborating alibi for the time period between nine and eleven that night. We believe if Sean is the killer, then the motive may have been jealousy. We learned from information we received from a publican in Ballygorman that Sean supposedly had an argument with Lizzy the previous Saturday night, she broke it off with him because he was jealous that she wanted a relationship with somebody else," Tom recalled.

"Joe Gallagher is a good man at listening into private conversations in his pub," Donal said angrily. "You don't have any proof that Sean is connected to the murder, only speculation as far as I can see and I just can't believe Sean could be a killer." he continued.

"We still don't have enough evidence to ascertain whether or not Sean is guilty, but one thing is for certain; the man spearheading the investigation is none other than Detective Inspector Harding. He was brought all the way from Galway, he's the best in the business. If Harding believes Sean has committed a crime, then no doubt he will manage to extract a confession out of him in no time at all. As they say in America, Sean will soon be singing like a bird." Tom smirked.

"That's totally outrageous, Sean is innocent, they have to let him go tonight or charge him, they can't hold him more than twenty-four hours," Donal demanded.

"How can you be sure he is innocent, Donal, how can you be certain of that since you are an expert on the law all of a sudden. Sean Breslin can be held for up to seven days without charging with an application to the courts which I can guarantee you now Inspector Harding is already working on and will get," Tom said with a confident expression.

Donal's heart sank, he had no answer as he sat back in the couch in a dejected manner, feeling frustrated and helpless.

"Look, Donal, there is nothing you can do. Let the investigation run its course, don't beat yourself up over it," Tom said feeling sorry for him.

"I can't just sit around and wait for them to pin this on Sean. I'm going to clear his name," Donal said as he stood up.

Tom leaned forward, his eyes narrowing. "And how do you intend to do that? Don't be so damn naïve."

Donal stepped towards the door and turned to Tom with a determined look in his eyes. "Well, I'm going to try," he said. Taking a deep breath, he forced himself to keep on moving forward. "I'm going, Tom, say sorry to Geraldine from me for rushing off."

As Donal left the house and got into his car, he felt a sense of foreboding. He knew the path ahead would be fraught with danger and uncertainty. He knew he would be going up against powerful forces – the police, the justice system, and the whispers of a small town that was quick to judge and could turn against him in an instant.

Yet despite all of this, Donal was determined to see his friend cleared. He knew Sean was innocent, and he would do everything in his power to prove it.

Chapter 18: Runnin' with the Devil

Sunday May 7th

James Murray trudged wearily through the wet and soggy field, his boots thickly encased in mud. He fought against the relentless wind with all of his might as he attempted to force the cattle back in through a gap, their loud mooing ringing out around him. Tom Burke, the owner of the cows, was at his side shouting orders at them as they ambled along. The sun had temporarily disappeared behind a cloud on the horizon and its weak light feebly illuminated their efforts to remove Tom's cattle from a neighbouring farm belonging to Kevin Glancy. Lucky for Tom, Kevin Glancy was a quiet man.

Tom Burke was a short fat man with a broad back and thick butty legs. His face was red due to high blood pressure and the pudgy skin on his face

James nodded. "Of course, Tom. Thanks again. I'll be in touch soon. Tell Anne that I said hello."

James slowly made his way across the expansive field, his head down and brow furrowed in thought, heading towards the gateway where he had parked his car. He desperately hoped that Tom's statement to the Gardai would provide a strong enough alibi for him should Sean Breslin get released by the Guards and they shifted their focus to him instead. Tom tried to quell the rising panic within, but it was becoming increasingly difficult; these were dark and uncertain times indeed.

Chapter 19: Hemispheres

Later that day

Donal McCabe and Fiona Donnelly strode hand in hand along the endless shoreline of Tullan Strand, a tranquil paradise set amidst the breathtaking rugged and beautiful coastline of Donegal. The crystalline waves of the azure sea danced their way to the sand, frothing and foaming into infinity with each incoming swell. The air was alive with a salty tang that filled their lungs. The early summer evening sun had emerged victorious over the stormy skies that had threatened to ruin their Sunday walk, casting its warm embrace across the entire beach. Yet, despite the beauty of the surroundings, Donal's mind was clouded with worry.

Fiona could feel the tightness in her boyfriend's grip, a sign of his growing anxiety. She carefully intertwined her fingers with his, offering a gentle reminder that she was still there for him. She intuitively knew it was the thought of Sean Breslin that had him so preoccupied and worried about what the future would bring for his friend in the coming days.

Fiona cast a concerned gaze at Donal, his head hung, and his desolate stare focused downward. “You are very quiet, Donal, is there anything I can say or do to make you feel better?” Fiona said.

Her voice was gentle and seemed to linger before finding its way to his ears. Donal remained silent but raised his head slowly, revealing the lost emotions in his eyes as he considered Fiona's words.

He gave a nod, his jaw clenched as he spoke. "Yes, and I don't know what to do. I'm sure of it, Fiona – Sean is innocent. But the Gardaí won't take on board anything we say." His words conveyed a deep anguish in his heart that Fiona could feel too; they were both desperate to find a way to prove Sean's innocence but were hampered by Garda indifference.

Fiona felt an anxious pit in her stomach as she asked the question, desperately hoping for an answer. "There must be something we can do to help him?" she implored.

Donal sighed in frustration, the sense of powerlessness he felt overwhelming. "I don't know what to do," he said. "I've tried talking to the Gardaí, but they won't even let me see him. Even if I could afford one, a top solicitor is out of my reach. I can't stand the thought of Sean being locked up for something he didn't do." He hung his head in defeat.

Fiona snaked her arm around Donal's torso, holding him close to her body. She stared into his eyes, conveying a message of hope and determination. "We'll find a way, Donal," she whispered softly.

Donal leaned into Fiona and tenderly pressed his lips against hers. He held her tightly, as if trying to convey all his gratitude for the past few days of unwavering support she had given him. He wanted to make sure Fiona knew just how much he appreciated her. "Thank you," he said in a gentle tone, his breath soft on her skin. "Thank you for your support these last few days – I really mean it, you are such a good person."

They strode onward in complete silence. As they kept walking, they tried to pay close attention to the distinct sounds of the strand, the ocean calling to them with its ever changing rhythm as it roared beneath the setting sun. The loud crashing of waves against rocky shorelines echoed throughout the air, a symphony of white within a glimmering spray. The piercing and chaotic screech of the seagulls echoed in the distance as they followed fishing boats into harbour, black specks against a seemingly endless sky. All the while their minds wandered about in deep thought, still preoccupied by deeper concerns.

Fiona's brow creased as she stopped walking, deep in thought. She had been wracking her brain for any possible solutions to help them but had come up empty. Then, like a bolt of lightning, an idea struck her and her eyes lit up with excitement. "I have an idea. I should have thought of this earlier. I have an uncle living in Dublin who is a retired detective," she said eagerly, hope ringing out strong in her voice. "Maybe he can help us, Donal."

Donal's expression held a hint of scepticism, conveying his uncertainty over Fiona's suggestion. He knew that a retired detective would most likely not want to involve themselves in an active Garda investigation, but he didn't want to make Fiona feel bad by dismissing her idea right away. "That's... a great idea, Fiona," he began slowly, carefully forming his words. "It could work – we don't have anything to lose."

Fiona could sense Donal's uncertainty and hesitancy, but she pressed on anyway. "I know it might seem like a ridiculous idea," she began, her voice full of hope and optimism, "but can you think of anything else we could do?" She looked at him hopefully, wanting to believe there was another way to make things work out.

“No, I'm all out of ideas. Can you ring your uncle, have you a phone number for him?” Donal asked.

Fiona looked thoughtful for a moment before responding, “Yes, I do believe I still have it somewhere at the house. I will make sure to get in touch as soon as I return home.”

“Terrific, well let's get back so,” Donal said impatiently, eager to give Fiona's idea a try, realising that they didn't have any other alternatives right now.

“We will but let's just enjoy this beautiful place for a few more minutes,”

Fiona said, her back to Donal as she faced the sea, her long blonde hair swept back by the wind. The sky was a fiery orange as the sun sank down to the horizon, painting the sea a deep red hue with streaks of pink and purple, its waters shining in the fading light of the day. Her face was lit up by the sunset, her eyes wide open as she admired the breathtaking scene, the magnificent beauty of the moment.

Chapter 20: Shattered

Monday May 8th

Detective Inspector Harding sat at the short wooden table, the only light in the room casting stark shadows across his face. His piercing gaze was fixed on the door, anticipating the entrance of his suspect. Finally, a few minutes later, detectives Dunne and Byrne ushered in a dishevelled Sean Breslin. He appeared exhausted and as if he had not slept at all during his time spent in custody over the weekend. His clothes that he had been wearing since Friday morning were tattered and creased. His bones ached from lying on the hard bed in his cell.

Sean slowly took his place across the table from Harding, the only sound a chair screeching against the tiled floor. Inspector Harding could sense the heavy atmosphere between them. The silence was filled with unspoken thoughts and a palpable tension that seemed to pervade the whole room.

"Good morning, Sean," Harding said in a tranquil tone as he welcomed him. "I hope you have taken the chance to reflect and contemplate on what we discussed on Friday night while you were spending time away from work in our excellent accommodation, supplied by the hard-working Irish taxpayers. I trust that you had a restful and refreshing weekend so that you are now invigorated and eager to take action today to help us to find justice for your girlfriend, Lizzy O'Dowd."

Harding fixed Sean in his gaze, scrutinizing him from head to toe. He could tell that it wouldn't take much for Sean to crack under the pressure; he was teetering on the edge, and with some additional strain over the next forty-eight hours or so, Harding felt confident that Sean would eventually confess to his transgression.

Sean said nothing in response, keeping his gaze directed at the table before him. He refused to meet the inspector's eyes, instead focusing on the grain of the wood and tracing it with his fingertip as if it held some secret he was desperate to uncover. The silence stretched on like an eternity while the inspector waited patiently for a response that never came.

"I want to show you something," Harding continued, taking out a clear plastic bag from his briefcase and holding it up so that Sean could see the contents. "Do you recognize this glass?"

Sean gave no response, his eyes fixed upon the glass intensely. His expression was one of puzzlement, his brows furrowed in thought and his lips slightly parted in contemplation. He remained motionless for a few moments, seemingly lost in a world of his own thoughts as he studied the glass before him.

"As you can see," Harding began, his finger gesturing to the glass, "this is a fine piece of Cavan crystal. It was discovered in Lizzy O'Dowd's kitchen. Take a closer look, Sean, and you'll notice that the surface of the glass has fingerprints on it; her fingerprints and your fingerprints."

Sean stared intently at the glass for a few more moments before finally raising his gaze to meet Harding's, his voice trembling slightly. "Yes, I drank from that glass when I was at Lizzy's house earlier on Wednesday evening, she offered me a whiskey after she invited me into her house after I had given her a lift. I told you this information already last Friday night."

Harding nodded, his eyes narrowed as if was bracing himself for what he had to say next. "That's what we thought. But there's more."

He reached into his briefcase and pulled out another plastic bag, this one containing a shining woman's earring with a vivid red love heart. The metal shimmered enticingly under the light, drawing his eyes to its intricate design. "Do you recognize this?" he asked as he held it up for Sean to examine.

Sean hesitated before responding, "I'm not sure."

"You are not sure." Harding raised an eyebrow and repeated cooly, "Well, it was discovered underneath the passenger seat of your car, and it matches one found on Lizzy's bedside locker," Harding said as he glanced down at the earring.

"Yes, Lizzy lost that earring in my car. We kissed for a while in my car before she got out. I remember her saying that I must have accidentally pulled off the earring when we were kissing and it fell on the floor of the car, she looked for it but couldn't find it," Sean said, his voice barely audible, slightly embarrassed to be recalling such an intimate event.

The evidence against Sean seemed to grow heavier by the moment, but Harding had one more piece of information tucked away, one last bit of knowledge that could send him to a fate from which he might not return. Harding steeled himself for what was to come and drew a deep breath before he began. His words were heavy with implication. "We have recently been informed by a witness that your car was spotted parked outside Lizzy's house at around 10 pm on Wednesday night, the time that we believe Lizzy was murdered." His voice was cold and detached as he watched Sean for signs of guilt or surprise, searching for any telltale reaction to confirm his suspicions.

"I wasn't there at 10 pm," Sean said, his voice rising in frustration. "I left Lizzy's house around 9 pm, I swear. I gave her a lift to her neigbour, Mrs Boyle. I drove straight home then because she didn't want me to wait, she said that she would be fine walking home."

Hardy furrowed his brow and looked at the suspect menacingly. "You've already given us a version of events, but I'm afraid your story simply doesn't add up," he said sternly, his eyes never leaving Sean's face. "I suggest you think hard about what you just told us and tell us again what really happened... make sure that it's true this time."

“Look, have you spoken to Mrs Boyle, she can tell you that Lizzy called to her house at 9 pm. Maybe Lizzy told her that I had given her a lift,” Sean said anxiously.

“Yes Sean, Detective Dunne has spoken to Mrs Boyle, an elderly lady whose memory is not quite what it used to be. Sadly, she could not recall if Lizzy had visited her on Wednesday night or not, due to her age and condition, God bless her soul,” Harding said.

Sean dropped his head in despair.

Harding arched his body forward like a predator going in for the kill on a wounded animal “Let’s, just stop wasting time now, Sean,” he said aggressively. “It’s obvious that your yellow Ford Escort car was parked at Lizzy O’Dowd’s house last Wednesday night. It was spotted there at 10 pm. Earlier At 9 pm Lizzy was observed in your car. Look, Sean, you were certainly there that evening and you killed Lizzy in a jealous rage because she wanted to end the relationship and start a new relationship with somebody else. You were obviously rough with her in your car before you went into the house, that is why her earring was violently pulled out of her ear.”

Sean indignantly declared, "That is not the truth. You are coming to the wrong conclusion. I was certainly not at Lizzy's house at 10 pm. How are you certain that it was my Ford Escort parked at her house, it’s a very common make of car." His voice rose with conviction and his eyes shone with a daring defiance as he stood up for himself.

Harding’s eyes locked into Sean's, his breath upon his face. "Then tell me,” he said, his voice low and menacing. "Where were you at 10 pm Wednesday night, since you have no alibi." He leaned even closer as if daring Sean to lie to him.

Sean paused before providing a response, considering his words carefully. "I was at home," he replied eventually, his voice barely above a whisper. "My mother had gone out to bingo and didn't get back until around eleven o'clock."

"Yes, yes, we've heard that baseless story before," Harding said as he slammed his fist on the table with a booming thud. “You have no alibi.” His gaze pierced Sean's soul as he spoke again. "You killed Lizzy and were home before your mother returned, isn't that, right? You cannot deny it."

Harding gradually reclined in his chair and drew in a deep breath, giving himself the momentary peace to calm himself. He tried to remain level-headed, but the evidence before him was undeniably convincing. He still had to tread carefully though, as there were still so many unanswered questions. His gaze scanned over Sean's face, analysing him for any more clues or evidence that could be used against him.

"Sean, we’re here to discover the truth. If you are innocent, we will leave no stone unturned in our quest for justice and to find the real perpetrator. However, for us all to achieve this aim, it requires your full cooperation," Harding said calmly as he began the routine of cleaning out and lighting his Petersen pipe.

With his eyes begging for understanding, Sean looked up at Harding and implored him. "I swear to you, I didn't take Lizzy's life," he said desperately. "I loved her."

Harding looked into Sean's eyes and saw the considerable pain he was in. He could only begin to imagine how difficult this situation must be for him, but he knew his duty, and he had to make sure it was carried out properly. He could feel the weight of responsibility on his shoulders as he steeled himself for what needed to be done.

"If you didn't take Lizzy's life, who did? All the evidence seems to be leading right towards you, and there is nobody else this case could point to," Harding said in a relaxed voice as he lit his pipe, the aroma of freshly lit tobacco wafting through the air. He looked at Sean with intense scrutiny and then slowly exhaled a puff of smoke, watching as it drifted away from him like an ominous cloud.

Sean opened his mouth to utter something, before reconsidering and slumping back in his chair. He was considering mentioning the name of

James Murray and the relationship he had with Lizzy, but he was scared that this would back up Harding's assumption that he killed Lizzy because he was jealous of her relationship with him.

Harding's eyes tracked every minutiae of Sean's body language, studying him intently. "Were you going to say something?" he asked, his voice deep and commanding. His gaze was penetrating, yet gentle at the same time as if he was trying to read Sean's innermost thoughts and secrets.

"No… no, nothing." Sean sighed.

"Okay, I see," Harding said as he put the plastic bags of evidence back into his briefcase, closed it with a loud click, and then stood up. He walked over to detectives Dunne and Byrne who were sitting down next to the wall and whispered to them from the corner of his mouth as he clenched the pipe in his teeth. "See what you can get out of him and remember, no marks on the face."

Harding left the room and closed the door behind him.

Chapter 21: Out the Door and Over the Wall

Later that day

Donal McCabe sat at his desk, enveloped by the stillness of the empty classroom. The day had been long, strenuous and difficult because his concentration was affected by his worries about Sean, but now the school day was finally over. As the last of his pupils departed from the school grounds, a comforting silence filled the room as he tidied up his desk. The silence was broken by a loud knock on the door.

Donal let out a heavy sigh, rose from his desk and made his way towards the door. He hoped it wasn't an angry parent all ready to give out about something he had said that day to her "darling" son. He approached the door with apprehension. When he opened it, to his surprise there was his work colleague Maureen Murray standing before him, her face drawn with exhaustion and her eyes swollen from tears she had recently shed.

"Donal," she murmured, her voice wavering slightly. "Can I come in?"

Donal was surprised to see Maureen look so upset and meek, she was generally so assertive and commanding. But now she stood before him with a certain vulnerability in her posture. He nodded in agreement and stepped to the side, allowing her access. Maureen walked slowly into the room, her feet dragging as if weighed down by invisible burdens. She stumbled over to one of the desks, collapsing onto the chair with a heavy groan.

"What's wrong?" Donal asked in a concerned tone.

Maureen took a deep inhale and exhale, her breathing heavy with anxiety. She forced herself to speak, the words tumbling slowly. "I'm in need of a break," she said weakly. "To be honest, I'm not mentally or physically prepared for work at the moment. Every time I try to focus on my teaching, my thoughts wander off elsewhere. It is not fair on the children."

Donal's forehead creased with concern as he contemplated her request. He could sense the trepidation in her voice, and the way she avoided eye contact even as she made the plea. It was uncharacteristic of Maureen, a fiercely hardworking and dedicated teacher who rarely asked for time off. For her to make such an unexpected request made him worry about her.

His eyes searched hers for an answer as he stepped closer, his voice soft and quiet. "Is everything all right, Maureen, is it your health, is it something serious... look, tell me that it is none of my business, I know that we don't always get on that well here at work, but if I can help you in any way, I'm here for you."

Maureen shook her head dismissively. "No, it's not my health," she said. "James and I are having problems. I think we need a break from each other."

Donal only had a passing acquaintance with Maureen's husband James, but he seemed like a decent sort, despite the whispers and rumours circulating around him. He looked at Maureen thoughtfully and said, "Well, if these are your personal matters then it's not my place to pry. Take as much time off as you need, no problem. As a matter of fact, I had a young female teacher just out of college call to see me last week, she asked me if there was any substitution work available. I told her that there wasn't, but I took her contact details just in case. I'm sure she could cover your classes until you are ready to come back."

Maureen clearly wasn't listening to what Donal said and she wiped tears from her eyes with a paper hanky as she spoke. "James has been acting strange lately," she sobbed. "Last Wednesday night, he came home late and I was already in bed. I could hear him banging about in the kitchen, but I didn't know what he was doing. He went to bed in the spare room. Later, when he was asleep, I went down to the kitchen and discovered what he had been trying to do. He had been trying to use the washing machine to wash his clothes, but he couldn't get it to work. I took his shirt out of the washing machine and noticed that it had blood on it."

Donal felt a chill run down his spine, as if a cold hand had brushed against it. He knew instinctively that whatever he was about to hear would not be good news. His lips formed the question that had been lingering on his mind. "What did you do?" he asked in a soft tone.

"I didn't say anything to him, because he has been very aggressive lately... oh, he never hit me, but he has a very intimidating and threatening way about him. His words can be cutting," Maureen said, staring at her hanky. "The next morning, when we were having breakfast, I noticed prominent scratch marks on his face. He said they came from falling into briars as he was trying to round up cattle for Tom Burke late the night before."

"Maybe that is where the blood stains came from on his shirt, maybe he was badly torn by the briars, and he bled onto his shirt," Donal suggested thoughtfully.

Maureen's eyes narrowed with suspicion as she spoke. "Perhaps, but I could smell ladies' perfume on his shirt, where did that come from?"

Donal felt completely out of his depth, the awkwardness emanating from him in waves. Looking down he shrugged in an uncertain gesture. Not knowing how to respond, he stood there and said nothing.

"I've suspected it for a long time, that James was having an affair," she said. "But this is the first time I've had proof, the perfume on the shirt. I have overheard all the gossip, people whispering behind my back in the village about James and Lizzy O'Dowd, but I didn't want to believe it... until now." Maureen's eyes filled with tears again as the realisation hit her like a wave.

Donal was still at a loss for words. He felt sorry for Maureen, but he didn't know what to say to ease her pain. All he could offer was a simple gesture of support, a tender yet comforting hand placed on her shoulder.

"Thank you, Donal," Maureen muttered through her tears.

After a moment of thought, Donal finally spoke. "You should definitely take some time off," he said, his voice soft and understanding. "Please take as long as you need – we only have about six weeks until the end of the school year. Why don't you come back in September when the next term starts? " Donal suggested.

Maureen gave Donal a grateful smile and said, "Thank you so much for listening to me and understanding my situation. I'm not sure if I will need that amount of time off, but I do appreciate it. I'll have to think it over."

"Well, it's entirely up to you, Maureen, whatever you need to do," Donal said as he tried to gauge her needs. "Have you a place to go, where will you stay?" Donal asked gently and waited patiently for a response.

"I'm staying with my sister Betty in Manorhamilton, here is her phone number if you need to contact me," Maureen said as she tugged at the pocket of her Aran cardigan and produced a wrinkled sheet of note paper and handed it to Donal.

Donal smiled warmly at Maureen. "Right, thank you, Maureen. You're always so dependable and reliable. Honestly, I don't know how I'd manage to run this school without you! But I suppose it's about time that I learned to stand on my own two feet – though everyone knows who the real boss around here is, eh, Maureen?" His gentle laughter was contagious and brought a smile to Maureen's lips in turn.

Maureen dabbed the remaining tears from her eyes before eventually mustering the emotional strength to rise from her chair. Allowing herself a few deep breaths, she slowly made her way towards the door. With a faint smile she turned to Donal and uttered a few final words. "Thanks again, I better get going, bye for now. Hope to be back as soon as I can," she said as she opened the door, took a final look behind her and walked out.

"Look after yourself, Maureen," Donal called after her, unsure if she had heard him.

Donal peered out the classroom window as Maureen drove off, a deep feeling of apprehension stirring in his chest. He had always admired her strength and tenacity, which seemed so formidable compared to his own. To see her so discouraged and beleaguered was truly worrying. She was usually composed and resolute, but now she looked small and exhausted. Watching her drive away with her shoulders slumped filled him with unease.

Donal busied himself tidying the classroom, putting away books and setting the desks in straight, orderly rows. Despite his best efforts to focus on his task at hand, Donal felt consumed by worry for Maureen and her dire situation. He wondered if James had any connections to the murder; was he somehow involved? His mind raced with all sorts of possibilities, each more worrisome than the last. He felt powerless to do anything but speculate and try not to think too hard about it.

After a quick stop to the local village store for some groceries, Donal made his way back home, only to find an unfamiliar car, a Red Datsun Sunny, parked in his driveway. He stepped out of his Fiat with a slight sense of unease, grabbing the bag of shopping from the back seat before cautiously walking over to investigate. As he got closer, a man emerged from the vehicle and made his way towards him.

Donal had never seen this person before and called out a tentative, "Hello, can I help you?"

"Hello, Donal. I'm Jack Devlin," the stranger said with a warm smile as he shook Donal's hand firmly. "Fiona Donnelly's uncle. I believe she asked me to come by at four o'clock?"

"Oh, yes, yes of course! It's wonderful to meet you, Jack – thank you for coming!"

Donal gave a polite nod in response and cast his gaze upon the man who had just stepped foot onto his driveway. Jack had a well-groomed and polished appearance. His strong jaw line was clean shaven, and his military style short hair was neatly combed and mostly grey, with only a few streaks of brown still visible. Although he appeared to be around sixty years old, he carried himself with a vitality and agility that belied his age. The light in his eyes still shone brightly as he spoke with great intensity.

Jack took a step back and gestured towards the front door. "May I come in, then? We have some urgent matters to discuss, I believe," he said in a polite but assertive tone. His gaze was intense as steel; it was clear that he meant business and he wanted to avoid small talk and get straight to business.

“Of course.” Donal's reply came out in a daze, still reeling from the news that Maureen had told him not long ago. He nodded and silently led Jack into his hallway as if lost in thought. Jack followed Donal into the kitchen, the former detective inspector walking confidently and swiftly with grace and vigour.

Donal busied himself with boiling the kettle for tea while Jack retrieved a small notebook and pen from his leather satchel. The soft glow of light illuminated their surroundings as they settled into the atmosphere of the room, ready to discuss what lay ahead.

"Well, Donal," Jack began, his eyes narrowing as he pored over the pages of his notebook. "Fiona has surely brought you up to date on my backstory. I served in the Gardai for forty years and was a detective inspector in Dublin for my last ten years before finally calling it quits last year. So yes, I know a thing or two about murder investigations, which is why this morning before I left Dublin, I contacted some of my old friends and received some intel on the Lizzy O’Dowd investigation and your friend Sean Breslin's role in it, and unfortunately, I've got some bad news for you. The head detective on the case is a fella by the name of Pascal Harding, an older and very adept inspector who hails from Galway. He's renowned for closing cases quickly, even if it means sometimes an innocent person takes the fall, and from what I can gather he is very close to charging Sean Breslin with the murder of Lizzy O’Dowd.”

As Donal heard the news despair washed over him, and his heart sank deep into the pit of his stomach. He was overwhelmed with worry, contemplating that it might already be too late to save Sean.

Jack continued, "I also discovered that two other detectives, Mick Dunne and Seamus Byrne, are on the case too. I used to work with Mick Dunne in the past and I can vouch for his detective skills; he's an expert at what he does but a rough-around-the-edges type of guy. No offense to him, but don't get on his wrong side or you'll face his wrath. He's a good man but excuse the language, he's a real hard bastard."

Donal heaved a deep sigh of exasperation as he slumped into his chair, trying to suppress the rising feeling of helplessness that was beginning to overwhelm him. His gaze flickered around the room, searching for an answer with which he could appease his worried mind, looking for hope where none seemed to exist. He finally asked in a ragged voice, "So what can we do? Is there any chance of getting Sean off?"

Jack paused for a few moments as he carefully considered his words before replying, "Donal, I have to be honest with you. I'm not entirely sure what to make of this situation. Interfering in an ongoing investigation is nothing to take lightly and I shouldn't really get involved. However, I promised to help Fiona out and she appears convinced that Sean is innocent, and she asked me to come here and help. So, I have to try to help my favourite niece. All I can do is try my best. I'll do what I can, but I can't promise anything, there's no guarantee of success." Jack said with a thin smile.

Donal could sense Jack's trepidations, but he was determined to press forward. "Thanks, Jack. We need your help. Sean is innocent and we have to do all we can to prove it." His voice was strong and unwavering as his earnest gaze met Jack's searching eyes.

Jack scrutinized Donal for an extended moment before finally offering a subtle nod. "All right, Donal. I'll do what I can." He cautioned, his voice low and sombre, "We have to be careful, however – we don't want to stir up any trouble with the local Gardai or muck up the investigation in any way."

"Have you any place to stay? You can stay here in the spare room if you want, it's the least I can offer you," Donal said.

"Thanks for the offer, Donal, but I have already got a room booked in McDaid's Bar over in the village. Apparently, Detective Dunne is staying there as well, so I'm hoping that since we have some history together he might be able to help me out in some way," Jack replied with a hint of optimism that his plan might work out.

"Well, if you change your mind there is a room here," Donal said.

"Thanks, Donal," Jack replied as he rose to his feet. "I think I'm going to get going, freshen up a bit, and then check out the village, chat with some of the natives, and see what I can find out. Call around to my room at McDaid's tomorrow around 4 pm and I will fill you in about anything I discover about the case. I'm in room number seven." He adjusted his coat and grabbed his satchel from where it hung from a nearby chair before heading towards the door.

Donal offered a smile and said, "Sure, I will of course."

The two men firmly clasped each other's hands in a gesture of agreement, holding the firm handshake for a moment before finally releasing. With that, Jack turned and began to make his way outside to his car to head towards McDaid's and his room to get some rest before the work that lay ahead.

Chapter 22: Street Legal

One hour later

Jack Devlin stepped out of the hot shower, droplets of water cascading off his body as he grabbed a towel and began to dry himself. Stepping up to the mirror for a closer look, he gazed upon his reflection. He saw the wrinkles around his eyes seemed even deeper than before, like a roadmap etched into his skin that showed all of life's experiences. His once-thick head of black hair had become almost fully grey, a sharp contrast to the youthful face he once remembered. He exited the en suite and made his way into the small but comfortable bedroom. There was an old armchair in the corner with a small round table next to it. A narrow single bed was pushed tight up against the wall. The bed had an old quilt and pillows with faded prints adorning them, a woollen blanket tucked in the corner. A small dresser stood next to the door, and a nightstand by the bed topped with an old lamp and a few books including the obligatory Gideon's bible. The walls were painted a bright yellow and decorated with traditional Irish artwork; the donkey bringing home turf from the bog, a red-haired boy in an Aran cardigan up on a cart, the usual standard fare. The window was covered with white net curtains that fluttered in the breeze as soft light streamed in upon the worn brown floral carpet that emitted a strong stench of cigarette ash.

After carefully adorning himself with grey jumper, white shirt, and black trousers, Jack opened the door to his room and made his way along the dark hallway towards the exit door. As he stepped out into the streets of Ballygorman, he was met with a warm embrace from a golden ray of sunlight. Wherever he looked, locals were milling about on their daily errands and shared friendly but curious glances in his direction. There was something about him that seemed to spark their interest.

Jack stepped into Doherty's, a small convenience store with a bright green sign above the door. Inside, he perused the shelves, his eyes tracing over the colourful and diverse array of items stocked on them.

The shopkeeper, Eddie, a middle-aged man with an affable smile, approached him. "Good evening, sir," he said kindly. "What can I do for you today?"

Jack gave him a warm smile in return. "Just looking around."

“You’re not local,” Eddie said as he glanced at Jack, giving him the once-over. “Are you in the area for a holiday? Maybe taking in the sights at Lough Melvin? Doing some fishing, perhaps?" The shopkeeper was clearly eager to hear about this stranger's story.

"Just here to visit my niece," Jack replied.

"Ah, so that's what brings you to our lovely village," Eddie said as he rubbed his hands together. "We have some great sights here as well – it's sure to be a refreshing getaway for you." The shopkeeper paused, his expression taking on a darker air. "You must have heard about the murder though – poor Lizzy O'Dowd was found dead in her house just last week. What a terrible business, the whole town is very upset about it."

Jack leaned in closer, eyes wide with curiosity. "I see," he said slowly, his voice very low. “Do you know anything about the case? Who is responsible for the crime?"

Eddie leaned in as well and lowered his own voice to an even softer level. "Well, they've arrested a local man named Sean Breslin." His face looked grim and forlorn as he spoke. “He has been confined in the Garda station for days now, and none of us have any clue as to whether he is really guilty or not. Lizzy O'Dowd was well-known for her unruly behaviour, always surrounded by numerous admirers who would visit her home at all hours. It could have easily been one of them who committed the crime, but nobody could tell for certain.”

"Oh, I see, well I hope they catch whoever is truly guilty soon," Jack said. He thanked the shopkeeper for his time and gave him a lingering nod before turning away from the store. As he stepped out into the street the sun was setting, casting long shadows on the pavement. The sounds of laughter and distant conversations echoed in his ears as he made his way back up the main street.

Jack needed more information, and he knew just the person to ask for it and where to find him. He took a deep breath before pushing open the heavy door of Gallagher’s pub and was almost immediately hit by a wall of stale beer stench so strong it almost felt like a physical punch in the face. The air was thick with cigarette smoke, making it hard to breathe as he stepped inside. Jack scanned the bar, here were only a handful of customers, but Jack's gaze quickly fell on one man seated at the corner of the bar – Mick Dunne, an old friend and former colleague. Mick was a detective and had worked under Jack in Dublin for many years before Jack retired. They hadn't seen each other in a while, but it would be good to catch up. Mick was sitting up at the bar, nursing a pint of Guinness.

Jack approached him and slapped him on the back. "Mick Dunne! How the hell are you?"

Mick Dunne swung around on his barstool in surprise. "Jack Devlin! Jesus, it's good to see you," he said with a wide grin, gripping him in an embrace.

Jack smiled and signaled to the landlord for two pints of Guinness. The conversation began to flow between them like water over a waterfall as they caught up on old times. They began chatting about their past experiences working together, becoming increasingly animated as they reminisced and reflected on the funny stories from that time. Laughing and speaking with an increasing level of excitement, it was evident how fondly they remembered their time spent side by side. Eventually, the conversation shifted to a more current subject matter.

"Pardon me for being so nosey," Mick began, leaning forward with intent curiosity, "but I'm wondering, what the hell brought you to Ballygorman? Are you here on holiday? I thought that Spain was more of your scene." A warm smile formed on his lips as he waited patiently for an answer.

Taking a sip of his drink, Jack replied, "Ah yes, just touring around western Ireland. I just stopped off to visit my niece, Fiona. She works here as a district nurse."

Mick tilted his head to the side in contemplation and slowly nodded in understanding. "Ah, I see," he said.

Jack's face was drawn tight with curiosity and anticipation as he posed the question, even though he already knew the answer. "And what about you? What brings you here?" His eyes were fixed intently on Mick and he waited patiently for his response, eager to hear what he had to say.

"I'm part of the investigation team into the murder of Lizzy O'Dowd," Mick said, his voice lowering.

Jack raised his eyebrows. "Really? I heard about that on the news. How's the investigation going?"

Mick took a long swig of his Guinness and tilted his head back. His expression turned sour as he slowly wiped away the droplets that escaped the corners of his mouth. "It's not going great, to be honest." He sighed as he looked around the bar to check if anybody was listening. "The detective inspector in charge is Pascal Harding, and he's in an awful rush to wrap up the case. He's convinced that a local man called Sean Breslin is the killer, but

I'm not so sure."

Jack drew closer, eyebrows furrowed in confusion. "Why are you uncertain?"

Mick took a deep breath and sighed as he replied, "Sean Breslin is the prime suspect. We've got reports that he was seen lingering near the house on the night of the murder, but I don't know if he did it yet," he said, shaking his head doubtfully. “He doesn’t seem the sort, but I suppose you never can tell.”

Jack studied Mick's face, searching for any hint of uncertainty. "So, you aren’t positive that he's guilty?"

Mick was hesitant, looking as if he were wrestling with a difficult decision. "I'm not entirely convinced," he said slowly, "but Harding is pressing to move ahead with charging him. He believes we have enough evidence to go forward."

Jack slowly brought the pint of cold Guinness to his lips and took an uneasy sip. He sat in deep thought for a moment, considering his options before lifting his gaze to meet Mick’s eyes. "Do you have access to the case files?" he finally asked, his brow creasing in concentration as he awaited his response.

Mick raised an eyebrow. "What the hell do you want the case files for?"

"I'm just curious," Jack said, trying to sound casual. "I haven't studied a good case file in years. Come on, Just humour me, Mick."

Mick's face was etched with trepidation as he replied, "I... I don't know, Jack. I could get in serious trouble if I do that. You know the score more than anybody.”

Jack placed his hand on Mick's arm, giving it a comforting squeeze. He looked into Mick's eyes, pouring assurances into the depths of his gaze. "Come on, old friend," he urged softly. "You know you can trust me. I won't tell anyone – I just want to take a look."

Mick let out a deep, resigned sigh as he tipped his beer up to his lips, taking another swig. After a few moments of silence, he finally spoke. "All right, all right. But just for a quick look. I'll go get them from the Garda

to be the result of being struck by a hefty brass poker?"

Mick shook his head again. "I didn't notice anything like that." His voice wavered with uncertainty.

Jack's gaze shifted to a picture, prominently displaying the kitchen table with a wide-brimmed fedora hat resting atop it like a crown. His curiosity piqued he asked in wonderment, holding up the photo so that Mick could see it, "Did this hat belong to Sean Breslin?"

Mick studied the photo for a moment before shaking his head. "I'm not sure, it may have done."

Jack leaned back in his chair, planting his fingers together thoughtfully as he considered his thoughts. "Sean Breslin might not be the killer," he uttered slowly, pondering the idea carefully. "We must delay Inspector Harding from pressing charges against him so that we have time to search for another possible suspect."

Mick gave a slight frown, his expression betraying his scepticism. He asked worriedly, "But what if we can't find another suspect? What then?" His eyes seemed to pierce through the air as he stared intently at his colleague, almost as if challenging him to come up with an answer.

Jack spoke with unwavering determination. His stare never faltered, his voice resounding with conviction. "Mick, you have to try," he said forcefully. "We owe it to Sean Breslin and ourselves to be certain about this – we cannot simply stand by and watch an innocent man be punished for a crime he might not have committed."

Mick sighed heavily but he eventually gave a resigned nod in agreement. "All right," he conceded. "I'll do my best to delay the inspector for as long as possible, but it won't be easy, he is a cranky old fucker."

“Okay, good man,” Jack said as he carefully placed the documents and photos back as he found them into the folder and handed them back to Mick.

“I'll let you know if I hear of any new developments,” Mick said as he walked towards the door.

“Thanks Mick, I will be here tomorrow if you need to find me,” Jack said.

After Mick left, Jack's mind overflowed with a flurry of thoughts and theories about the murder case. He paced back and forth, unable to release himself from the burden of needing to understand what had happened. With each thought that passed through his mind, he couldn't shake off the feeling that something was amiss in this case, like a missing puzzle piece.

Chapter 23: Along the Red Ledge

Tuesday May 9th

Donal McCabe drew a deep breath and paused, his hand poised to rap on the door of number seven in the lodging house above McDaid's pub. The air was thick with dampness and cold from inadequate heating. His knuckles rapped lightly against the wood three times.

The door creaked as it inched open, and out of the slice of light that fell into the dark hallway stepped Jack Devlin, a wide smile painted across his face. "Come in, Donal," he said cheerily, taking a step back to give him room to pass.

Donal followed Jack into a cramped room that seemed to serve as both his living quarters and his office. With note paper stacked neatly on top of the dresser and small round coffee table, it was apparent that the space had been used for much more than just sleep. The air was heavy with the pungent odour of tobacco smoke, and Donal noticed multiple stained ashtrays around the room. Jack gestured for Donal to take a seat on the bed, while he settled himself into the worn green armchair and took a large inhale from his cigarette.

Donal peered at his companion inquisitively, an expectant glint in his eyes as he posed the question. "Did you manage to find out anything useful?" he enquired, hopeful for a positive response.

Jack inclined his head in acknowledgment. "After studying the case files of the Lizzy O'Dowd murder last night, I'm very confident that your friend Sean Breslin is not guilty of this heinous crime," he said with conviction. His words were spoken with such determination and authority that there was no mistaking his belief that Sean had been wrongfully accused.

Donal's brows shot up into his hairline in disbelief. "What makes you so sure? And I'm very curious as to how you got your hands on the case files."

Jack leaned back in his chair and exhaled a deep sigh. "The case files were hard to come by, but it's the autopsy report that matters. It stated that there were traces of human skin and blood underneath the victim's nails, indicating that she had been trying desperately to claw at her attacker's face to ward him off. A brass poker was also discovered lying beside her body which I believe she used as a weapon in her attempts to defend herself." He paused, expression solemn as his gaze drifted off in the distance. After a few moments passed, he spoke again. "Mick Dunne, one of the detectives on the case, informed me that Sean Breslin had no visible signs of being attacked – no scratches or nail marks upon his face and no bruising to be found anywhere on his body – which would suggest he hadn't been hit by the poker."

Donal inclined forward, curiosity flooding his features. "So," he prodded, voice laced with intrigue, "what does that mean?" He remained still as a statue as he eagerly awaited the answer to his question.

Jack raised his shoulders in a nonchalant shrug. "It points to the fact that Sean Breslin was not the killer of Lizzy O'Dowd. There are also whispers doing the rounds of a secret romance she was enjoying with someone other than him. Did you ever hear about that?"

Donal paused thoughtfully, considering his words before speaking. He took a deep breath, exhaling slowly. "Yes... I did hear some rumours, yes."

Jack nodded. "That's what I thought."

All of a sudden, a thought entered Donal's head. "This might be worth investigating. My colleague at work, Maureen Murray, told me yesterday some information about her husband James Murray that may be relevant. She mentioned to me how she had found blood on his shirt last Thursday morning when she was doing the laundry, the morning after Lizzy had been murdered. Maureen revealed that the shirt also carried a suspicious scent, one of women's perfume. Along with this, she noticed a series of red scratch marks on her husband's face that morning. He claimed that he got them from falling into briars in a ditch as he was driving cattle, but she didn't buy it. She went on to say that his personality seemed to have changed drastically since the previous Thursday – becoming more aggressive and irritable – so she was forced to leave him. She said that she had enough and suspected for a long time that he was having an affair." It was a strange coincidence; too coincidental for Donal to ignore.

Jack sat upright in his chair, his voice a low murmur of urgency. "Donal, I'm certain that James Murray might be able to provide some clues related to the murder. I will contact Detective Dunne and suggest that James Murray should be brought in for questioning. He could have some valuable information that could help us crack this case wide open and hopefully get your friend Sean released."

Donal nodded vigorously in agreement. "Thank you so much, Jack. I can't express how lost and helpless I felt before you showed up. I was absolutely certain Sean was doomed."

Jack exhaled a heavy sigh, his face drawn in worry. "No, we're not quite there yet, Donal," he said, his voice tinged with apprehension. "Inspector Harding is a stubborn old codger, as stubborn as an old mule, as the Yanks say – once he has his mind set on something, good luck trying to convince him otherwise." His gaze flicked towards the window. "He might still stick to his guns even through all this. He doesn't like to be undermined or admit that he was wrong about his initial judgment."

“I certainly hope not,” Donal declared, his face displaying a hint of worry.

“Me too,” Jack agreed, nodding in agreement.

Donal rose from the bed. "Very well," he said, his voice measured and resigned. "If it's what you think is necessary to get your source in the investigation involved, then I won't hold you up." He paused for a moment before continuing, "Do whatever you think is right."

"Sure," Jack responded. "I'll let you know if I hear anything."

Donal gave a small nod of understanding, then headed for the door. "Thanks, and best of luck to you," he offered as he exited the bedroom.

Twenty minutes later at another knock at the door, Jack made his way across the room and slowly twisted the door handle. As he opened it, a faint smirk tugged at his lips as he caught sight of who was standing outside. "Speak of the devil and he will appear...come in, Mick," he said warmly as he motioned him inside with a wave of his hand. "You must be psychic," he said with a chuckle. "I was just thinking about you and considering if I should venture down to the bar or possibly even the Garda station to look for you." Jack’s laughter echoed off the walls, but it was not returned by Mick who instead looked on bemusedly, his features arranged in a puzzled expression as he stepped into the room and Jack closed the door behind him.

"What's the news, Mick?" Jack asked with a hint of anticipation.

Mick sighed deeply, the weight of his words hanging heavily in the air. His eyes were tired, but his face was determined as he spoke. "With a hell of a lot of effort, I managed to convince Harding to hold off on pressing charges against Breslin for another twenty-four hours," he said. "It wasn't easy though, he's utterly convinced that Breslin is responsible and wants this case wrapped up as soon as possible. He was almost finished preparing the necessary paperwork to send a file to the Director of Public Prosecutions and I think he is fuming with me.”

“Well, you were successful in stalling him, that’s the main thing, well done, Mick,” Jack said as he congratulated his friend with a friendly pat on the shoulder. "Now, I have learned today that it appears very possible there is another local man, James Murray, who had been having a relationship with the murder victim and I think it would be worth talking to him," Jack suggested before going into further detail about the specifics of what he had learned.

Mick's eyes widened in surprise as Jack relayed the information to him. He shook his head in thought. "Well that sure sounds like we have another suspect on our hands," he concluded, conviction in his tone. He ran a hand across his bald head, looking off into the distance. "And it might just save my skin, it will prove to Harding that I was right to stall charging Sean Breslin."

Jack nodded in agreement. "Without a doubt. If James Murray had anything to do with this, then it is of the utmost importance that you bring him in for questioning," he said in a definite tone.

Mick sighed heavily. "It's a long shot though, Jack. We don't have any concrete evidence."

"The blood on his shirt," Jack remarked gravely.

"Yes, but where is the shirt?" Mick inquired.

"Leave that to me," Jack replied. "Mick, you have a duty to pursue every lead, no matter how small. You owe it to the murder victim and her family members to find the truth."

Mick cast a serious look in Jack's direction. "You're right," he said firmly. "I'll arrange to have James Murray brought in for questioning tomorrow morning." He spoke with authority and conviction, and Jack felt relieved that his plan had been accepted.

As Mick rose from sitting on the bed, Jack's voice rang out in the silence. "Mick, just one more thing before you go. We have to exercise caution when dealing with this. If the reporters catch wind of it, we may be facing a lot of unwanted attention." He gave Mick a stern look to emphasize his point; this was not something that should be taken lightly.

Mick nodded, a deep sigh leaving his lips. "I understand, Jack," he said, his expression grim and determined. "I'll take care of it with the utmost discretion." He gave one last nod of acknowledgment before turning around and walking out the door, closing it quietly behind him as he left.

Chapter 24: Give 'Em Enough Rope

Wednesday May 10th

Detectives Mick Dunne, Seamus Byrne, and Garda Sergeant Pat O'Donnell arrived at James Murray's farmhouse at 7:30 on Wednesday morning. The sun was barely peeking through the clouds, casting a pale light over the verdant fields and rolling hills that surrounded the village of Ballygorman. The air was crisp, and a light breeze swept through the fields, rustling the tall grass and carrying the scent of fresh manure. The front garden of the Murray house was unkempt, with weeds growing in between the cobblestones that led to the front door.

Mick Dunne knocked on the back door and waited, his heart pounding with anticipation because he knew this was a pivotal moment in the investigation and that the fate of an innocent man hung in the balance. He was aware they were taking a big risk by questioning James Murray, but it was the only new lead they had, and the stakes were high. If they couldn't find any evidence against Murray, Sean Breslin would be charged with murder later that day.

After a few moments, the door creaked open.

"Good morning, I am Detective Mick Dunne, standing behind me are Detective Byrne and Sargeant O'Donnell. Are you James Murray?"

"Yes, I am," James finally replied after a long, probing stare.

Dunne stepped forward, his authoritative voice cutting through the silence. "Mr. Murray, we need to talk to you," he said firmly.

James eyed the three men with wariness as they approached him slowly. He nervously inquired, "What about?"

"We're investigating the murder of Lizzy O'Dowd," Mick replied. "We need to ask you a few questions."

James immediately felt the weight of the words, as if a heavy blanket had just been thrown over him. His face turned pale and his heart sank. He knew that he couldn't avoid the scrutiny of the law forever, despite the fact that he had been plotting so hard to avoid it. James tried to steady the tremor in his voice as he replied, "Of course, officers. Please come in." He stepped aside and gestured for them to enter his home, anxiety churning in his stomach as he watched them cross the threshold.

The three officers trailed James into his parlour. Since Maureen had left him, the kitchen was an utter disaster area full of unwashed pots, pans and plates and he felt too embarrassed to bring them in there. The parlour, on the other hand, had fortunately been kept tidy since it was the 'good room' that was never really used. It was sparsely furnished with a few armchairs arranged around a small fireplace, its mantle lined with trinkets and knick-knacks. On the walls hung paintings of charming pastoral scenes and family portraits.

"Would you like a cup of tea?" James asked, trying to appear calm and hospitable.

Mick Dunne looked the man straight in the eye and said firmly, "No, thank you. We're here on official business, Mr. Murray. We don't have time for small talk, we need you to accompany us to the Garda station at Ballygorman for questioning." His voice was serious and stern, yet respectful. He wanted the man to understand he had no choice but to comply with their orders.

James stood still for a moment then finally nodded in agreement. He silently walked with the officers outside towards the car and climbed into the back seat without a word of protest. The car's engine came to life, and they began their journey to the station, haunted by a heavy silence that permeated inside the vehicle. The wind rustled outside as they sped down the road and James's focus was distant, fixated on something far away from this moment – some unknown place he longed to be.

As they walked into the Garda station, James was led to a small interview room. Detective Inspector Pascal Harding was seated inside waiting for them, his stern face betraying the intensity of his focus. He had already drawn his own conclusions and seemed certain that Sean Breslin was the guilty party in this case, viewing James as nothing more than a distraction to be tolerated before he could set off on the right path again.

Mick Dunne pulled out a chair and sat next to Harding, their eyes locking on James. Harding adjusted his tie, cleared his throat and then began. "I'm certain you understand why I've called you here today, Mr. Murray," he said as James pulled out a chair to sit down at the table. "We're conducting an investigation into the unfortunate murder of Lizzy O'Dowd, and we believe that you may possess some valuable insight that could assist us in our inquiries. My name is Detective Inspector Pascal Harding and you have already spoken to the man next to me, Detective Sergeant Mick Dunne. Since it was his notion to bring you here this morning for a... chat, he will also be partaking in the questioning. If you are willing to cooperate with us, if you can answer the questions honestly and thoroughly, then this whole process should be concluded swiftly and without any major issues."

James sat with a slight smirk on his face. "Look, I know why I'm here," he said as he crossed his arms over his chest defensively. "But I don't know anything about that poor woman's death. Why would somebody want to kill Lizzy?"

"That's what we're trying to figure out," Mick said, his voice stern, holding a resolute seriousness. "We're asking everyone who knew her to come in and answer some questions, to provide us with their insights so we can try to discover what actually happened on Wednesday night, May 3rd." His gaze shifted across the room as if he was looking for someone or something to give him direction.

"Ah, I understand," James responded, his gaze shifting between the two detectives like a ship in choppy waters. He nodded slowly before continuing, "I'm more than happy to help in any way that I can."

"Okay, that's terrific, Mr Murray, let's get started so. If you wouldn't mind, could you tell us where you were on the night of the murder? This would have been last Wednesday night, May 3rd, between 9 pm and midnight," Harding asked with a stern but sympathetic voice, getting straight to business, not wanting to waste any more time than necessary on the interview.

Mick's eyes bore into the suspect, analysing every flicker of emotion that crossed his face. He waited patiently for a response, pen poised above his notebook ready to take down whatever information he provided.

James sat uncomfortably in his chair, nervously running a hand through his ever-thinning hair. A distant look came over him as he began to recount the events of that fateful night. He paused for a moment to collect his thoughts before continuing with the story, taking a deep breath before beginning. "I was at Tom Burke's farm. Tom is a neighbour of mine."

Mick's gaze was intense and unwavering as he carefully posed the question. "Can you give us the names of the witnesses who can verify that?" His voice was measured and calm, but there was a note of urgency beneath it that betrayed just how important this information was to him. He waited for an answer with eager anticipation.

"Tom Burke, obviously. He can vouch for me." James wore a fake smile and spoke the name confidently, expecting it to be enough to prove his point.

"What exactly were you doing at Tom Burke's farm that night?" Harding asked, the question hanging in the air for a few moments, like the smoke from his Peterson pipe.

"Well, poor old Tom is a very careless and lazy farmer," James explained. "He doesn't bother to fence his land properly and of course as a result his cattle are always breaking out. I was over with him on Wednesday night helping him get his cattle back in from Kevin Glancy's land. I was just being a good neighbour, just doing my duty."

"Do you really think that it was necessary to do such a job in the dead of night?" Mick asked sceptically. "It gets dark around 9:30 these evenings. Couldn't it wait until morning when there'd be more light, to see what you were doing?" The gruffness of his voice echoed off the walls around him.

"It was awkward in the dark all right, but we had flashlamps and thankfully a bright full moon," James replied with a nod. "Tom wanted to get his cattle off Kevin Glancy's land before he noticed they were there, the next morning."

Mick Dunne bent forward, his gaze piercing as he intensely examined James's face. "So, you are telling me that you were assisting Tom Burke with the cattle on the night of the murder?" His voice held a slightly menacing edge, suspicion radiating from his eyes as he awaited a response.

"That's right," James replied, his eyes darting nervously around the room.

"Pardon me for asking, but when were you finished with your task?" Harding inquired, carefully jotting down a few notes in his notebook. He glanced over the page thoughtfully. His eyes eventually fixed on his page and his pen as he awaited a response, an earnest expression etched on his face.

"It was a late hour, Tom Burke had some difficulty managing one of the cattle – a heifer if my memory serves me right – and it took longer than we thought to round the last of them up. It must have been somewhere close to midnight when we finally finished up." James's voice quivered nervously as he recounted what happened.

"And you're sure you didn't see or hear anything suspicious while you were out there?" Mick interjected, his eyes holding James's gaze unwaveringly, waiting for an answer, the tips of his fingers tapping rhythmically on the table as he studied James's face intently.

"Well, around 10 pm as it was getting dark, Tom drove me back to my house and I collected two flashlamps. We passed Lizzy O'Dowd's house on the way back at around 10:15 and Tom mentioned that he noticed a yellow Ford escort outside Lizzy's house. I didn't see it, I was looking down at one of the flashlamps to see if it was working," James replied.

"Yes, Mr. Burke did indeed report that to us last Sunday," Harding responded thoughtfully as he sat back in his chair to allow his colleague Mick Dunne to continue with his questioning. "Did you observe any other peculiar incidents, or notice anyone moving about in the vicinity? Could you have seen any cars driving off or heard any odd sounds, like a scream perhaps that had caught your attention?"

James's throat tightened, and his mouth became parched of moisture. He shook his head. "Nothing like that, just me and Tom and his herd of cattle." Despite the warmth in the room, an icy chill ran through him at the thought of what had actually happened with Lizzy that night. The images were too much to bear, so he quickly pushed them out of his mind and focused on what was in front of him.

"Did you have any sort of relationship with Lizzy O'Dowd?" Mick asked, growing impatient, almost as if the answer he sought had been evading him for far too long.

James considered his reply carefully before speaking. "We were neighbours," he began slowly. "I helped her out around the house after her husband John passed away, doing whatever small tasks I could manage. That's all it was." There was a pause in the air as if he could feel the unheard questions still lingering in the atmosphere. He shifted slightly, unsure how to respond to their unspoken inquiries.

"Is that true?" Mick continued. "We've been hearing that you've been sneaking out to spend time with her, even though you're a married man." His accusatory words hung heavily in the room, leaving no place for doubt of his displeasure.

Harding turned his head sharply towards Mick, eyes blazing with rage, as he tried to make sense of the questions being posed and pondered whether it was appropriate for his colleague to be asking such things.

Mick cut off Harding just as he was about to say something, not wanting to miss the opportunity to air his trepidations. "Come on, James, we all know you were more than just good friends with Lizzy. We all know the two of you have a past together," he said quickly.

"And what makes you think that?" James replied, his voice even but his temper rising. A swell of indignation surged inside him at the detective's brusque attitude, though he attempted to maintain his composure and suppress any signs of agitation. A battle raged within him, between asserting himself and politely abiding by the rules, and it was only through sheer force of will that he managed to remain stoic in the face of what he considered blatant disrespect.

Mick rolled his eyes and snorted indignantly. "Come on, everyone in town knows about it," he said with a hint of disbelief dripping from his voice. James's face grew serious, his brow creasing in frustration as he shook his head slowly. "That's a terrible accusation to make," he started, the anger evident in his tone. "You should never listen to the stupid rumours around this town." His gaze was intense as he questioned Mick. "Who told you that rubbish?"

"It doesn't matter who said it," Mick replied sharply. "What about the scratch marks on your cheeks? How did you get them, looks to me like they are scratch marks from a person's long fingernails. Had you a row with your wife or somebody else?" His voice was full of accusation as he eagerly awaited a response.

"I fell into a ditch of briars while I was herding cattle for Tom Burke," James replied. "It was dark, so it was hard to see where we were going."

"And the bruise on your left temple," Mick asked as he pointed at the black swelling and discoloration on the side of James's forehead.

"From the same fall on Wednesday night, I hit my head against a gatepost. Accidents do happen, the joys of farming." James smiled wryly.

Mick let out a sceptical sigh and said, "It all seems a little too convenient, don't you think?" James shifted in his chair, his eyes flickering nervously around the room in search of an answer. He stammered for a moment and then let out an exasperated groan. "You can think what you want but it's the truth," he said in an angry tone. "Look, this is all pointless. I didn't kill Lizzy – I swear it!" His voice was filled with desperation as he tried to plead his innocence.

"But you had an inkling that something wasn't right, didn't you?" Mick Dunne said sharply. "You must have picked up on the murmurs and whispers that echoed through the streets of the town. And yet, despite all of this, you stayed silent; it wasn't until we brought you in here today that you opened your mouth."

"I didn't know anything. I heard some rumours, but I didn't want to get involved. I didn't think it was my place and what information did I have that you didn't know before? Tom Burke already told you about the yellow Ford Escort outside Lizzy's house on Wednesday night," James replied.

Harding decided to begin to wrap up the interview, believing that it was futile to continue to question James anymore.

"We're simply trying to narrow down our list of suspects, Mr. Murray. I trust you understand," Harding said in a measured tone as he fixed his gaze on James for an extended time. "Very well, James. We'll let you go now, we have taken up enough of your time. We really appreciate your cooperation this morning. Just so that we can have a complete record, we will take your fingerprints on the way out. It's only protocol to make sure you are not involved."

James nodded, relief washing over him. Slowly, he rose from his seat, feeling the trembling of his legs as he attempted to steady himself. "That is perfectly fine," he replied in a voice barely audible above the sound of his unsteady breath.

As James Murray departed the Garda station, Detective Harding whirled around to face Mick Dunne, his face contorted in rage. His cheeks were flushed a deep and fiery red, his brow furrowed in fury. "What the hell was that all about, Dunne? We just wasted an entire hour of our time on that ridiculous exchange!" Harding's voice boomed around the station like thunder rumbling across a stormy sky.

Mick could feel Harding's tobacco-stained spit and breath on his face. Mick Dunne squared his shoulders and maintained an unwavering stance, standing his ground against his superior. "I don't think it was a pointless pursuit, sir. I can smell something amiss about James Murray's story. And those scratches on his face only serve to bolster my suspicion."

"Those scratches? He said he got them from a briar patch while helping Tom Burke with the cattle. That's a plausible explanation, isn't it?"

Mick's eyebrows rose in suspicion. "Maybe, but what about the deep purple bruise on his temple? He said he accidentally bumped it on a gatepost, but that story just seems dubious to me. I can't help but wonder if there was something more malicious behind the incident."

"Or it could be exactly what he said it was," Harding said, his voice steadily rising again. "We have absolutely not a shred of evidence, no proof to connect James Murray to the murder, Dunne. None whatsoever. We have a suspect in custody, that is Sean Breslin, and I want to charge him, and I will charge him. So just do your job, Detective."

Dunne's face grew taut with frustration, his eyes narrowing in anger and lips pursing together in a thin line. He wanted to argue his point further, but he knew it was futile. Taking a deep breath, he attempted to compose himself. "Yes, sir," he replied. "I understand." His voice was strained and he could feel the irritation threatening to bubble up once again as his boss began speaking again.

"Excellent. Now let us begin constructing a formidable legal case against Breslin for the courts," Harding demanded.

As the detectives sauntered away from the interrogation room, Dunne couldn't shake his uneasy feeling that they had just let a possible killer slip through their fingers. He knew Harding was being pressed to hurry and close this case, but he entertained doubts that maybe some crucial evidence was going unnoticed. Doubts lingered in his mind that perhaps an urgent need for speed due to financial constraints had caused them to miss something vital.

Mick Dunne quickly spun around to face Detective Byrne once Harding had rounded the corner and was out of earshot. He gazed directly into Byrne's eyes, searching for any hint of what his next move should be. Byrne remained expressionless as he held Mick's gaze and slowly stepped back, allowing him enough space to take in a deep breath before continuing down the hallway.

"I'm not sure where we're headed with this, Seamus," Mick said, as he rubbed his bald head.

"What do you mean?" Seamus asked. "I mean that we're so fixed on Breslin as the prime suspect for Lizzy's murder that we aren't considering any other alternatives," Dunne explained. "What if James Murray really did have something to do with it?”

Byrne looked sceptical, narrowed his eyes, and shook his head. "Come on, Mick. You know as well as I do that we don't have any real evidence to link James Murray to the murder. Harding's right, we've got Breslin in custody. So let’s focus on getting a conviction for him and not waste our time chasing wild theories, and leads with no real substance. Look, if we get this all tied up tomorrow, we can be back in Dublin on Friday to see our wives and kids and get out of this boring hole of a spot."

Dunne exhaled deeply, a sigh of longing for the familiarity of Dublin and his family, yet still with the glimmer of hope that there was something more to this case. He felt a slight stirring in his heart, a feeling that if he just looked hard enough, he might yet find what it was he sought.

Chapter 25: Pump it Up

Four hours later

Detective Mick Dunne gripped the steering wheel tightly as he drove the short distance from Ballygorman Garda station to the car park at Lough Melvin. His knuckles grew whiter as he felt a wave of anger and frustration wash over him, considering the possibility that an innocent man might be charged with the crime simply because the top brass wanted a result and wanted the case wrapped up irrespective of the consequences. He couldn't shake the feeling of unease and it had intensified, almost gnawing at him since he received the phone call an hour ago from Jack Devlin. What could be so urgent that Jack would ask him to meet immediately, Mick wondered as he pulled into the car park with his mind full of questions and his heart racing.

His eyes swept around the area, eventually focusing on the two cars parked nearby – a Fiat Mirafiori and a Datsun Sunny. He carefully manoeuvred his own vehicle into place beside them before stepping out and making his way over to where Jack was engaged in conversation with another man. The breeze from Lough Melvin gently rustled their clothes.

As he approached, Jack turned upon hearing Mick's heavy footsteps on the gravel and introduced him to the stranger. "Mick, this is Donal McCabe. He's a teacher at the local primary school and a close friend of Sean Breslin."

Mick glanced at the man before him with an air of caution, his eyes darting around to take in every detail. He hesitantly raised his hand towards Donal's, a subtle tension lurking behind his gaze which revealed that there was something troubling him. As they shook hands, Mick felt he was being sized up in return.

"What's going on, Jack?" Mick asked, getting straight to the point. His eyes scanned the area for any indication of what Jack could be up to. "What brings you to a place like this, why did you want to meet me here?" He looked expectantly at his friend, curious as to what he was planning.

"It's quiet here, there are too many eyes and ears in the village." Jack's face grew tight and his expression solemn, making it clear that what he was about to say should not be shared lightly. "More importantly, you brought James Murray in earlier this morning for questioning."

"We did," Mick responded with a heavy sigh, his chest heaving in resignation. He let out a tired breath that seemed to echo the defeat in his voice, as if all his efforts had been for nothing. He shook his head slowly and sunk into a defeated silence, sadness reverberating from deep within him.

"And you didn't keep him for very long, did you?" Jack said, his tone laced with a touch of disappointment. "He must have arrived at the Garda station at around eight in the morning and was brought back home again by ten o'clock, just two hours later."

"How do you know all that?" Mick inquired; curiosity laced with surprise in his words.

Jack responded with a smirk, "I was parked just down the street from the Garda station, taking it all in." He continued casually, his voice conveying an air of confidence that could not be denied. "I had a perfect view of everything as it happened."

"Oh, right," Mick said.

"So, fill me in, what happened in the interview room?" Jack asked, curiosity brimming in his voice.

"I think that James Murray is guilty, he was lying through his teeth," Mick asserted. "He had the scratch marks on his face and the bruising on his temple which would fully corroborate what you said about Lizzy fighting back with her nails and the poker before she was murdered. He gave us some cock and bull story about falling into a ditch of briars to explain the cuts on his cheeks."

"Did he have an alibi for the night Lizzy was murdered?" Jack posed the question.

"He said that he had been helping his neighbour Tom Burke round up cattle that had broken out of his farm between nine and twelve on the night Lizzy was killed. This seems incredibly hard to believe, considering it was pitch-black outside after 9:30 pm," Mick replied.

"But I don't get it, if you were so certain he was lying why did you let him go?" Jack quizzed.

"Because damn Inspector Harding is convinced that Sean Breslin is the murderer, and nothing will change his opinion. The poor fella will be charged this afternoon if Harding has his way," Mick replied angrily.

"Oh Christ, what can we possibly do?" Donal asked, feeling a sense of hopelessness come over him as his mind raced for an answer.

"We must take action to exonerate Sean," Jack declared resolutely. "I have an idea of where we can begin, and Mick, I need you to talk to Tom Burke, the person responsible for supplying James Murray with a fraudulent alibi on the night of Lizzy's death. See if you can get him to confess."

Donal listened intently, hanging on every word, feelıng a glimmer of hope. Maybe there was a chance to clear Sean's name after all.

Mick hesitantly nodded, taking a deep breath. "I can try," he replied.

Jack gave him an encouraging look and placed a hand on his shoulder. "You will, Mick, put the fear of God into him, inform him that he is breaking the law and could experience serious punishment for the crime."

"The main problem is that there's simply no solid evidence to link James Murray to the murder," Mick said as he shook his head and rubbed his hands against the sides of his thighs in frustration. "If only we had something."

"We might have something," Donal interjected as soon as Mick had finished speaking, his brow creasing in earnest concentration.

"What is it?" Mick inquired, intrigued by the sudden spark of enthusiasm on Donal's face.

"The bloody shirt that James was wearing from the night of the murder, his wife Maureen discovered it the next morning. I'll contact her and see if she can find it, hopefully she didn't wash it already," Donal said.

"Right, can you get onto that straight way," Jack ordered in an authoritative tone.

"I can, I'll ring her from the phone box when I get back to the school." Donal nodded in agreement and replied with certainty.

"Okay, you better get going so," Jack suggested.

"Wish me luck," Donal said as he took a deep breath and made his way to his car.

"Good luck to you Donal and to you Mick, I'll be back at McDaid's if you need me," Jack shouted, watching the two men walk across the gravel coated car park.

"Hey Donal, have you any idea where Tom Burke lives?" Mick asked as he trailed behind him.

"I could give you directions, but you will probably get lost, he lives up a maze of laneways off the main road. Look, follow me, I'll lead you to his house, it will only take five minutes."

"Right, lead the way," Mick said and jumped into his car.

After a short journey that traversed winding byroads and narrow lanes, they arrived at Tom Burke's farm. Donal adeptly manoeuvred his car around the farmyard, before turning his attention to finding the nearest telephone box back in Ballygorman in order to call Maureen Murray.

Mick slowly stepped out from his car, and as he looked up towards Tom

Burke's house his mind churned with the uncertainty as to the kind of demeanour Tom would adopt upon seeing him.

He knocked on the door, and after a few moments he heard muffled footsteps from the other side. The door opened, revealing a middle-aged rotund man with a red face that was flashing alarms of high blood pressure.

"Can I help you?" Tom said, eyeing Mick suspiciously, his gaze travelled slowly over his face, scrutinising every inch of it.

"Good afternoon, sir. I am Detective Mick Collins, can you confirm that you are Tom Burke?"

Tom nodded nervously, his eyes wide with surprise, and he hesitated for a moment before replying, "Yes."

"I need to ask you some questions concerning the recent murder of Lizzy O'Dowd," Mick said. "Can I come in?"

Tom's complexion grew a shade paler, his eyes darting feverishly around the yard outside. He seemed to be contemplating slamming the door in Mick's face and making a run for it, but he eventually reconsidered that idea. His thoughts had been scribbled hastily on his face, anxiety and paranoia written like chapters in a book.

"Step in," he said gruffly, stepping aside to let Mick through.

As he entered the house, he was met with a murky darkness that was oppressive, the atmosphere thickened by the heavy curtains that blocked out any light that could have drifted in from outside. Everything was muted in shades of grey and black. Mick could smell the strong scent of cabbage boiling and spuds frying in lard, along with a mustier scent that was most likely caused by years of accumulated dust and dirt. He also detected a pungent smell of mould and mildew from the dampness that had seeped into the walls.

They settled down at a small, worn out and shaky kitchen table. Mick had to hastily brush away the crumbs of bread, potato skins and granules of sugar scattered across its surface before placing his notebook on top. He ran his hands along the edge of the table, feeling the bumps and grooves as he studied each tiny imperfection in detail.

"Right, Tom, let's get started," Mick began. "First of all, you made a statement in Ballygorman Garda station last Sunday evening in which you claimed that at approximately 10 pm on Wednesday, May 3rd you noticed a yellow Ford Escort parked outside the home of the murder victim, Lizzy O'Dowd. Is that true?"

Tom shifted in his seat uncomfortably, refusing to meet Mick's inquisitive gaze as he murmured an uncertain, "Yes." His throat felt constricted, and the words were forced out of him, less a confirmation and more a surrender to Mick's assertion. He felt his hands trembling slightly and he tensed, worried that Mick would notice him fidgeting. Mick did notice and pressed him for more information. "This morning I, alongside Inspector Harding, sat in an interrogation room with your neighbour, James Murray. We asked him questions pertaining to the murder of Lizzy O'Dowd - questioning his whereabouts between 9 pm and midnight on the night she was killed. Where was James that night, Tom?"

"He was with me... helping me... with the cattle," Tom replied, hesitating before answering, beads of sweat forming along his forehead as fear started to creep in.

It was clear he had something to hide. Mick could sense it. "Are you quite certain that it was on Wednesday night, May 3rd?" Mick queried, doubt evident in his voice. Tom shifted his weight uneasily and ran a hand through his hair before hesitantly mumbling out a reply. "Yes... I'm pretty sure."

Mick raised an eyebrow sceptically. "You're 'pretty sure'? Not completely certain?" he asked with an air of disbelief. Tom paused apprehensively. "Yes, last week... last Wednesday night," he began uncertainly, his voice lacking its usual confidence. His gaze shifted away for a moment before making eye contact again as he spoke. "I'm not sure of the date," he admitted.

"Right," Mick replied simply, a knowing gleam in his eye as his lips curled into a slight smirk. "It was dark for moving cattle and it took you three hours, a right pain in the arse, that job in the dark I'd say," Mick said.

Tom was at a loss for words, his mouth opening and closing like a gasping fish, unable to find the right phrase to describe the situation. Referring to it as merely 'difficult' seemed like a gross understatement. After several moments of uncomfortable silence, he finally managed an ineloquent reply. "It was... it was surely difficult."

"How could you see what you were doing?" Mick inquired.

"Well...sure we...just had to manage the best we could," Tom replied with a shrug.

"Did you bring flashlamps or torches with you?" Mick asked, his voice filled with anticipation.

Tom shook his head regretfully and replied, "No, we didn't have a thing with us."

Mick turned to Tom, a curious gleam in his eye. "Well, according to James Murray you had two flashlamps," he said.

"Oh yes, we did, that's right. I had forgotten that," Tom replied as he stared over at the window.

"Where did you come across them?" Mick queried.

Tom had his head cocked to one side as he replied cautiously, "What do you mean?"

"The flashlamps, where did you get them?" Mick asked.

"Oh, I got them from my shed, out the back," Tom replied.

"Well, that is strange," Mick exclaimed, "because James said he got them from his shed at his homeplace."

Tom paused for a moment as the recollection of what James had told him registered in his mind. "Oh yes," he continued with a nod, "that's right."

"So, you didn't get them from your shed, yet you just said that you did." Mick raised an eyebrow in disbelief.

"Oh, I forget that it was James that got them from his shed," Tom said, scratching the back of his head.

"So, let me get this clear then. James Murray had flashlamps with him when he arrived here at 9 pm," Mick said in a demanding voice.

"That's right." Tom wrung his hands, unable to meet Mick's stern gaze as he confirmed his statement.

An uncomfortable silence hung in the air, heavy with the implications of what had been said. It was clear that Tom had something to hide, something that he didn’t want Mick to discover.

“He came prepared, that’s for sure,” Mick remarked, breaking the short silence.

“He did surely, that’s right.” Tom nodded.

“So, James was here with you, helping you with cattle from 9 pm to 12 pm.”

“That’s right, yes,” Tom affirmed.

“Are you absolutely certain of that, Tom?” Mick questioned. “You and James were together for the entire three hours, right?”

Tom inhaled deeply before exhaling and replied in a quiet voice, “Yes, I'm completely sure.”

“So, I can’t understand, I can’t make any sense of this, maybe I’m getting daft in my middle age or something. How were you driving by Lizzy O’Dowd’s house and somehow noticed a yellow Ford escort there at 10 pm on Wednesday night, May 3rd, if you were here at that time helping James Murray gather up your cattle from a neighbour’s field. How could that be even possible, how could you be in two places at the same time? Explain that to me, Tom, please, because I am really confused now,” Mick said his tone growing more forceful as he sensed that Tom was lying to him.

Tom's gaze remained fixated on the tabletop before him. He wouldn't answer, his silence only adding to the tension that hung in the air like a heavy fog. Every second felt like an eternity as the weight of Mick’s stare seemed to press down on him.

"Tom, explain that to me," Mick implored, repeating the query. Tom's face was a portrait of confusion, his eyes shifting frantically from side to side as he tried to think of an answer. Eventually, his voice cracked as he uttered the words, "I... don’t know." Tears began to brim in his eyes and slide down his cheeks, cascading down with the force and speed of a river. He looked away ashamedly like a child who had just been found out.

Mick knew now that Tom was broken and in a vulnerable state and he went in for the kill, time to put the fear of God into him as Jack Devlin had suggested. "Have you provided James Murray with a false alibi, Tom? Can I remind you that it is a criminal offence to do so," Mick said as he took a small book out of his inside jacket pocket and began to read from it. "Under the Criminal Justice Act of 1967, it is an offence to obstruct, pervert or defeat the course of justice, this includes providing false information or misleading the authorities in relation to a criminal investigation, such as by providing a false alibi. Under the 1967 Act, a person convicted of perverting the course of justice could face imprisonment for up to two years. In more serious cases, the penalty could be more severe."

Tom's face hardened as he wiped away his tears with the tattered sleeve of his coat, not uttering a single word in reply. The detective pushed in closer and spoke slowly, emphasizing each of his words. "Do you understand what that means, Tom? You could be sent to prison for two years if you don't reconsider your statement, but if you agree to cooperate, we can offer you some leniency."

Mick's voice was steady and measured as he spoke, his tone firm but gentle. "Tom, I need to know the truth about James Murray. Did he really help you herd up cattle on the night Lizzy O'Dowd was murdered?" The kitchen echoed with silence as Mick waited for an answer. Meanwhile, his eyes wandered over Tom's face searching for signs of hesitation or deceit in his expression. Still no reply came.

Tom shifted uncomfortably in his seat, his eyes darting around the room. Mick could see the sweat beading on his forehead. Finally, Tom spoke, his voice barely above a whisper. "I'm sorry, I lied. James wasn't with me that night. He forced me to provide him with an alibi. He made me do it."

Mick sat upright, his eyebrows lowering as he tightly pursed his lips. He stared intently at Tom, his eyes narrowing with suspicion. "Tom," he began in a stern and urgent tone, "are you absolutely certain that's the only thing James instructed you to lie about?"

No response from Tom.

"What else did he tell you to lie about, Tom?"

Tom took a deep breath, unsure of what to say. His face contorted in concentration as he tried to recall the exact words that were spoken. Finally, he replied, “He told me to report to the Gardai that I noticed a yellow Ford Escort car parked outside Lizzy's house that night, a car like Sean Breslin’s.”

“The night Lizzy O’Dowd was murdered?” Mick asked.

Tom paused for a moment, his expression strained as he searched for the right words. “Yes, that night,” Tom finally said, his voice barely audible.

Mick's heart began to pound in his chest as he wondered what else James might be willing and capable of. He looked at Tom thoughtfully, searching for any sign that he was hiding something. "Is there anything else you need to tell me, Tom," Mick said quietly, "now that you have the chance to get it off your conscience?"

Tom timidly nodded, his eyes wide with fear. His voice shook as he spoke. "That's all I know, I swear it. He made me do it. I didn't want any trouble." There was something about the way he said it that made his words sound desperate, like he was begging for mercy. He seemed to shrink into himself with each passing moment.

Mick gave Tom an affirming pat on the shoulder as he tried to console him. "I understand, Tom. You did the right thing by being honest with me. Now, I need you to accompany me to the Garda station so that you can tell my superior, the detective inspector, what you told me. Will you do that for me?"

Tom hung his head in silent agreement and gave a slight nod of affirmation. Mick rose from the table, his mind racing with newfound possibilities as he escorted Tom to the back seat of his car. As he drove back to the Garda station in Ballygorman, he replayed every word of the conversation with Tom in his mind, trying to piece together the details that would be crucial in building a case against James. He thought about the bloody shirt that his wife, Maureen had found in the washing machine, wondering how they could use it as evidence. He thought about the lies that James had told during his initial questioning, and wondered what other secrets he might be keeping.

Mick noticed Inspector Harding immediately when he arrived at the station. He was pacing back and forth, his brow knitted with worry and tension.

"Where have you been, Dunne?" Harding said firmly. His piercing gaze seemed to bore into Mick's very soul as he waited for an answer.

"I went to talk to Tom Burke," Mick replied. "And I have some new information that I think you need to hear."

"Who?" Harding asked.

"Tom Burke, the farmer that James Murray was supposedly working with on the night of the murder," Mick said.

"Oh yes, yes, Tom Burke, what about?" Harding asked impatiently.

"Well if what he told me is true, then we need to talk to James Murray again," Mick said with certainty.

Harding raised an eyebrow, his interest piqued. "Go on."

Mick recounted to Harding, with every detail and nuance, everything Tom had mentioned, observing as his features gradually grew heavier and graver with each passing second. He could sense that Harding was filled with disappointment and vexation at Tom proving him wrong about James Murray. His expression was a mixture of frustration and chagrin, fumbling for the right words to express his displeasure.

"Tom Burke is waiting out in the car. I'll bring him in so you can hear his side of the story and get a better understanding of what I just told you," Harding said.

His boss nodded approvingly and replied simply, "Okay, bring him in."

After Mick had escorted Tom Burke to the interview room, he made his way out to the corridor, settling down on an old chair by the doorway. He reached into his pocket and pulled out a cigarette, lighting it and consuming it rapidly. He took a deep breath before pulling out two more cigarettes, chain smoking them one after another in an attempt to calm himself as he waited. Eventually, after what felt like ages, Harding stepped out.

With a keen sense of anticipation, Mick turned to the inspector and asked in a hushed voice, "Well, Inspector, what do you think?"

The law enforcement officer's forehead tightened as he contemplated the situation at hand. Then finally, after some moments of silent contemplation, he spoke with firm authority. "I think that you are right, Mick. We need to bring James Murray back in for questioning and we need to do it quickly."

Mick gave a decisive nod, his mind already whirring with plans and possibilities of what would come next. He was certain they were edging closer to the truth, and he was determined to see this through until the very end.

Chapter 26: If You Want Blood

Later that day

James Murray sat in the chair as if he was unconcerned, confident and relaxed. But underneath the small table his hands trembled as he faced Detective Inspector Harding and Detective Mick Dunne for a second time that day in the dimly lit interrogation room of Ballygorman Garda station. His pulse raced, each beat like a drum echoing through his veins.

Mick Dunne, his face set with a look of stern determination as he spoke. His voice was strong and firm, as if nothing could sway him from the path he had chosen. "James," he said, "we've got a problem here. Tom Burke just told us that you asked him to lie for you, to provide you with a false alibi on the night in question. You weren't with him that evening, were you?" He fixed James with an unwavering gaze, his expression leaving no doubt that he considered James to be a liar.

James shifted in his seat as he desperately searched for a convincing explanation. He knew he had to be careful with his words. "Look," he began hesitantly, "I can explain why I wasn't with Tom, but it's complicated. I needed him to tell that lie, to cover for me so that no one would get hurt."

Detective Dunne's eyes were narrowed as he interjected, his voice rife with disbelief, "And what reason would that be, James?" His incredulity seemed to hang in the air and his entire posture expressed his doubt as he waited for James's response.

James gulped, his gaze shifting quickly between the detectives. He hesitantly opened his mouth to speak, each word reluctantly spilling out like raindrops. "I... I was with somebody else that night, a woman, but I couldn't tell anyone about it because it would break my marriage apart. I was so scared that I asked Tom to cover for me and say he was with me instead. That I was helping him with his cattle."

Detective Dunne's eyebrows arched in disbelief. "So, you expect us to believe that story now. James, that is complete horseshit, we know it and you know it, will you just cop yourself on."

James's voice wavered as he spoke. "I swear, it's the truth. I never meant for any of this to happen. I just... I got caught up in a moment of weakness."

Mick readied his pen, the end hovering impatiently over the notebook in front of him as he prepared to write down the details. He ran his hand across his bald head and looked up to meet James's eyes. With a raised eyebrow and an expectant expression, he asked, "So what's her name? And where does she live?"

"Who?" James inquired, as Mick cackled in amusement. "This charming woman you were so intimately involved with on the evening of Wednesday, May 3rd?" he clarified with a wry smile. His tone held a subtle hint of disbelief.

James scratched his head in confusion. "Well, I'm not sure where she lives," he said slowly. "I met her in a bar in Sligo town. She told me she was from London, just over on holiday here." He scratched his head again as he pretended to remember more details about the mysterious woman. Mick rolled his eyes and let out an incredulous laugh. “That’s convenient,” he muttered sarcastically. "So did the two of you go back to a hotel or anything? Could anyone confirm that you were actually together?" His tone was filled with doubt and suspicion as he looked at James searching for answers.

"No, I don't think so," James replied thoughtfully. Mick raised an eyebrow, quirking his lips in a half-smile that didn't quite reach his eyes. "Jesus, James, I'll give you one bit of credit, you are quick to spin an auld yarn... Anyway, go on, so where exactly did you and this scarlet woman from London have your so-called romance?" he pressed with a slight edge to his voice before taking a sip of his water.

"Oh, in her car," James replied, his curt words echoing off the walls of the room. A smirk curled on Mick's lips as he nodded understandingly and answered, "Right," with a confirming voice.

Harding, who had been uncharacteristically quiet until then, leaned back and the expression on his face hardened. His eyes levelled with James's, almost daring him to say something that could prove to be another lie. "James," he began slowly, enunciating each word carefully, "you have lied to us multiple times already. How can we possibly put any trust in anything you say?"

James's eyes flew around the room, a look of intense desperation and pleading on his face. His strong facade was beginning to crumble, the mask of confidence that he had so carefully maintained slipping away. "Please," he begged earnestly, an edge of desperation in his voice, "just give me a chance to explain."

Before either detective could respond, a loud knock on the interview room door interrupted the tense atmosphere. Dunne and Harding excused themselves and stepped outside, leaving James alone with a uniformed officer, uncertainty gnawing at his insides like a hungry snake.

Minutes felt like hours, every passing second of agonizing waiting dragging on for an eternity. James's guilt and fear intensified with the oppressive silence that filled the room, almost tangible in its intensity. Finally, Dunne and Harding returned – a much anticipated and dreaded sight – Harding carrying a large plastic evidence bag tightly in his grip.

Harding walked slowly towards James and as he drew nearer, each step was like a heavy burden on James's conscience.

Harding's eyes drilled into James's soul, the guilt and accusation thickening the tense atmosphere. With a slow and controlled motion, he placed a large evidence bag on the table, revealing the bloody garment within.

Harding presented a white shirt to James, searching his eyes for recognition. "Do you recognise this shirt, James?" he asked. James stared down at the garment for a few moments, rubbing it between his fingers as if in an attempt to recall memories connected with it. He let out an uncertain breath. "I'm not sure," he muttered hesitantly.

"You should recognise it because it is yours. Your long-suffering wife, Maureen, is currently in the front office of this Garda station, and she has been very cooperative. She was the one who brought in this shirt, and she told us that she heard you down in the kitchen after midnight in the early hours of May 4th, just a few hours after Lizzy was senselessly murdered. She said that she heard you banging about for a long time and then you went to bed in the spare room.

She went downstairs after you were asleep and discovered that the noise you were making came from your ridiculous attempts to try to work the washing machine, something that you obviously had no experience of using before. She opened the door of the washing machine and discovered this blood-stained shirt. You were clearly trying to wash the blood away, but you failed. She said there was also a strong smell of ladies' perfume on the shirt, and she suspects it came from you being up close with Lizzy O'Dowd the night before. She said that she was well aware for a long time of your affair with Lizzy, but she was so afraid of you, she never mentioned it," Harding said angrily.

"James, this is an undeniable piece of evidence, a damning testament to your involvement in the murder of Lizzy O'Dowd."

James's heart plummeted to his feet as he stared at the incriminating evidence, his mind spinning rapidly for an explanation that would remove the blame from him. Desperation and terror surged within him, accompanied by hot tears which rolled down his face unchecked. "But... but the blood on the shirt," he gasped brokenly, as if in a last effort to salvage himself from this nightmare. "I told you it was mine. Look," he continued breathlessly, desperation lending power to his words, "look, that woman from London I met in Sligo, she got a bit rough, and she tore into my cheeks with her fingernails as we were... making love. She was a bit weird, to be honest."

Detective Dunne's voice echoed around the room like a harsh winter wind, devoid of emotion. With the precision and ease of a scalpel, he dissected James's story, revealing its frail threads and inconsistencies. "First it was an alibi with Tom Burke as your accomplice," he said coolly, "then the affair you'd been having – and now this. Can you explain to us why your wife found a blood-stained shirt hidden away if it was merely from scratches?"

James was lost in thought, trying to find a way out of his predicament but it seemed hopeless. Suddenly, he had a moment of clarity, and he knew that there was no way out, game over.

"Well, James," Harding said in a stern voice as he pounded the table with his fist, "what do you have to say for yourself?"

James's voice quivered unsteadily as he stumbled over his words, his mind a heavy fog of guilt and sorrow. "I... I can't explain," he muttered in anguish. "I'm so sorry. I never meant for any of this to happen. It was all an accident, I just gave her a shove and she toppled backwards, striking the edge of the coffee table. I didn't mean for it to end like that."

Harding fixed his gaze on James as he asked in a grave tone, "Are you telling us, James, that you committed an act of violence against Lizzy O'Dowd in her home during the night of Wednesday, May 3rd?" He waited for a response, his eyes never leaving James's face as he spoke.

"It was a moment of madness," James confessed. "I didn't mean for it to happen, I just tried to kiss her, and she scratched at my face and suddenly I found myself pushing her away without even realising what I had done." He hung his head low in shame, eyes cast downward and a heavy guilt settling on his conscience.

The room descended into an oppressive hush as Harding's stern visage momentarily softened, a hint of understanding and relief washing over his features. He slowly uttered the words, "James Murray, I arrest you on the suspicion of murdering Lizzy O'Dowd. You have the right to remain silent; anything you say may be used against you in a court of law." His deep voice reverberated through the silence, hammering home the brutal nature of his statement.

Mick Dunne left the room for a moment before re-entering with a pair of handcuffs. The sound of them locking into place was like a thunderclap, echoing around the room and sending shivers down James's spine. A sense of finality descended upon him. The weight of his confession hung in the air, intertwining with the suffocating reality of his actions. There was no turning back now. He had confessed, revealing the darkness that had lurked within him.

His once-confident façade now shattered, leaving only the fragments of a broken man in its wake. As he was led away by the detectives, he glanced back at the blood-stained shirt, a stark reminder of the irreversible choices he had made. The sight caused him to shudder with fear and regret, his future now painted by despair and shame.

Outside the interview room, the station was alive with activity. Officers strode purposefully past each other, their footsteps echoing in the corridors as they collectively shouldered the heavy burden of justice. Meanwhile, up high in its isolated hillside perch, the small town of Ballygorman went about its day unaware of the darkness that had been uncovered within its walls. The evening sunlight gleaming through the window did nothing to hide the insidious truth behind what had just occurred inside that very room.

The investigation into the murder of Lizzy O'Dowd had been a gruelling and exhausting ordeal, but one that finally revealed the truth. As James Murray was led away in handcuffs, his confession ringing out into the night air like a death knell, it became quickly apparent that in some souls lay a capacity for darkness and deception; after all, to assume that this unassuming individual was capable of such atrocity seemed unthinkable at first glance. Yet here he stood – branded by murder.

EPILOGUE: DUST IN THE WIND

Saturday May 13th

Late afternoon light bathed the sleepy town of Ballygorman in a pleasant golden hue as May's bloom carried the promise of summer. Sean Breslin found himself drawn towards the quiet sanctuary of St Mary's graveyard. The silence was gently broken only by whispers of a faint breeze rustling through the branches of tall trees, crests softly swaying like slow moving waves in an ocean. He drifted down this path until he stood at its entrance. With heavy steps, Sean slowly traversed the wrought-iron gate, its hinges squeaking faintly as it opened and closed. He stopped in his tracks for a brief moment, taking in his surroundings. The gravestones stood still before him like old sentinels of a forgotten past, their weathered faces etched with stories of long-forgotten lives lived and loves lost. He could feel his heart racing faster as he carefully scanned each grave, looking for the final resting place of Lizzy O'Dowd.

Eventually, he found it. His chest tightened with a sudden rush of emotion as he stood in front of the grave, and Sean's breath caught in his throat. Loss threatened to consume him, his body trembling with grief. He knelt before the grave, taking in the freshly laid earth that still bore evidence of recent sorrow. The sun had yet to dry out some of the tears that had fallen upon its surface.

His hands trembled as he gently laid the vibrant bouquet of wildflowers on the mound, their petals of pink and purple a living tribute to her life-giving beauty. He paused for a long time, remembering every detail of her face and how far too soon it had been taken from him. A lone tear rolled down his cheek as he prayed.

The weight of his grief pressed upon him, and Sean closed his eyes, seeking solace in the sacred space. Memories of their laughter, their dreams, and their stolen moments flooded his mind as he quietly spoke to her.

As the words lingered in the air and then faded into the ether, Sean ran some of the dark soil from the grave through his fingers, and then with a heavy sigh he rose from his knees, his gaze lingering for a moment longer on the grave. He felt a strange mix of peace and sadness, a bittersweet acknowledgment that life must continue despite the ache within his heart. Sean knew that while the pain of loss would always remain, he had the strength to find beauty amidst the shadows.

Donal McCabe sat at a worn wooden table in Gallagher's bar next to Fiona Donnelly, across from them Jack Devlin, Sean Breslin and Paddy Farrell. As the group gathered, laughter echoed throughout the room, but the events of the past ten days still hung in the air. It was a night of respite and celebration, their spirits buoyed by the release of Sean from Garda custody and the resolution of the false accusations that had plagued him. Their glasses brimming, ready to embrace the joys of camaraderie and the end of a dark chapter in their lives. Now they basked in the warmth of their joy, finding succour in each other's presence.

Laughter and light filled the air, blending with the clinking of glasses and the crackle of the fire that danced in the hearth, painting their faces with soft shadows.

Donal raised his glass in a toast, a broad smile on his face. "Well, Sean, it's good to have you back where you belong," he declared with joy.

His companions eagerly joined him in the toast, their voices harmoniously chanting 'To Sean!' in unison as their glasses clinked together like tiny bells.

Sean's eyes glittered with gratitude at the show of support from his friends and he nodded solemnly in response, overwhelmed by emotion. "Ah, lads, I can't thank you enough for standing by me," Sean said, his voice filled with sincerity.

Fiona leaned over to Sean, her voice filled with concern as she spoke. "We've all been so worried for you, Sean, but we knew that the truth would eventually come out – we just had to trust in that." Looking into Sean's eyes, she saw the gratitude radiating from him and smiled softly in response.

"Thank you, Fiona. I'm blessed to have you all in my corner," Sean replied.

Paddy interjected with a devilish grin on his face. "It had us wondering if you were actually leading a double life as the world's greatest criminal mastermind!"

The group erupted in raucous laughter. The boisterous sound filled every crevice of the bar, merging with the traditional music that flowed from the corner. Its joyful melody carried through the air like a balm that washed away their worries. In that moment, they were transported to a place where burdens were shed, and the scars left by recent events seemed to dissolve away.

As the night progressed and their glasses emptied and refilled, the conversation danced from one topic to another, their stories became a tapestry of their experiences, memories and dreams, blending the past and present as if it was a form of catharsis, an emotional purging. Conversation flowed like a meandering river, touching on topics both mundane and transcendent. They entertained each other with stories of their mischievous adventures as children, the hilarious pranks they played on unsuspecting neighbours, and the dreams that still glimmered like distant stars in their hearts. They reminisced about the people they'd met throughout life and everything that brought them to where they were now – an unexpected but pleasant moment shared between friends.

Sean leaned back in his chair, his gaze wandering to the ceiling as he spoke, his voice full of wonder and anticipation. "You know, someday I'd love to travel the world, experience different cultures in the far east and see wonders beyond North Leitrim."

Fiona's eyes lit up, her voice overflowing with enthusiasm. "Oh, Sean, I can already picture you exploring ancient ruins in the far east."

Donal chortled heartily, shaking his head as he remarked, "Don't listen to that lad Sean. He hasn't ever been any further east than Mullingar!"

"Feck off, McCabe, who asked you for your opinion anyway," Sean replied with disdain, his lip curling in mock disgust.

"Ah, the world has so much to offer, Sean, so much to experience. I've seen my fair share of it. I've had the great fortune to travel to some amazing places. You should travel. Pack your bags. You only get one crack at this life, enjoy it," Jack said wistfully.

Paddy looked up at his friend with a mischievous smirk as he spoke his words. "Well, don't ask me to go with you Sean – someone has to stay here and keep this place looking pristine while you gallivant around the world."

"Jasus, you're killed sweeping those footpaths every day, Paddy," Sean joked.

Their banter continued as the time grew late, and they soaked up the last moments of the evening. The clock hanging on the wood panelled wall to the right of Donal McCabe ticked away, its loud and melodic "tock, tock, tock" ringing through the room like an incessant reminder of time passing by. Its antique design was one that had seen many years, its metal hands and numbers covered in a thin layer of dust. The pendulum swung back and forth in a mesmerising fashion, creating an almost soothing rhythm that was hard not to focus on, a sharp noise compared to the other sounds that filled the room. It sounded like a knife against bone.

Tock, tock tock.

It was definitely a tock and not a tick. It was not a thin tick sound but a heavy, slow and deep tock. Like the sound resonating from the throat of a primeval beast it was loud and overbearing. The pendulum swung over and back within the Gustav Becker casing and the clock defiantly tocked.

Tock, tock, tock.

It was fourteen minutes to twelve on a May Saturday evening.

The End

Printed by Amazon Italia Logistica S.r.l.
Torrazza Piemonte (TO), Italy